AF263006

MAURA-ANN CAIRNS

The Bride of Marchetti

First published by Maura-Ann Cairns 2026

Copyright © 2026 by Maura-Ann Cairns

All rights reserved. No part of this publication may be reproduced, stored, or transmitted in any form or by any means, electronic, mechanical, photocopying, recording, scanning, or otherwise without written permission from the publisher. It is illegal to copy this book, post it to a website, or distribute it by any other means without permission.

This novel is entirely a work of fiction. The names, characters, and incidents portrayed in it are the work of the author's imagination. Any resemblance to actual persons, living or dead, events, or localities is entirely coincidental.

Maura-Ann Cairns asserts the moral right to be identified as the author of this work.

First edition

This book was professionally typeset on Reedsy.
Find out more at reedsy.com

Contents

I

Dedication

They'll call him a monster.
But you'll turn every page anyway, won't you, tesoro?

Lorenzo Marchetti

II

Content Warning

This story explores dark and unsettling themes, including forced marriage, power imbalance, coercion, emotional manipulation, confinement, violence, and explicit sexual content.
The romance in this book is intentionally dark, featuring characters who make morally questionable choices in situations where consent and control are compromised.

Reader discretion is advised.

III

playlist

Bella Ciao - Fonola Band
You Can Be So Cruel - Royal Blood
I Hate Everything About You - Three Days Grace
Cruel Lover - ARI LEE
Animals - Maroon 5
Do You Really Want To Hurt Me - Nessa Barrett
Gangsta - Kehlani
Teeth - 5 Seconds Of Summer
Woo - Rihanna
Moth To A Flame - The Weeknd
Falling - Chase Atlantic
Talking Body - Tove lo
Hands On Me - Ariana Grande
Streets - Doja Cat
Back To Black - Amy Winehouse
Hotel - Montell Fish
Stand By Me - Ben E. king

1

Chapter One: Dakota

Italy smelled like espresso and broken promises.

I shifted my camera bag on my shoulder as I followed my father through Rome's narrow streets, watching his bald head gleam under the August sun while he checked his phone. Again. Fourth time in ten minutes.

"Dad, seriously." I dodged a couple taking selfies by the fountain. "You drag me to Italy for 'business' but won't tell me what kind of business requires your daughter as a plus-one?"

"Dakota. Not now." That tone. The one that said the conversation was over before it started.

I'm twenty-one with a photography degree and work in two legitimate galleries, but Robert Phillips still treats me like I'm sixteen and asking to borrow his car.

My father has always been secretive about his work. Vague explanations. Locked office doors. Phone calls at midnight that he took in hushed tones, emerging twenty minutes later with his jaw tight and his eyes distant. My mother, Aurora, learned years ago to stop asking questions. Now she just smiles that brittle smile, kisses him goodbye, and refills her wine glass.

I never learned to stop asking.

We turned down a side street where the buildings pressed in close, all terracotta and sun-bleached cream, ancient stone worn smooth by centuries. My photographer's eye catalogued everything—the play of light and shadow, the cobblestones polished by a million footsteps, laundry strung between windows like prayer flags.

"Where are we going?"

Dad's jaw clenched. "A café. I'm meeting someone. You'll wait outside."

"Wait outside? Like a dog?"

"Dakota—"

"Fine. Whatever." I pulled out my camera, the vintage Nikon that cost three months of my life. If I was being dragged across the world for some cryptic meeting, I'd at least get decent shots.

The café appeared ahead, tucked into a corner with dark green awnings and wrought-iron chairs arranged in that deliberately careless way expensive places do. My father's shoulders tensed as we approached. He tugged at his collar even though it wasn't hot.

Robert Phillips was nervous.

I'd never seen my father nervous.

"Stay here." He didn't look at me. "Don't wander off."

"Yes, sir," I said, dripping sarcasm.

He disappeared inside, leaving me alone on a Roman street corner with my camera and the growing certainty that something was very, very wrong.

I found a small pink building down the street—cotton-candy pink that shouldn't exist in real life but did, vivid and surreal against the muted tones around it. Bougainvillea spilled from window boxes in violent purples and reds. I photographed it, capturing the way afternoon light turned the windows to liquid gold.

Photography was my language. Through the lens, everything made sense.

I was lining up a shot of a dog sprawled on the cobblestones when someone slammed into my shoulder.

Hard.

I stumbled, nearly dropping my camera, and whirled around ready to fight. "Hey! Watch where you're—"

The words died.

The man standing before me was tall. Stupidly tall. Six-foot-three, maybe six-foot-four, all lean muscle and expensive fabric. Dark hair that looked artfully messy in a way that definitely cost money. And his eyes—hazel, catching the light like whiskey in cut crystal—fixed on me with utter contempt.

Like I was gum on his shoe.

"Stai attenta." His voice was low, cold, a knife sliding between ribs. "Piccola turista stupida."

I didn't speak Italian, but I knew a dismissal when I heard one. My spine went steel-straight. "Excuse me? You ran into me."

His eyes narrowed. He said something else in rapid Italian, paired with a dismissive hand gesture that made my blood pressure spike.

"If you're going to insult me," I snapped, "at least do it in English so I know exactly what kind of asshole you are."

For a moment, he just stared. Then, slowly, his mouth curved into a smirk that had nothing kind in it.

"Americana," he said, like it was a curse.

"Yeah. And proud of it. Problem?"

"You should watch where you stand." His English was perfect, accented in a way that probably made other girls weak in the knees. It just pissed me off. "These streets are not safe for little girls playing tourist."

"Little girl?" My voice went sharp. "That's rich coming from someone who apparently can't walk in a straight line."

His jaw tightened. A muscle ticked below his cheekbone. Up close, I could see a scar under his right eye, pale against tanned skin. It should've made him look damaged. Instead, it made him look dangerous.

"You have quite a mouth on you," he observed, voice soft in a way that felt like a threat.

"And you have a problem with personal space. We all have our flaws."

Another flash of that cruel smirk. He took a step closer. Testing me. I forced myself not to back down, even as my heart hammered so hard I could feel it in my throat.

"What's your name, americana?"

"None of your business."

"Rude and American. How predictable."

"Judgmental and insufferable. How European."

Something flickered in his eyes. Not quite amusement. Something darker. "You should be careful who you speak to this way. In this city, that mouth could get you killed."

"Is that a threat?"

"Advice." His smile was all teeth. "Though I doubt you're smart enough to take it."

We stood there, locked in something that felt like a fight but looked like something else entirely. I could smell his cologne—bergamot and something darker, addictive. I hated that I noticed. Hated the way my pulse kicked up for reasons that had nothing to do with fear.

"Dakota!"

My father's voice shattered the moment. I turned to see him emerging from the café, face ashen, and behind him—

Oh, God.

An older man in a three-piece suit, sharp brown eyes, expression that radiated power and cruelty in equal measure. The kind of man who'd never been told no in his entire life.

"Lorenzo!" The man's voice cracked like a whip. "Vieni qui!"

Lorenzo.

He gave me one last look—something cold and calculating sliding behind those hazel eyes—before turning toward the older man. My father grabbed my elbow hard enough to bruise.

"We're leaving. Now."

"Dad, what—"

"Not here." His eyes darted between Lorenzo and the older man, who were speaking rapid-fire Italian. "Hotel. We'll talk at the hotel."

I looked back once. Lorenzo was staring right at me, and his expression had gone arctic. Those whiskey eyes tracked me like I was prey.

Like I was a problem that needed solving.

My father dragged me into a side alley, finally releasing my arm. He exhaled shakily, running a hand over his face.

"Dad." I kept my voice level. "Who the hell were those people?"

He hesitated. "That was Alonzo Marchetti."

The name meant nothing to me. "Okay. And?"

"And we're in trouble, Dakota." His voice sounded hollow, scraped raw. "We're in so much fucking trouble."

I stopped walking. "What kind of trouble? Who is Alonzo Marchetti?"

My father looked at me then, really looked at me and I saw something in his eyes I'd never seen before.

Terror.

"The kind that doesn't go away," he said quietly. "And Alonzo Marchetti is…" He shook his head. "We need to get back to the hotel. I have to call your mother."

We walked in silence, but my mind was spinning. Robert Phillips, who'd never been rattled by anything in my life, was afraid.

*

Back at the hotel near the Spanish Steps, I paced while Dad made his call behind closed doors. I could hear his voice through the walls, low, urgent, desperate.

I pulled out my camera and scrolled through the photos. The pink building. The woman with the pigeons. And then—

I stopped.

In the reflection of the pink building's window, barely visible but definitely there: Lorenzo. Hands in his pockets, eyes fixed on me.

He'd been watching me before he "bumped" into me.

It hadn't been an accident at all.

"Dakota." My father emerged, somehow more pale than before. "Sit down."

I sat on the bed's edge, camera clutched in my hands like a weapon. "Talk."

He poured himself whiskey from the minibar. Two in the afternoon. My father never drank during the day.

He downed it in one swallow.

"The business I do." He stopped. Started again. "It's not consulting."

"Yeah. I figured."

He ignored me. "I work for certain people. Powerful people. People who don't forgive mistakes."

My stomach dropped. "What kind of people?"

"The kind you don't say no to." He poured another drink. "I've done well for them. Made them money. But recently…" His hand shook. "A deal went bad. Money was lost. A lot of money."

"How much?"

"Enough that an apology won't fix it."

I stared. "What does this have to do with me?"

He couldn't look at me. "They want collateral. Insurance that I'll make it right."

"Dad—"

"They want you, Dakota."

The words hung in the air like smoke. I waited for the punchline. But he just stood there, knuckles white around the glass.

"What?" The word barely came out.

"Alonzo Marchetti wants you to marry his son." My father's voice had gone mechanical. "Lorenzo. He's twenty-six. Heir to the family. Currently unmarried."

"No." I stood. "Absolutely fucking not."

"It's temporary. A few years. Long enough for me to fix this, prove my loyalty. Then you can divorce—"

"Are you insane?" My voice cracked. "You're trying to sell me to the mob?"

"I'm trying to keep you alive!" His voice broke. "Do you understand what these people do? If I say no, they'll kill me. They'll kill your mother. They'll kill you. At least this way—"

"At least this way I'm only forced to marry a stranger who looked at me like I was trash?"

"You think I want this?" His hands shook. "You think I didn't spend that entire meeting trying to find another option?"

"There's always another option!"

"Not with them. Not with the Marchettis." He sank into a chair, suddenly looking ancient. "They own Rome, Dakota. Politicians, police, judges. All of them."

I felt sick. "How long have you worked for them?"

"Does it matter?"

"It fucking matters!"

He flinched. "I started when you were fifteen."

The room tilted. Six years of lies. Six years of my life built on whatever this was.

"Does Mom know?"

"No. God, no. I kept her out of it. Both of you." He laughed, broken and bitter. "Fat lot of good that did."

I wanted to scream. Throw something. Break something. Instead, I just stood there, camera in my hands, the weight of it suddenly unbearable.

"When?" Barely a whisper.

"When do they want an answer?"

His phone buzzed. Whatever color remained in his face drained completely.

"Dad?"

He turned the phone toward me with trembling hands.

A photo. No words.

Me and Lorenzo on the street. That exact moment we'd been facing each other, locked in battle. Someone had been photographing us while I'd been photographing Rome.

A second message came through.

Tomorrow. 6 PM. Villa Marchetti. Don't be late.

"I'm so sorry, baby girl." My father's voice cracked.

But I wasn't listening. I was staring at that photo, at the way Lorenzo's eyes were fixed on mine, and remembering what he'd said.

That mouth could get you killed.

He'd known.

The entire time we stood there trading insults, he'd known exactly who I was.

Which meant our meeting hadn't been accidental.

It had been a test.

And apparently, I'd passed.

2

Chapter Two: Lorenzo

The American girl had no idea she was being watched.

I stood at the second-floor window of the pink building—one of our safe houses, deliberately forgettable—and observed her through the curtains. She moved like someone who'd never had to look over her shoulder. Camera up, framing shots like this crumbling neighborhood was something worth capturing.

Naive.

My phone buzzed. My father: *È lei?*

Sì, I typed back. *She's here.*

Dakota Phillips. Twenty-one. Fresh out of some American university with a useless photography degree. Her file sat in my jacket pocket—thin, unremarkable. The story of someone who'd never mattered until her father fucked up badly enough to land on our radar.

My father's instructions were simple: assess her. See if Robert Phillips' daughter could handle what was coming, or if she'd shatter the second reality hit.

Alonzo Marchetti didn't invest in broken things.

I'd argued against this entire plan. There were cleaner ways to handle the situation. But my father was immovable, his logic cold and airtight: marriage created permanent leverage. Kill Robert, lose his Pentagon connections. Kill his family, make enemies of his government contacts. But marry his daughter? That made him family. That made him ours.

And I was the lucky bastard who got stuck with it.

Test her, my father had said. *See what she's made of.*

I checked my watch. Robert Phillips would be sitting across from my father right now, sweating through his expensive suit while Alonzo explained exactly how much money had vanished and what that meant for his future.

I left the window and took the stairs down, footsteps silent on old wood. The street was warm when I stepped outside, afternoon sun beating down on cobblestones worn smooth by centuries.

Time to see if Dakota Phillips would crumble or fight back.

The collision was calculated—my shoulder met hers at precisely the right angle to make her stumble without actually hurting her. I'm not a savage.

Her reaction was instant. Not fear. Not apology.

Pure, unfiltered rage.

She whirled on me, and before she even processed my face, I saw it—that flash of genuine anger, raw and honest.

Then she looked up.

I waited for recognition. For the softening, the stammered apology, the instinctive retreat people made when they realized who I was.

It didn't come.

Instead, her spine went straight. Her chin lifted. Those dark eyes met mine with something that looked dangerously like defiance.

Interesting.

I insulted her in Italian. Called her a stupid little tourist. Watched her face flush even though she couldn't understand the words.

Then she said something that genuinely shocked me.

"If you're going to insult me, at least do it in English so I know exactly what kind of asshole you are."

The words landed like a slap.

Asshole.

She'd called me an asshole.

To my face.

I stared at her, caught off guard for the first time in years. People didn't talk to me this way. Not in Rome. Not anywhere. I was Lorenzo Marchetti—heir to an empire built on blood and fear, the son who made problems disappear.

And this tiny American nobody with her camera and her tourist clothes had just called me an asshole.

She kept going too, that mouth firing off responses faster than I could catalog them. Sharp. Unfiltered. She crossed her arms when I stepped closer, holding her ground even though I could see her pulse hammering in her throat—a tell her pride refused to acknowledge.

The whole thing lasted maybe two minutes. Two minutes where Dakota Phillips proved she had more spine than sense, more courage than survival instinct.

She had absolutely no idea what she was walking into.

I asked for her name. She refused. Called me judgmental and insufferable when I pointed out how predictably rude Americans were.

The girl had fire, I'd give her that.

But fire without control was just destruction waiting to happen.

"You should be careful who you speak to this way," I told her, letting each word sink in. *"In this city, that mouth could get you killed."*

She asked if it was a threat.

I told her it was advice.

What I didn't tell her: it was also a warning she wouldn't understand until it was too late.

"Dakota!"

Her father's voice shattered the moment. I saw genuine terror flash across Robert Phillips' face as he emerged from the café, my father following with that expression that meant the deal was done.

"Lorenzo!" My father's voice cracked like a whip. *"Vieni qui!"*

I gave the girl one last look—let my eyes trace over her face with cold assessment, memorizing details the way I did with all my problems.

She stared back. Christ, there was still no fear. Just confusion and anger and something that almost looked like challenge.

Brave little fool.

I turned and walked toward my father, sliding my hands into my pockets.

"Well?" My father asked in Italian, voice low. *"Your assessment?"*

I glanced back. Her father had grabbed her elbow—too hard—and was dragging her away with desperate urgency.

"She's disrespectful," I said flatly. *"Argumentative. No sense of self-preservation whatsoever."*

"So she has spirit."

"She has a death wish."

My father's mouth curved into something that wasn't quite a smile. *"Good. She'll need it, being married to you."*

The words hit like a fist to the gut, even though I'd known they were coming.

"Padre—"

"The discussion is over, Lorenzo." That tone. The one that meant argument was pointless. *"Robert Phillips owes us three million euros and his life. He has neither. What he does have is connections in the American defense sector that we need, and a daughter who can ensure his cooperation."*

"Then put a gun to her head. It's cleaner."

"It's also temporary." My father straightened his cuffs. *"Fear fades. Family is forever. You marry the girl, Robert becomes invested in our success. His contacts become our contacts. His access becomes our access."*

The logic was sound. I hated that it was sound.

Robert Phillips had embedded himself deep in Pentagon procurement over fifteen years. Not as a major player—he was too small for that—but as a facilitator. Someone who could smooth contracts, redirect attention, make inconvenient questions disappear. He'd been useful. Profitable.

Then he got careless with our money, and now we needed insurance he'd fix it.

"There are other ways—"

"None that serve us as well." My father met my eyes, and I saw the steel that had built our empire staring back at me. *"You've had twenty-six years of freedom, figlio mio. But you're a Marchetti. The family requires this of you."*

I wanted to argue. Wanted to explain that I'd avoided entanglements for good reason, that the things I did—the things I was—weren't compatible with having someone close enough to be used as leverage against me.

But I knew my father. Once he made a decision, the only thing left was obedience.

"How long?" I asked, voice carefully neutral.

"As long as it takes to secure what we need from Robert. Two years minimum. Five at most." He checked his watch. *"The wedding will be in three weeks. Civil ceremony, quiet. We'll make the appropriate announcements afterward."*

Three weeks.

I pictured those defiant eyes across a breakfast table from me every morning. That sharp tongue making comments about my hours, my work, the blood I sometimes came home with on my cuffs.

My mother would have opinions about this arrangement. She always did — about everything I did, every decision my father made, every woman who'd ever been foolish enough to get close to this family. God help Dakota Phillips when those two finally met.

"She called me an asshole," I said, the words coming out harder than I meant.

My father raised an eyebrow. *"And?"*

"No one talks to me that way."

"Then teach her not to." He clapped a hand on my shoulder, the gesture almost paternal despite the cold business we'd just concluded. *"Make sure she understands her place before she embarrasses this family."*

He walked past me, back toward the car waiting at the end of the street.

I stood there on that sun-bleached Roman street, fury and frustration coiling tight in my chest.

Fine.

If I had to marry Dakota Phillips, if I had to bind myself to some American girl with more courage than common sense, then she'd learn exactly what she'd walked into.

I pulled out my phone and found the surveillance photos. The perfect shot — me and Dakota locked in confrontation, her face tilted up with that defiant expression that made something dark twist in my chest.

I sent it to Robert Phillips' number. No message. Let him show his daughter exactly how thoroughly we'd orchestrated this. Let her sit with it tonight — the realisation that nothing about today had been accidental. That I had been watching her long before she ever saw me.

Then I typed the second message: *Tomorrow. 6 PM. Villa Marchetti. Don't be late.*

As I hit send, I made myself a promise.

Dakota Phillips wanted to stand up to me? Wanted to prove she wasn't afraid?

Fine.

Let her try.

They all learned eventually. One way or another.

Robert Phillips would have some explaining to do tonight. I almost pitied him — almost — having to look his daughter in the eye and tell her exactly what he'd traded her for.

Almost.

3

Chapter Three: Dakota

I was pushing cold eggs around my plate when my father finally emerged from his room.

Twenty minutes of moving scrambled eggs in circles. My appetite had died somewhere around 3 AM when the reality of my situation really sank in. The hotel breakfast buffet mocked me—fresh pastries, fruit, cheese, meat. All this food for a girl who'd just been sold.

My father moved like he was trying to be invisible. He poured cornflakes with shaking hands, pieces scattering across the table. He sat down across from me, leaving an entire chair between us as a buffer.

"Still mad at me?" he asked.

I set down my fork. It hit the plate with a sharp clink that made him flinch.

"Mad?" The word came out flat. *"That's what you think this is?"*

"Dakota—"

"I'm not mad, Dad. Mad is what I get when you forget my birthday or eat my leftovers." I met his eyes. *"This is something else entirely."*

His face crumpled. Tears welled up—actual tears.

I had never seen my father cry.

Not when his own father died. Not when he lost his job. Not even when I broke my arm at seven and he had to carry me screaming to the ER.

"I'm so sorry, baby girl." His voice cracked. *"I didn't want this. I swear I didn't want any of this."*

Part of me wanted to reach across the table. The part that used to curl up in his lap when I was little and believed my dad could fix anything.

I stayed frozen.

"Then why?" My voice came out quieter than I meant. *"Why work for them at all?"*

"The money." He couldn't look at me. *"Your mother's lifestyle. Your college tuition. The house, the cars—I thought I could control it. I thought I was smarter than them."*

"And instead you got me sold off like property."

He flinched hard. *"I don't want to wake up and find you dead, Dakota. I don't want to come home and see your mother murdered in our bedroom. They showed me pictures."* His hands shook worse. *"Pictures of what they do to people who cross them. Bodies that—"* He broke off. *"If I say no, we're all dead within a week. This keeps you breathing. Keeps your mother safe."*

He wasn't asking for forgiveness.

He was asking me to sacrifice myself so he could live with his choices.

"When do we leave?" I asked finally. *"For the villa."*

He checked his watch. *"Eight hours."*

I pushed back from the table, chair scraping loud in the quiet room.

"Then I'm going to pack." I paused at the door. *"And Dad? Don't ask me if I'm still mad. Because the answer is going to be yes for a very, very long time."*

Those eight hours passed like a slow suffocation.

I sat on the edge of the hotel bed and stared at my suitcase for most of it. Packed it. Unpacked it. Packed it again. Took my camera out and held it for a while, like it could anchor me to the person I'd been forty-eight hours ago — the girl who'd landed in Rome thinking the worst thing waiting for her was a boring business trip.

Eventually I zipped the bag shut and didn't open it again.

The drive to Villa Marchetti took forty minutes through winding roads that climbed into hills outside Rome. My father drove in silence, white-knuckling the wheel. I kept my eyes on the window, watching the landscape shift from urban sprawl to countryside dotted with cypress trees.

We arrived with the afternoon still stretched long and golden ahead of us

— hours before the dinner we'd been summoned to, which somehow made it worse. No rushing, no urgency. Just time to sit with what was coming.

When the villa came into view, I understood why they called it that instead of just a house.

Three stories of cream stone and white pillars rising from the hillside like something out of a movie. Windows reflected the late afternoon sun, turning them to sheets of molten gold. Classical proportions that screamed wealth so old it didn't need to announce itself.

Then I saw the cars.

A sleek black BMW. A champagne Rolls-Royce. And a matte black Ducati that looked like barely contained violence on two wheels.

I'd bet my camera that was Lorenzo's.

My father pulled our rental sedan up behind them. We looked pathetic in comparison.

Before he could turn off the engine, a man in a black suit emerged from the entrance.

"Mr. Phillips," he said in accented English. *"Welcome to Villa Marchetti."*

He took my suitcase. I grabbed my camera bag — that stayed with me, always.

"Mr. Marchetti is expecting you in the study."

The interior was all marble and gold. The chandelier probably cost more than my education. The paintings weren't prints — they were originals, the kind you see behind velvet ropes.

My footsteps echoed. We passed room after room — a library with shelves reaching the ceiling, a sitting room with furniture too precious to actually use, a dining room with a table that could seat twenty. On a console table near the staircase sat a vase of white peonies, freshly arranged, petals still perfect. Someone had placed them there that morning. Someone who lived here and cared how things looked.

I wondered if that was her — the woman whose existence hovered at the edges of everything I'd been told about this family. Lorenzo's mother. Alonzo's wife. Whoever she was, she hadn't been mentioned once, and somehow that silence felt more unsettling than anything else.

We climbed a curved staircase. The man stopped at a heavy wooden door, knocked twice, sharp and precise, then opened it without waiting.

"Mr. Phillips and Miss Phillips," he announced.

The study was dark wood and leather. Bookshelves on two walls. A massive desk with nothing on it except a single folder and an expensive pen.

Behind the desk sat Alonzo Marchetti.

Charcoal three-piece suit. Silver hair perfectly styled. Sharp brown eyes tracking us like prey.

"Robert," he said, accent thicker than his son's. *"Miss Phillips. Please, sit."*

Two chairs faced the desk, angled toward each other. Lower than his. Forcing us to look up.

My father headed straight for them. I stayed standing.

Alonzo's eyebrow rose. *"Miss Phillips. Sit."*

"Where's Lorenzo?"

The words came out before I could stop them. My father made a sound like a kicked dog.

"My son is attending to business. He will join us shortly." A pause, weight behind it. *"Now. Sit."*

I sat.

Alonzo opened the folder with deliberate slowness. *"Let us discuss the terms."*

"Terms?" My voice came out steadier than I felt. *"I thought the terms were simple. I get sold, you get your money back, everyone pretends this is normal."*

"Dakota—" my father started, but Alonzo raised one hand and he shut up immediately.

"Your father explained the situation?" Alonzo looked at me.

"He explained that he screwed up and I get to pay for it. Yeah, we covered that."

Something flickered in those sharp eyes. He pulled out a document and slid it across the desk. *"The marriage contract. Read it carefully."*

Dense legal text in English and Italian. My entire life reduced to bullet points.

"The ceremony will be in three weeks. Civil. Small. You will move into Villa Marchetti following the wedding and reside in Lorenzo's wing."

Lorenzo's wing. Because apparently this place had wings.

"You will fulfill the role of Lorenzo's wife publicly. Family functions, business dinners, united front." He paused. *"Privately, you and my son will come to your own arrangements."*

The careful phrasing made my skin crawl.

"How long?"

"Minimum two years. Maximum five, depending on your father's ability to fix his mistake." Alonzo's gaze shifted to my dad. *"If Robert performs adequately, the marriage can be dissolved quietly."*

"And if he doesn't?"

"Then it becomes permanent."

The words settled like stones in my stomach.

"Additional terms. You will not leave the grounds without permission or escort. You will not contact friends or family beyond supervised calls. You will not discuss family business with anyone."

He paused, almost as an afterthought. *"My wife will want to meet you before the wedding. She's involved in the household — you'll find she has opinions about most things."* Something in his expression softened almost imperceptibly. *"She is not your enemy, Miss Phillips. I'd remember that."*

I didn't know what to do with that. A mother. A real one, living in this house, who had opinions. Who wasn't my enemy, which implied she'd had the chance to form a view of me already.

Before I could ask anything, the door opened.

The temperature dropped.

I didn't need to turn around to know who it was. The whole room shifted — even Alonzo straightened slightly. The air thickened, charged with something dangerous.

"Ah, figlio," Alonzo said, warmth creeping into his voice. *"We were just reviewing the contract."*

I turned.

Lorenzo stood in the doorway like he owned everything in it. All black — fitted pants that probably cost more than my car, a black button-down with sleeves rolled to his forearms, exposing tanned skin and the edge of a tattoo.

No tie. Top button undone.

He looked like sin dressed for a funeral.

Sharp jaw covered in dark stubble that was somehow perfectly groomed to look careless. Dark hair pushed back from his face, just long enough to grab. Hazel eyes that shifted between green and gold depending on the light, framed by lashes that had no business being on a man who radiated this much danger.

But it was the way he moved — predatory, controlled, every step deliberate. Violence wrapped in expensive clothes.

A silver ring glinted on his right hand. His knuckles were scarred.

Those eyes found mine immediately. Recognition flashed, then assessment, then pure contempt settling like a mask.

"Americana," he said, making it sound like an insult. His voice was dark honey and broken glass.

"Asshole," I shot back.

The corner of his mouth twitched. Not a smile — something sharper.

My father whimpered. Alonzo actually laughed.

"Yes," he said. *"This will be interesting."*

Lorenzo crossed to his father's desk and leaned against it instead of sitting. Casual, but I could see the tension in his shoulders. Coiled energy ready to strike.

He smelled like expensive cologne and cigarette smoke and something darker I couldn't name.

"Has she signed?" Lorenzo asked, eyes locked on mine. Up close, I could see a thin scar cutting through his left eyebrow.

"We were just getting to that." Alonzo slid the pen toward me. *"Miss Phillips?"*

I looked at the contract. At the pen. At my father, who couldn't meet my eyes. At Alonzo, watching with clinical interest. At Lorenzo, whose expression promised nothing but pain.

"And if I refuse?"

Lorenzo moved so fast I flinched. He leaned down, one hand braced on each arm of my chair, caging me in. His face was inches from mine.

"Then I make sure your father understands exactly what happens to people

who waste my family's time." His voice was soft, conversational, absolutely terrifying. *"I'll start with his fingers. One joint at a time. And I'll make you watch."*

My heart slammed against my ribs. I could feel the heat radiating off him, see the absolute lack of mercy in his eyes.

"Lorenzo," Alonzo said mildly. *"Step back."*

He didn't move for three more heartbeats — long enough to make his point. Then he straightened slowly, deliberately invading my space on the way back up. He returned to the desk, but his eyes never left mine.

"Your son has a flair for drama," I said, proud my voice barely shook.

"My son has a flair for results," Alonzo corrected. *"Now sign the contract, Miss Phillips. Unless you'd like to find out if he's bluffing."*

The weight in his voice made it clear — Lorenzo wasn't bluffing.

I picked up the pen.

My hand shook, but my signature came out clear. Dakota Marie Phillips in black ink.

"Excellent." Alonzo pulled the contract back. *"Lorenzo will show you to your room."*

"What?" My head snapped up. *"I need to go back to the hotel—"*

"You need to understand that this is your home now." Lorenzo pushed off the desk. *"You live here. With me."*

"I didn't agree to—"

"You just signed a contract that says otherwise." He tilted his head, studying me like I was an insect he was about to crush. *"Come on, principessa. Let me show you your cage."*

I stood on shaking legs, camera bag clutched to my chest. My father finally looked up, eyes red.

"Dakota, I—"

"Don't." My voice cracked. *"Just don't."*

Lorenzo was already walking away, not waiting. The message was clear — I didn't have a choice.

I hurried after him, hating how small I felt trying to match his stride.

We climbed another staircase to a hallway that felt different. More lived-in.

Personal. The walls were darker, the artwork more modern and disturbing — abstract pieces that looked like violence frozen on canvas.

His wing.

Lorenzo stopped at a door near the end, pulled out a key, unlocked it with a sharp twist. He pushed it open but didn't go in, just leaned against the frame, watching me.

The room was massive. A huge bed with white linens that looked obscenely soft. Floor-to-ceiling windows overlooking the grounds. A sitting area with a velvet couch, a clean-lined desk.

Beautiful.

A cage.

"This is your room," Lorenzo said, still blocking the doorway, forcing me too close. *"Mine is across the hall."*

He reached out suddenly. I jerked back. His jaw tightened, something dangerous flashing in his eyes.

"Calma," he murmured.

Then his hand was at my throat.

I froze.

His fingers didn't squeeze, didn't hurt — just rested against my pulse point, feeling my heart race. His thumb brushed my jaw, almost gentle.

"There's a lock on your door," he said softly, eyes on where his hand touched my skin. *"Use it. Every night. Because some nights I drink, and some nights I'm angry, and I can't promise what I'll do if I find your door open."*

Not a threat.

A warning.

He dropped his hand and stepped back, leaving cold where warmth had been.

"Bathroom's through there. Your things arrive within the hour. Dinner's at eight. You're expected." He turned to leave, paused. *"And principessa? That fire in your eyes, that defiance — it's going to get you hurt. My father wants you alive, but he never specified in what condition. Remember that."*

"Is that a threat?"

He turned back, pure darkness in his expression. *"It's a promise. You hate me? Bene. Good. Hold onto that. Because the alternative—"* His eyes dragged down my body slowly, deliberately, making me feel stripped bare. *"—would be far more dangerous for both of us."*

"I'm not afraid of you."

Lorenzo moved so fast I didn't see it. Suddenly he was in my space, one hand wrapped around the back of my neck. Not tight, but possessive. Controlling. He leaned down until his lips brushed my ear.

"Bugiarda," he whispered. *Liar. "I can feel your pulse racing. I can see you trying not to tremble. You should be afraid of me, piccola. I'm the monster your father sold you to."* His breath was warm against my skin. *"And unlike him, I don't pretend to be anything else."*

He released me and walked away, footsteps echoing.

The door stayed open.

I stood there trembling, watching him stop at the door across the hall. He looked back once, expression unreadable in the dim light.

"Welcome to Villa Marchetti, moglie." Wife. The word dripped with contempt. *"Try not to make me kill you before the wedding."*

Then he disappeared into his room.

I stumbled inside and went straight for the lock.

It clicked.

From both sides.

He hadn't lied — I could lock him out. But the fact that he had a key, that he could come in whenever he wanted and had warned me to lock the door anyway, was somehow more terrifying than if he'd just imprisoned me.

I sank onto the bed, camera bag clutched to my chest.

Through the windows, Roman countryside stretched forever, beautiful and completely unreachable.

My throat still burned where his hand had been. Not from pain — from the phantom heat of his touch, from the dark promise in his eyes, from the way my body had betrayed me by responding even as my mind screamed danger.

That girl from two days ago — the one who thought the worst thing that could happen was a boring business trip — was gone.

In her place: Dakota Marchetti.

I wasn't her yet.

Three more weeks.

But I would be.

And Lorenzo Marchetti — beautiful, dangerous, terrifying Lorenzo — was going to make sure I paid for every second of it.

I touched my throat where his hand had been.

I could still feel the warmth.

I hated that I could still feel it.

4

Chapter Four: Lorenzo

I didn't knock.

The door to Dakota's room swung open under my hand, the lock disengaged, which meant she'd forgotten. Careless. I filed that away and stepped inside.

There she was, face-down on the bed, shoulders shaking with sobs she thought no one could hear.

Something twisted in my chest. I crushed it immediately.

"Get up."

She lifted her head, eyes red and swollen, mascara streaked down her cheeks. For a second, she looked young. Vulnerable. Then her expression went hard.

"You don't knock?"

"My house. My rules." I leaned against the doorframe, arms crossed. *"You've been in this room for two days. That ends now. Get dressed — we're leaving in ten minutes."*

"God, you're such an—" She grabbed the pillow and hurled it at my head.

I caught it one-handed without looking away. *"Careful, principessa."*

"Or what?" She shoved past me, all fury and motion, her shoulder slamming into my chest hard enough that I felt it. She snatched a tissue from the bathroom. *"Where the hell are we going anyway?"*

"Rome."

Her hand froze halfway to her face. *"What?"*

"You heard me. Father's orders. He wants you seen in public. Wants the engagement announced properly." I pushed off the doorframe. *"So get dressed. Something pretty. You're going to smile and pretend you're not miserable."*

I watched her process it, the realisation that she had no choice, no say, no way out. The fight drained from her eyes, replaced by something worse.

Resignation.

"Of course," she whispered.

I should have left then. Instead, I stayed in the doorway, watching her grab clothes from the closet with shaking hands.

"You have eight minutes now," I said, and left before I could do something stupid like apologise.

*

Rome should have been beautiful.

The late afternoon sun painted the ancient streets gold, tourists flowing around us like water around stones. The air smelled like espresso and fresh bread and centuries of history.

Instead, we walked in hostile silence.

Dakota's camera hung around her neck, and she clicked it constantly — capturing everything except me. Every angle deliberately excluded me from the frame. Every shot a small act of defiance.

"You done playing photographer?" I asked after she stopped for the fifth time to shoot some meaningless fountain.

"I'm working."

"You're stalling."

"Maybe I just don't want to walk next to you." She didn't look up from her viewfinder. *"Ever think of that?"*

"Every second, piccola. Trust me."

She finally lowered the camera, and the look she gave me could have stripped paint. *"Don't call me that."*

"What? Little one?" I stepped closer, crowding her space. *"Does it bother you?"*

"Everything about you bothers me."

"The feeling's mutual."

We stood there on the cobblestones, tourists flowing around us, locked in our mutual hatred like it was the only honest thing between us.

Then someone called my name.

"Lorenzo!"

I knew that voice. Fuck.

Demitry was weaving through the crowd, that easy grin already plastered on his face, expensive sunglasses pushed up into his dark hair. Of course. Of all the streets in Rome, he had to be on this one.

"Cugino," I said flatly.

He clasped my shoulder, pulling me into one of those half-embraces that were all show. Then his eyes slid past me to Dakota, and I watched his expression shift into something I recognised too well.

Interest. The predatory kind.

"And who is this?"

"No one," I said at the same time Dakota said, *"Dakota."*

Demitry's grin widened. He took her hand — just took it, smooth as silk — and pressed a kiss to her knuckles that lasted a second too long.

"Bellissima," he murmured, eyes never leaving hers. *"Demitry. Lorenzo's cousin."*

Dakota actually smiled. At him. A real smile, the first one I'd seen since she'd signed that contract.

It made something dark and ugly unfurl in my chest.

"He doesn't mention much," she said, cutting her eyes at me. *"I'm starting to think he doesn't mention anything."*

"Lorenzo? Mention things?" Demitry laughed, his thumb brushing across her knuckles before he released her. *"He's been a closed book since we were boys. Some things never change."*

I stepped closer, inserting myself into their moment. *"We're busy, Demitry."*

"Busy? In Rome?" He spread his hands, still focused entirely on Dakota. *"Impossible. The city is meant to be savoured, not rushed. You must let me show you the real Rome, bellissima. Not whatever grim tour Lorenzo has planned."*

"We're fine," I said, my voice dropping into something harder.

"I'd love that," Dakota said at the exact same time, chin lifting in challenge.

Demitry laughed, delighted. *"Trouble in paradise?"*

"There's no paradise," Dakota muttered, but she was still looking at him. Still smiling like he was fresh air after being locked in a tomb. Like he was everything I wasn't.

My jaw clenched so hard I felt my teeth grind. *"We have plans."*

"Plans can change, cugino." Demitry's eyes found Dakota's again, warm and inviting. *"What do you say? Have you seen the Trevi Fountain?"*

"No, actually." She glanced at me, something defiant and reckless in her expression. *"Sure. Beats whatever he had planned."*

I smiled — cold and sharp enough to cut. *"Lead the way then, cousin."*

But when Demitry turned, already chattering about the fountain's history, I caught Dakota's elbow. My fingers wrapped around the bare skin just above her wrist, and I felt her pulse jump.

I leaned in close, my mouth nearly touching her ear. *"Don't get comfortable with him."*

She yanked her arm free, leaving my hand empty and still warm from her skin. *"Jealous?"*

"Of Demitry?" I let my eyes drag over her slowly, deliberately. *"Hardly."*

"Could've fooled me." She walked ahead, falling into step beside Demitry like they were old friends, leaving me standing there like an idiot.

And when she took his arm — her fingers curling around his elbow, her body angled toward his — I made myself look away.

I followed behind them through the winding streets, watching Demitry make her laugh, watching her come alive in a way she never did with me. Every smile she gave him felt like a blade between my ribs.

I told myself I didn't care.

I was a shit liar.

The Trevi Fountain was packed with tourists, all of them throwing coins and taking photos and believing in fairy tales.

Demitry kept Dakota close, one hand hovering at the small of her back — not quite touching but claiming the space anyway. She didn't pull away. Didn't tell him to fuck off the way she did with me.

She was listening — actually listening — her head tilted in that way she never did when I spoke. Like his words mattered. Like she wanted to hear them.

"The legend says if you throw a coin over your left shoulder, you'll return to Rome," Demitry was saying, voice pitched low and intimate. He pressed a euro into Dakota's palm, his fingers lingering against her skin. *"Make a wish, bellissima."*

She turned toward the fountain, and I watched her close her eyes for just a second before she tossed the coin over her shoulder. It arced through the air, catching the light, and disappeared into the water with a small splash.

"What did you wish for?" Demitry asked, leaning in like they were sharing secrets.

Dakota glanced back at me — just a flicker, so fast I almost missed it. *"If I tell you, it won't come true."*

"Ah, but I can guess." Demitry's smile turned knowing. *"Freedom, perhaps?"*

Her smile faltered. *"Something like that."*

That was it. That was fucking it.

I stepped forward, inserting myself between them with enough force that Demitry had to step back. *"We need to go."*

"Already?" Demitry's eyebrows rose, but there was something sharp in his eyes now. He knew exactly what he was doing. *"But we just got here."*

"Now."

Dakota crossed her arms, and I could see the fight building in her. *"You don't get to just—"*

"Actually, I do." I turned to Demitry, my cousin, my blood, and let him see exactly how done I was with his little game. *"Appreciate the tour, cugino, but we have a dinner reservation."*

"We do?" Dakota said flatly, eyes boring into mine.

"We do now."

Demitry laughed, but it had an edge now. *"Lorenzo, when did you become so possessive? I'm just showing the lady around."*

"The lady is my fiancée."

Dead silence.

Dakota's eyes went wide, then furious. I'd just announced it publicly, made it real in a way the contract hadn't.

"Fiancée?" Demitry's smile sharpened, turning calculating. *"Lorenzo, you devil. You kept this quiet."*

"Not anymore." I grabbed Dakota's wrist, my fingers wrapping around it tight enough to feel her pulse hammering. *"We're leaving."*

"Get your hand off me," she hissed.

"Walk."

I didn't stop until we were three blocks away, tucked into a narrow side street away from the crowds. Away from Demitry's knowing eyes and Dakota's fake smiles.

Dakota ripped her arm free the second we stopped, her skin flushed with anger. *"What the hell is wrong with you?"*

"What's wrong with me?" I stepped closer, backing her against the weathered stone wall. *"You were practically throwing yourself at him."*

"I was being nice! You should try it sometime."

"Nice." I laughed, bitter and harsh. *"That's what you call it? The way you were looking at him? Taking his arm? Letting him touch you?"*

"He was being a gentleman. More than I can say for you."

"A gentleman." I braced one hand on the wall beside her head, the other by her shoulder, caging her in. *"He was working up to asking for your number. Probably your room key too. That's who Demitry is. That's what he does."*

"So what if he was?" She lifted her chin, defiant even now, even trapped. *"At least someone wants—"*

She cut herself off, but too late.

At least someone wants me.

The words hung between us like a confession.

"You think I don't—"

I stopped. My breath was coming too fast. I was too close to her, close enough to see gold flecks in her eyes, close enough to smell her perfume mixing with the Roman evening air.

"You don't what, Lorenzo?" Her voice was softer now, confused. *"Finish the damn sentence for once."*

The sun was setting, painting the alley in gold and shadow. She looked impossibly beautiful trapped between my arms and the wall — beautiful and furious and completely untouchable.

And I wanted to touch her so badly it felt like violence.

"You want to know what I think?" I leaned in until my forehead almost touched hers. *"I think you smiled at him because you knew it would piss me off. I think you let him flirt with you because you wanted me to react. And I think it worked."*

"That's not—" But her breath hitched.

"I think," I continued, voice dropping lower, rougher, *"that you hate me so much you'd let my cousin charm you just to prove a point. Just to show me you have choices."*

"I do have choices."

"No." I let my hand slide from the wall to her jaw, tilting her face up to mine. *"You don't. Neither of us do. And that's the problem."*

Her pulse was racing under my thumb. *"Then why do you care who I smile at?"*

"Because—" The word came out jagged. *"Because you're mine now. I didn't ask for this. I don't fucking want this. But you signed that contract, and so did I, and until one of us is dead or free, you're mine. Not Demitry's. Not anyone else's. Mine."*

"I'm not a thing you can own."

"No." My thumb brushed across her bottom lip, and I felt her sharp intake of breath. *"You're so much worse than that. You're a complication. A liability. And I don't trust you. But I don't trust him near you even more."*

"Why?" The word was barely a whisper.

"Because I know him. I know what he sees when he looks at you — an in. A weakness. A way to get under my skin." I pulled back slightly, let my hand drop. *"And it's working."*

"Maybe I want it to work."

"Then you're more naive than I thought." I pushed off the wall, putting space between us before I did something we'd both regret. *"Demitry doesn't want you. He wants to win. And you're just the prize in whatever game he thinks we're*

playing."

"*And what about you?*" Her voice was hollow now. "*What do you want?*"

You. To not want you. To go back to before your father walked into our lives. To stop seeing your face every time I close my eyes.

"*To survive the next two years without killing anyone,*" I said instead. "*Including you.*"

"*How romantic.*"

"*This isn't a romance, principessa. It's a sentence. For both of us.*"

She pressed her lips together, and I could see her trying not to cry again. Trying to be strong. It made me feel like the monster I was.

"*We're going back to the villa,*" I said, gentler than I meant to.

"*Of course we are.*" Her voice cracked. "*Because God forbid you actually finish a sentence. God forbid you ever tell me what you're really thinking.*"

I'm thinking you looked beautiful in the sunlight. I'm thinking I wanted to break Demitry's hand when he touched you. I'm thinking I'm going to hell for dragging you there with me.

I started walking. After a moment, I heard her footsteps behind me — reluctant, angry, but following.

Always following, because she didn't have a choice.

Neither of us did.

And maybe that's what I hated most — not her, but the fact that I was starting to want her to follow me for a different reason entirely.

The drive back was silent.

Dakota pressed herself against the passenger door like she could merge with it, camera clutched in her lap, staring out the window at the darkening countryside. I kept my hands on the wheel, knuckles white, trying to strangle the steering wheel instead of my own thoughts.

The lady is my fiancée.

I'd said it like a brand. Like a declaration of ownership. And the look on her face — shock, then fury, then something that looked almost like betrayal — had been seared into my brain for the entire drive back.

"*You had no right,*" she said finally, her voice cutting through the silence.

"*I had every right.*" The words came out sharper than I meant. "*You're going to be my wife."*

"Only on paper." She turned to glare at me, and even in profile I could see the fury radiating off her.

"That's all that matters."

"To you, maybe."

"To everyone." I flicked my eyes to her for just a second — long enough to see her flinch. *"Or did you think Demitry was being friendly out of the goodness of his heart? He saw an opportunity. A way to get under my skin. And you let him."*

"He was treating me like a person instead of a—"

"Instead of what?" My voice dropped, something dark and vicious crawling up my throat. *"Instead of what you are? My father's solution to your father's problem? A debt paid in flesh?"*

The words hit her like a physical blow. I watched her turn back to the window, saw her blink hard against tears she was trying to hide.

Christ. I was a bastard.

"You're a bastard," she whispered, like she'd read my mind.

"And you're stuck with me, principessa." The endearment came out like a curse. *"So you might as well stop looking at other men like they're your way out. There is no way out."*

Silence crashed back down, thick and toxic.

The rest of the drive passed like that — her pressed against the door, me gripping the wheel, both of us trapped in the consequences of our choices.

When we reached the villa, I'd barely slowed down before she yanked her seatbelt off and shoved the door open.

"Dakota—"

But she was already out, stumbling onto the gravel in her rush to get away from me. I watched her walk faster toward the house, shoes crunching on stone, not looking back.

I parked properly and followed her inside.

She was already halfway up the marble staircase when I entered the foyer. Taking the steps two at a time like the house was on fire.

"Dinner is at eight," I called up to her, my voice echoing in the cavernous

space. *"You're expected. My mother made sure the kitchen prepared something."* I paused, letting that land. *"She's been asking about you. Don't make me explain your absence."*

Dakota stopped on the landing.

I watched her grip tighten on the bannister — not the reaction I expected. Not anger this time. Something more complicated crossed her face, something almost like curiosity breaking through the fury, before she shut it down.

"I'm not hungry."

"That wasn't a request."

She turned slowly to look down at me from the landing, and whatever question she'd been about to ask about my mother died behind her eyes, replaced by the easier armour of contempt.

"You know what, Lorenzo?" She smiled, all teeth and no warmth. *"Go to hell."*

Then she turned and walked away with measured steps — not running, because that would give me the satisfaction.

Her door slammed hard enough that I heard it from the entrance hall.

I stood there for a long moment, staring up at the empty landing, waiting for the satisfaction of winning that round.

It didn't come.

Instead, there was just the echo of that slam and the memory of her voice: *Go to hell.*

I was already there, principessa. Had been since the day I'd agreed to this.

I pulled out my phone and typed a message to Demitry:

Stay away from her. This isn't a request.

His response came immediately:

Possessive and in denial. This is going to be fun to watch, cugino.

I shoved the phone back in my pocket and headed to my study instead of upstairs. Put distance between myself and her closed door before I did something stupid like knock. Like apologise.

Like tell her the truth — that watching Demitry touch her had made me want to break things. That I'd dragged her away not because of duty or appearances, but because I couldn't stand the way she'd smiled at him.

That she was right. I was a bastard.

But at least I was an honest one.

I poured myself a drink and stared out the window at the dark countryside, trying not to think about my mother setting a place at the dinner table for a girl who was currently locked in her room hating everything about this house.

She'd have to meet her eventually. They both knew it. The whole household knew it.

Tomorrow, probably. Or the day after.

Whenever Dakota stopped running long enough to stand still.

I tried not to think about the way she'd looked at me on those stairs — like I was both the problem and the only person who might understand it.

Good.

She should hate me.

She should lock me out.

Because I was starting to realise that the monster she needed protection from wasn't Demitry.

It was me.

5

Chapter Five: Dakota

The silence in the car was suffocating.

I kept my eyes on the window, watching Rome blur past in streaks of amber streetlight. Lorenzo's hands gripped the steering wheel like he was trying to strangle it, knuckles white, that silver ring catching the light every time we passed under a lamp.

The lady is my fiancée.

He'd said it like a threat. Like a brand. Like a declaration of war. And for half a second before those words, I'd seen something crack through that cold mask — something dark and possessive and completely dangerous.

Jealousy.

The humiliation of it burned like acid, being claimed in front of Demitry like I was property, like Lorenzo had every right to put his hands on me and mark his territory. I wanted to claw the feeling off my skin.

"You had no right," I said finally, my voice cutting through the silence.

"I had every right." His accent sharpened the words into weapons. "You're going to be my wife."

I turned to glare at his profile, all sharp angles and clenched jaw in the dashboard light. "Only on paper."

"That's all that matters."

"To you, maybe."

"To everyone." His eyes flicked to me for just a second, dark and burning.

"Or did you think Demitry was being friendly out of the goodness of his heart? He saw an opportunity. A way to get under my skin. And you let him."

"He was treating me like a person instead of a—"

"Instead of what?" Lorenzo's voice dropped dangerously low. "Instead of what you are? Your father's debt. My father's solution. A problem dressed up in pretty packaging."

The words hit like a physical blow.

I turned back to the window, blinking hard against the sudden burn behind my eyes. I would not cry. Not in front of him. Not again.

"You're a bastard," I whispered.

"And you're stuck with me, *principessa*." The endearment landed like a curse. "So stop looking at other men like they're your way out. There is no way out."

The rest of the drive passed in toxic silence.

When we reached the villa, I didn't wait for him to park properly. The second he slowed enough, I yanked my seatbelt off and shoved the door open, stumbling out onto the gravel.

"Dakota—"

I walked faster, shoes crunching on stone, not looking back. The villa loomed above me — cream stone and golden windows. Beautiful and hateful. My prison wearing the face of paradise.

I made it through the front door and headed straight for the stairs, taking them two at a time.

"Dinner is at eight," Lorenzo called from below, his voice echoing off the marble. "You're expected."

"I'm not hungry."

"That wasn't a request."

I stopped on the landing, gripping the bannister until my knuckles ached. Slowly, I turned to look down at him.

He stood at the bottom of the stairs, arms crossed, face carved from ice. But his eyes — those hazel eyes, were burning.

"You know what, Lorenzo?" I smiled, all teeth and no warmth. "Go to hell."

I turned and walked to my room with measured steps. Not running. Running would give him the satisfaction.

I slammed my door hard enough to rattle the frame.

For a long moment I stood there breathing hard, waiting for him to follow. Waiting for his footsteps on the stairs, for his fist on the door, for him to make good on whatever unspoken threat was simmering between us.

Nothing.

Just silence.

I locked the door and sank onto the bed, heart still hammering.

Then I started planning.

He wanted to break me down, make me compliant, turn me into another possession. But I'd survived eighteen years with a gambling addict for a father. I could survive Lorenzo Marchetti. I just had to be smarter.

The bathroom. We shared a water heater, old villa, old plumbing. Run a bath long enough and there'd be no hot water left for his precious morning shower.

His study. All dark wood and obsessive order. I'd seen him adjust a pen on his desk three times until it was perfectly aligned.

The kitchen. Coffee at seven every morning, I'd already clocked the routine. Good beans and regular beans in identical containers, side by side.

It was petty. Childish. Probably stupid.

Perfect.

A knock on my door pulled me back.

"Miss Phillips? Dinner will be served in one hour."

The housekeeper. Maria, I thought.

"I'm not coming down."

A pause. "Mr. Lorenzo said—"

"I don't care what Mr. Lorenzo said."

Silence. Then retreating footsteps.

I grabbed my camera and scrolled through today's shots. The fountain. The cobblestone streets. The way afternoon light fell across ancient stone.

And Demitry, laughing at something I'd said, warm and genuine and nothing like the cold contempt I got from Lorenzo.

He wanted to fuck you, Dakota.

I stared at Demitry's smile for a long moment. Then deleted it.

Twenty minutes later, another knock.

"Miss Phillips. Dinner is ready."

"I said I'm not coming."

"Mr. Marchetti is waiting."

"Then Mr. Marchetti can wait a little longer." I turned on music, American pop, bright and obnoxious and nothing like this house. Not too loud. Just loud enough to make a point.

A pause. "I'll inform Mr. Marchetti of your… decision."

The way she said it made my skin prickle. Like I'd just signed my own death warrant.

My phone buzzed. Unknown number.

I should have let it go to voicemail.

"Hello?"

"Dakota." Lorenzo's voice, cold and sharp. "Get downstairs."

I sat up straighter. "Are you seriously calling me from inside the house?"

"I'm giving you one chance to do this the easy way."

"Or what? You'll break down my door? That'll look great in front of the staff."

A dark laugh, humorless and cutting. "The staff work for my father. They'll do what they're told and forget they saw anything. They've forgotten worse."

The casual certainty of it sent ice crawling down my spine.

"I'm not one of your soldiers. You can't order me around—"

"You signed a contract."

"Under duress!"

"You signed." His voice dropped lower, something coiling beneath the surface. "Which means you follow the rules. Family dinners. Dutiful fiancée. You do what you're told."

"Then I guess I'm breaking the rules."

I hung up.

My hands were shaking as I set the phone down. I'd just hung up on Lorenzo Marchetti in his own house. The man who'd threatened my father's fingers. The man who'd warned me that defiance had consequences.

The man whose touch I could still feel on my throat.

He didn't come.

Fifteen minutes passed. Then thirty.

I started to think maybe I'd won this round.

Then my door handle rattled.

"I know you're in there, *principessa*." His voice was too calm. Too controlled. "This is childish."

I stayed silent, heart hammering.

"Fine." A pause. "Stay in your room. Skip dinner. But tomorrow? No more access to the grounds. No camera privileges. That garden you were so interested in, every door stays locked. You'll stay in this wing. This room, if necessary."

I yanked the door open.

He was leaning against the opposite wall, arms crossed, expression maddeningly calm. He'd changed, still all black, but a fitted t-shirt now, sleeves pushed up to show tattoos snaking down his forearm. His hair was slightly mussed, like he'd been dragging his hands through it.

His eyes, though. Banked fire. Waiting for oxygen.

"I hate you," I said clearly.

Something flickered across his face, too fast to catch. "The feeling's mutual, *americana*."

"Then why do you care if I come to dinner?"

He pushed off the wall and closed the distance between us until I had to tilt my head back to meet his eyes. Close enough that I caught his cologne, and underneath it, cigarettes and something darker.

"Because my father expects it." His voice was low, intimate in its threat. "Because appearances matter. Because whether you like it or not, you're part of this family now. Which means you play by our rules."

"And if I don't?"

His hand came up. I flinched back. But he only tucked a strand of hair behind my ear, fingers barely grazing my skin. The gentleness was somehow worse than any threat would have been. worse than any threat.

"Then you'll wish you had." He let his hand fall. "You think locking your door keeps you safe? *Piccola*, I have keys to every room in this house. The lock is a courtesy. Don't mistake it for protection."

"Is that a threat?"

"It's a promise." He stepped back and I could breathe again. "Now. Walk downstairs with me like a civilised person, or I carry you down over my shoulder. Either way, you're coming to dinner."

I believed him. That was the terrifying part, I completely believed he'd do it.

"Fine," I bit out.

"Good girl."

The words sent a shiver down my spine that had nothing to do with fear.

We walked to the dining room in hostile silence, his hand hovering at the small of my back — not quite touching, but close enough that I felt the heat through my shirt.

The dining room was dimly lit, candles casting dancing shadows. Two places set — close, intimate. A couple's dinner that neither of us wanted.

Lorenzo held out a chair.

I took the other one.

A muscle jumped in his jaw. He sat down with infuriating grace, like nothing I did could truly touch him. But I'd seen that flash. I filed it away.

Small victories.

The food was excellent, pasta in a cream sauce, fresh bread, wine that probably cost more than my camera. Under different circumstances, I might have loved it.

Now it tasted like ash.

"Demitry will call," Lorenzo said.

I looked up. "What?"

"My cousin. He'll try to contact you." He swirled his wine, watching me over the rim. "When he does, you won't answer."

"You don't get to tell me who I can talk to."

"Actually, I do. No unsupervised contact, that's part of the arrangement." His smile had edges. "Including charming cousins playing hero."

"The arrangement where you bought me."

His eyes flashed. "The arrangement where your father's debt was forgiven. Where your mother gets to keep breathing." A beat. "Or shall I let my father handle it the traditional way? One phone call."

The threat sat between us, quiet and absolute.

"At least Demitry smiled at me," I said. "At least he treated me like I was worth talking to. Like I was more than a problem to be solved."

Lorenzo's grip tightened on his glass. For a second I thought it might shatter.

"You want pretty lies?" His voice was flat. "Sweet words? That's not what I am. This—" He gestured between us. "—this is reality. Demitry's charm is a game. This is honest. I don't like you. You don't like me. But we're stuck, so we might as well stop pretending otherwise."

"Fine. I don't like you."

"I don't like you either."

"Great."

"Wonderful."

We stared at each other across the candlelight, and the air between us felt electric — charged with anger and something else I refused to name.

By dessert, tiramisu I barely tasted, the fight had drained out of me. Too tired to even maintain my anger properly.

"We're going to have to do better than this," Lorenzo said, quieter now.

"Excuse me?"

"This. The hostility. The defiance." He leaned back, studying me. "It won't work long-term."

"Then let me go."

"Not an option."

"Then this is what you get." I held his gaze. "You want me to smile and play pretend? Give me a reason to."

Something moved across his face. "My father is watching. The staff are watching. Eventually we'll need to present a united front."

"For you or for me?"

"Both." A pause, and for just a moment, something almost human crossed his expression. "You think I wanted this? A wife? Especially one who looks at me like I'm the devil himself?"

"Then why agree to it?"

"Because—" He stopped. Jaw tight. Then he stood abruptly. "This conversation is over."

"Typical. Walk away when it gets real."

His chair scraped back. Suddenly he was beside me, hand on the back of my chair, mouth at my ear.

"You want real?" His voice came out rough. "Real is that I could have said no. Let my father deal with your family. Walked away clean. I didn't." A breath. "Real is that I'm trying to keep you alive in a world that would swallow you whole. Real is that every time you push back, you make it harder for both of us."

The warmth of his breath against my skin. The tension radiating off him, fury held by the thinnest thread.

"So forgive me," he said, voice dropping to something almost raw, "if I don't have pretty words. If I can't pretend this is anything other than what it is. A nightmare. And we're trapped in it together."

He pulled back.

I stood on shaking legs. "Thank you for dinner. Let's never do this again."

I walked out before he could answer. Before the tears tightening in my throat could escape.

Made it to my room before the shaking caught up with me.

I locked the door and slid down to sit on the floor, back against the wood, and waited for my heartbeat to slow.

Through the door, footsteps. Stopping just outside. Standing there.

Then Lorenzo's voice, so quiet I almost missed it:

"Lock's still there, principessa. Use it."

His footsteps retreated down the hall.

I sat in the dark with my fingers pressed to my throat, where he'd touched me that first day, and tried to remember why I hated him.

It was getting harder.

Tomorrow I'd swap his coffee beans. Tomorrow I'd remember he was the enemy. Tomorrow I'd rebuild my walls.

But tonight, sitting on the floor with his words still in the air — *I'm trying to keep you alive* — I let myself wonder if maybe the monster was more complicated than I'd thought.

Then I remembered the casual violence in his eyes. The cold contempt. The way he'd called me a complication like I was furniture.

No. He was still the monster.

I just had to keep reminding myself of that.

6

Chapter Six: Lorenzo

The shower was cold. Not cool. Not lukewarm. Fucking freezing.

I stood under the spray for exactly five seconds before slamming my palm against the tile hard enough to hurt. "*Cazzo,*" I muttered, shutting it off.

We'd replaced the water heater two years ago specifically because the old one couldn't handle the whole villa. This wasn't a malfunction. This was deliberate.

I dried off with rough movements, jaw so tight I felt my teeth grind. I pulled on black pants and a black shirt, skipping the tie. It was barely seven AM, three days since Dakota had arrived in Rome, and I was already fantasizing about wringing someone's neck. Someone with defiant eyes and an American accent.

The bathroom mirror was fogged. I wiped a clear spot and caught my reflection—dark circles I couldn't hide, tension in my shoulders I couldn't shake.

I hadn't slept. I kept replaying the way her pulse had jumped under my hand last night when I'd tucked her hair back. The way I'd stood outside her door for a moment too long, listening to the silence on the other side.

I shook my head, dispelling the thought. What she felt was irrelevant. What I felt was even more irrelevant.

*

I headed downstairs to the kitchen. Maria was already working, humming softly as she prepped vegetables.

"*Buongiorno*, Lorenzo. Your coffee?"

"*Per favore*." I moved to the espresso machine, then stopped. My single-origin Ethiopian blend—shipped from a specialty roaster in Milan—was gone.

"Maria. Where are the coffee beans? The ones in the blue bag."

Understanding dawned on her weathered face. "Ah. The *signorina*… she made coffee earlier. She said she needed the best we had. I believe she used the whole bag."

I found the bag in the trash. Empty. Eight hundred euros worth of coffee used for a single morning. The regular beans sat untouched on the counter, mocking me.

I made my espresso with the cheap shit, each movement controlled. I didn't break anything. I just stood there while the machine hissed, feeling my irritation build into something darker.

This was war. And Dakota Phillips had just fired the first shot.

Something was off the moment I entered my study.

The books on the shelf—alphabetical yesterday—were now sorted by color. A fucking rainbow of spines transitioning from red to blue. My pens were on the wrong side of the desk. My chair had been lowered by exactly half an inch.

I pulled up the security footage and scrolled back to 6:30 AM. There she was: Dakota, in pajama shorts and an oversized shirt, hair messy. She'd moved with methodical precision, testing the chair height herself to make sure it was *just* annoying enough.

Then she'd smiled—small and satisfied.

I should have been furious. I *was* furious. But underneath it, something else stirred. Admiration. Most people in her position would be crying in their rooms. Dakota was choosing to fight.

It was reckless. Ultimately futile. But I could respect the impulse.

My phone buzzed around nine. Demitry.

"*Cugino*! Is married life not agreeing with you?"

"Fiancée. And it's complicated," I snapped.

"She's beautiful, Lorenzo. But does she know what she's gotten into? Because she seemed quite unhappy yesterday. And unhappy wives have a tendency to look for sympathy in the wrong places."

The implied threat was clear. "If I find out you've so much as sent her a fucking emoji, we're going to have a problem," I said, my voice dropping an octave.

"Possessive," he chuckled. "I'm just making sure you're not making a mistake. We both know how your father handles mistakes."

I hung up. Demitry wasn't wrong—Dakota was a liability. Every moment she spent resenting me was a moment she might do something catastrophically stupid.

Around two, a message came from Maria: *The signorina tried to access the east garden. Found it locked. She seemed very upset.*

I stared at the screen. I hadn't locked it. My mother's garden was the one place on this property that felt alive. It was wild, overgrown with the roses she had planted before her health began to fade. Now, she rarely left her suite in the north wing, but the garden remained her sanctuary.

I typed back: *Why is it locked?* Maria: *Your father had it locked. Security concerns.*

My father didn't miss anything. He'd seen Dakota with her camera and decided she was getting too comfortable.

At five, I found myself standing outside the garden gate, keys in my hand. Dakota's camera would have captured the golden hour light here perfectly. I was sliding the key into the lock when a cold, measured voice stopped me.

"Lorenzo."

My father stood at the end of the corridor, hands clasped behind his back. "The American girl. She's been mapping exits. Learning the layout."

"She's taking photographs, Father."

"She's a risk. I saw the footage from yesterday. The way you looked at her—that is not the look of a man doing his duty." He stepped closer. "The garden stays locked. Her camera stays in her room after six PM. And you will attend dinner with her every night until I'm convinced she understands her position."

"And if she asks why?"

"Tell her the truth." He smiled. "That guests don't get keys."

He walked away, his footsteps echoing. I stood there, staring at the roses my mother used to tend. Dakota would have seen the beauty in the abandonment.

I could unlock it now. But fighting my father over Dakota would mean admitting she mattered.

And she couldn't matter. Not yet.

Back at my desk, I pulled up the security footage from 2:00 PM. I watched her reach the gate, hopeful. She tried the handle twice, then just stood there, fingers wrapped around the iron bars, staring at the flowers she couldn't reach.

She didn't cry. She just looked at something beautiful she couldn't have. Then she walked away, and the hope died in her eyes.

I closed the laptop and poured a drink. I told myself I'd done the smart thing. I told myself I didn't care that I'd just watched something break inside her.

I was getting better at lying to myself. But not good enough.

7

Chapter Seven: Dakota

I woke up smiling, but by 10:00 AM, the smile was dead.

Lorenzo hadn't just retaliated; he'd reconstructed the villa's physics to spite me. Breakfast had arrived at 6:45 AM. The garden was padlocked. Even Maria looked at me with a pained, "inventory-purposes" apology when I asked for a snack.

It was the fourth day of my life in Rome, and I was starving, bored, and seeing red.

I'd spent the afternoon in his study, a reckless ten-minute heist with a hairpin and a pounding heart. I didn't just want to move his pens today. I wanted to draw blood. I found a manila folder marked *Confidenziale* and shoved three heavy, stamped documents under my shirt.

Now, sitting in my room as the sun began to dip, I felt the first chill of regret. The Italian words, *Contratto, Urgente,* looked terrifyingly official.

A sharp knock at the door made me jump, nearly knocking the stolen papers off the bed.

"Signorina?" It was Maria. "Mr. Lorenzo and his father are expecting you downstairs in twenty minutes. For dinner."

My stomach did a nervous flip. "Dinner? I usually eat in here."

"The Master has requested your presence. And… the Signora will be joining as well."

The Signora. Lorenzo's mother.

I shoved the documents deep under my mattress, my hands shaking. I'd wanted a war. It looked like I was getting a formal invitation to the front lines.

*

The dining room was a cavern of marble and gold, lit by a chandelier that looked heavy enough to crush a car.

Lorenzo was already there. He looked… wrecked. His black shirt was untucked, his hair a mess, and his eyes were vibrating with a frequency that made the hair on my arms stand up. Beside him sat a man who could only be his father, Alonzo—a statue of a man with eyes like polished flint.

But it was the woman at the head of the table who stopped my breath.

She was frail, her skin like fine porcelain, but her eyes were the exact shade of Lorenzo's—a dark, haunting amber. She wore a silk shawl and watched me with a curiosity that felt unnervingly kind.

"Dakota," Lorenzo said. His voice was a serrated blade. He didn't look at me; he looked *through* me. "Sit."

"Bianca," the woman whispered, reaching a thin hand toward me. "Please. Sit by me, child."

"This is my mother," Lorenzo said, his jaw clenching so hard I heard the bone pop. "Mother, this is Dakota Phillips."

The dinner was a nightmare of clinking silver and suffocating silence. Lorenzo's father watched me like I was a bug he was considering stepping on. But every time I looked at Lorenzo, I saw him sweating. He looked like he was dying.

"You look pale, Lorenzo," Alonzo remarked, cutting into a piece of veal. "Something weighing on your mind? A loss, perhaps?"

Lorenzo's glass hit the table with a crack. "Nothing I can't handle, Father."

He turned his gaze to me. It wasn't hatred. It was *terror*. Pure, unadulterated fear. He knew the papers were gone. He knew if his father found out he'd lost a Russian contract because his "fiancée" was playing games, blood would be spilled before the dessert course.

"Dakota," Lorenzo said, his voice dropping to a whisper that didn't reach his father. "A word. In the hall. *Now*."

He practically dragged me into the corridor, slamming the heavy oak doors shut. He pinned me against the cold stone wall, his hands braced on either side of my head.

"Where are they?" He didn't scream. It was worse. It was a death-rattle whisper.

"Where are what?" I tried to lift my chin, but my knees were water.

"Don't fucking play with me! Not here! Not with him behind that door!" He leaned in, his forehead dropping to rest against mine. He was shaking. Lorenzo Marchetti was actually shaking. "The Russian contracts. The originals. If they aren't on my desk in five minutes, my father won't just lock your garden, Dakota. He will bury you in it. And he'll put me right next to you."

The air left my lungs. "I… I didn't know. I thought they were just business papers."

"Everything is business!" He gripped my shoulders, his fingers digging in. "You want to hurt me? Fine. Burn my clothes. Break my car. But don't touch the family's lifeblood. You have no idea what these people do to men who lose their signatures."

I saw it then—the world he lived in. It wasn't a game of "rearranging pens." It was a ledge, and I'd just pushed him off it.

"Under my mattress," I whispered.

He exhaled a breath that sounded like a sob of relief. He stayed there for a second, his face inches from mine, his eyes dark with a mix of fury and something that felt dangerously like a plea.

"Go to your room," he rasped. "Lock the door. Do not come out until I tell you."

"Lorenzo—"

"Lock it, Dakota! For your own sake." He looked back at the dining room doors, where his mother and father sat. "Because if I have to choose between my father's wrath and protecting you again, I don't know if I can do it twice."

I turned and ran. I didn't stop until I heard the click of my lock.

Downstairs, the Signora would be waiting for her dinner to continue. But in my room, staring at the empty space under my mattress where I'd just handed over my only leverage, I realized the war had changed.

I wasn't a prankster anymore. I was a liability.

And in Lorenzo's world, liabilities didn't get to grow old.

57

8

Chapter Eight: Lorenzo

I made it three steps down the hallway before I had to stop and press my palm against the cold, indifferent marble of the wall.

My hand was shaking.

I stared at it, my own goddamn hand, trembling like an amateur who'd never handled pressure. I'd killed my first man at nineteen without a flicker of hesitation. I'd sat through interrogations that would make a priest weep. But Dakota Phillips had undone me in a five-minute confrontation in a hallway.

"I hate you." "I know."

The words were a blood-oath between us now. But as I stood there, the silence of the villa ringing in my ears, I could still smell her—that scent of vanilla and defiance. I could still feel the phantom heat of her body pressed against the stone where I'd pinned her. My entire world had narrowed down to the pulse hammering in her throat and the terrifying realization that I hadn't wanted to pull away.

I'd wanted to sink into her. To let the war consume us both.

"Cazzo," I breathed, pushing off the wall.

I forced myself toward my father's study. The three documents were clutched in my hand like evidence of my own failure. Downstairs, the dinner had ended in a suffocating tension that only a Marchetti household could produce. My mother had been led back to her wing, her haunting

58

amber eyes lingering on me with a pity that felt like a physical weight. My father, Alonzo, was waiting.

I didn't knock. I walked in, laying the recovered contracts on his desk.

Alonzo didn't look up immediately. He finished his grappa, the ice clinking against the glass—a sound that usually signaled someone was about to lose a limb. When he finally looked at me, his eyes were flat and arctic.

"Missing," he said, his voice a low vibration. "You told me they were *missing*, Lorenzo. And then you produce them in the middle of a family dinner like a magic trick. How does a Russian contract vanish from a locked study?"

"Dakota took them. She picked the lock."

The silence that followed was heavy enough to crack the floorboards. My father stood, moving with the predatory grace of a man who had never known a day of peace. He picked up the primary contract, his thumb brushing over the signatures.

"The American girl," he mused. "Your fiancée. A girl who has been in this house for four days and has already compromised our most sensitive security. Do you understand the implications, *figlio?*"

"She didn't know what they were. She was playing a game of retaliation for the garden—"

"This is not a game!" Alonzo slammed the glass down, the amber liquid splashing onto the desk. "Ignorance is not a shield; it's a liability. If those signatures hadn't been found—if the Calabrians thought we were mishandling their business—blood would be on the floor before morning. Yours, likely."

He stepped into my space, his presence a suffocating shadow. "You're letting emotion cloud your judgment. You look at her and see a beautiful girl. I look at her and see a leak. A crack in the foundation. One that needs to be filled with cement."

"I'll increase security," I said, my jaw clenching so hard I felt the bone pop. "Additional cameras. Restricted access. She won't leave her wing without an escort."

"That is a start. But it isn't a lesson." Alonzo's eyes narrowed. "She needs to understand that in this family, we don't pick locks. We don't steal. And we certainly don't embarrass the Master at his own table. Perhaps a night in the cellar would clarify her perspective? Or a more… physical reminder of her place?"

A violent, possessive snarl rose in my throat, barely suppressed. "No. She is my responsibility. I will bring her under control my way."

Alonzo studied me, his gaze calculating. He saw the tension in my shoulders. He smelled the perfume on my shirt. A slow, cruel smile touched his lips. "You're protecting her. Why? Is the contract suddenly more than business to you?"

"I'm protecting the arrangement," I lied, the words tasting like ash. "If we break her too soon, she's useless to us. We need her compliant for the wedding, not traumatized."

"Fine," Alonzo said, turning back to the window. "You have one week. One week to turn that wild animal into a Marchetti wife. If she steps out of line again—if she so much as breathes the wrong way—I handle it. And my way leaves marks that never fade. Understood?"

"Understood."

I left the room, the air in the hallway feeling suddenly thin.

I didn't go to my bedroom. I went back to my study—the room she'd violated. It felt different now. The books were still sorted by color, a rainbow of defiance that mocked my need for order. I sat in the chair she'd lowered, the height making me feel off-balance, and pulled up the security feed.

I told myself I was checking the perimeter. I told myself I was looking for security gaps.

But I clicked the feed for her room.

She was there. She hadn't gone to bed. She was sitting on the floor with her back against the door I'd told her to lock, her knees pulled to her chest. In the grainy infrared light, she looked like a ghost. Her shoulders were shaking.

She was crying.

I watched her for an hour. I watched her until my eyes burned and the guilt in my stomach turned into a dull, throbbing ache. I'd spent my life watching people—watching for lies, watching for weapons, watching for weaknesses. But watching Dakota Phillips fall apart in the dark was the most difficult thing I'd ever done.

I reached out, my finger tracing the outline of her shadowed figure on the monitor. I could see the way her hair fell over her face, the way she tucked her hands into her sleeves for warmth. She looked so young. So misplaced among the marble and the blood-stained history of this villa.

I'd justified the cameras. I'd called them a security measure. But as I watched her sob into her knees, I knew the truth.

I was obsessed.

I was addicted to the way she looked at me with pure, unadulterated hatred, because at least it was *something*. It was better than the hollow, terrified stares of the women my father usually brought around. Dakota was fire, and even as she burned my world down, I wanted to stay in the heat.

Lock your door, I'd warned her.

The lock was for her. But it was also for me. Because some nights, the man I was supposed to be—the cold, calculating heir, lost the war to the man who wanted to break down that door and promise her the world just to see her smile.

I closed the laptop with a sharp snap, the screen going black.

One week.

I pulled a key from my desk drawer, the key to the east garden. I looked at it for a long time, the cold metal biting into my palm. I wouldn't give it to her today. I couldn't. Not after what she'd done.

But as I stood up and walked to the window, looking out at the roses she couldn't reach, I realized I was no longer just her captor. I was her shield.

And in seven days, I would either have to break her myself, or watch my father do it for me.

I knew which one I'd choose. And I knew she'd hate me for it even more.

9

Chapter Nine: Dakota

Five days.

I hadn't spoken to Lorenzo in forty-eight hours, not since the night of the stolen documents, when he'd backed me against a stone wall and looked at me like he wanted to either devour me or delete me from existence.

The villa had become a game of shadows. I'd see him disappearing around corners or hear the growl of his BMW at midnight. But today, something had changed. I walked to the east garden, expecting the usual resistance of the heavy iron gate.

It swung open with a silent, well-oiled glide.

No explanation. No note. Just the roses, the fountain, and the freedom of the one place he knew I wanted. It wasn't an apology, Lorenzo Marchetti didn't seem the type—but it was a white flag.

"Signorina?" Maria appeared at the garden archway. "The Signora Bianca is in the sunroom. She requests your presence for a fitting."

"A fitting?" My stomach tightened.

"The wedding is in two weeks, Signorina. There is much to be done."

Two weeks. The anchor dropped in my chest, heavy and cold.

The sunroom was filled with ivory lace and the scent of expensive lilies. Bianca sat in a high-backed chair, looking elegant in cream silk, though her hands trembled slightly as she adjusted her pearls. She looked like a queen whose throne was made of glass.

"Dakota," she said, her voice warm but thin. "Come. The seamstress is waiting."

For two hours, I was pinned and tucked. Bianca watched with a keen, hauntingly familiar gaze—Lorenzo's eyes, but softened by decades of whatever this life did to a woman.

"You're very quiet, *cara*," Bianca said as the seamstress moved away to fetch more pins.

"It's a lot to take in," I managed, staring at my reflection in the floor-to-ceiling mirror. I looked like a bride. I looked like a lie.

"Lorenzo is quiet, too," she murmured. "He hasn't slept. I hear him pacing in the wing above mine. He thinks he is being subtle, but I am his mother. I see the way he looks at the security monitors. I see the way he tenses when your name is mentioned."

She stood slowly, walking over to adjust the lace on my shoulder. "He is fighting something he doesn't understand. And when a Marchetti man cannot control something, he becomes… difficult."

"He's obsessed with control," I whispered.

"No," Bianca corrected gently, her eyes meeting mine in the mirror. "He is obsessed with *you*. And that is far more dangerous for a man like him."

Dinner that night was a staged performance for Alonzo.

The air in the formal dining room was so thick with tension I could barely swallow the wine. Lorenzo sat across from me, a silhouette in all black, his jaw covered in a rough shadow of stubble. He looked exhausted. He looked like he was vibrating at a frequency that could shatter the crystal chandelier.

He didn't look at me. Not until his father spoke.

"The wedding preparations are on schedule," Alonzo remarked, cleaning his blade with a napkin. "The Calabrians and the Russians will both be in attendance. It will be a show of absolute unity."

"Unity," Lorenzo repeated, his voice like gravel. He finally looked up, his hazel eyes locking onto mine.

It was a collision. My heart hammered against my ribs, an erratic, panicked rhythm. For four days, we'd stayed apart, but the proximity was a match tossed into a room full of gasoline.

"Lorenzo," Bianca said softly, sensing the shift. "Perhaps you could take Dakota to the Borghese Gallery tomorrow? She needs to see something of Rome besides these walls."

"The gallery is closed," Lorenzo said, his voice flat. A blatant lie.

"It is not," Bianca frowned.

"It is for us," Lorenzo snapped, his eyes never leaving mine. "She stays here. It's safer."

Alonzo's eyes sharpened. "Safer for her? Or for your focus, Lorenzo?"

Lorenzo's glass hit the table with a crack. "Excuse me."

He stood and walked out, his footsteps echoing like gunshots.

I found him twenty minutes later. I was heading to my room when I saw the door to his study ajar. I should have kept walking. I should have remembered the documents, the threats, the cold showers.

But I stopped.

He was standing by the window, his back to me, his hands buried in his pockets. The room was dark except for the glow of the security monitors on his desk.

One of the screens showed my bedroom. Empty.

"Why are you watching an empty room, Lorenzo?" I asked, my voice trembling.

He spun around. In the dim light, he looked wrecked. His tie was gone, his top buttons undone. "You shouldn't be here, Dakota."

"You unlocked the garden."

"It was a mistake." He stepped toward me, and I didn't move. I couldn't. "Everything in the last five days has been a mistake. My father is right. I'm distracted. I'm compromised."

"Because of me?"

He laughed, a harsh, jagged sound. He was in my space now, his heat radiating off him in waves. "Because I can't stop checking the feeds to see if you're breathing. Because I can't sit at a table with you without wanting to flip it over just to get to you. Because I'm losing my goddamn mind."

"Then let me go."

He grabbed my arms, his grip firm but not hurting. He leaned in, his forehead dropping against mine. "I can't. That's the problem. I'm obsessed, principessa. And in my world, obsession is a death sentence."

He smelled like sandalwood and desperation.

"Lock your door tonight," he rasped, his breath ghosting over my lips. "Lock it and don't open it. Because I'm at the end of my rope, and if you stay out here… if you look at me like that for one more second…"

"What?" I whispered.

"I won't be the one protecting you anymore," he growled. "I'll be the one you need protection from."

He let me go so abruptly I stumbled. He turned back to the window, his shoulders shaking with the effort of restraint.

I ran to my room and turned the lock. The click was the loudest sound I'd ever heard.

I was in trouble.

10

Chapter Ten: Lorenzo

I hadn't slept in five nights.

Every time I closed my eyes, I saw the security feed. Dakota sitting in the garden, her knees drawn to her chest as though she could make herself small enough to disappear. Dakota pacing her room in the dark hours before dawn, her bare feet silent on the marble floors. Dakota's dark hair spilled across white pillows, her face slack with a sleep that looked more like surrender than rest. I was becoming a ghost in my own home, haunted by a girl who occupied the room directly across the hall and every corner of my mind I had no business letting her into.

My father's warning from three days ago rang in my ears like a funeral bell: *"You have one week to bring her under control. Or I handle it my way."*

I knew what his way looked like. I had seen it. I would not let that happen to her.

The clock was ticking. And then, my mother's text arrived.

Charity gala tonight. You and Dakota. 7pm. The emerald dress is in her room. No arguments. — M

My mother, Bianca, was the only person in the world who could command me with a single text and receive instant obedience. She understood optics the way a general understands terrain. She knew that with the wedding only ten days away, the city was already whispering. Hiding Dakota made her a victim; showing her off made her a Marchetti. And a Marchetti, above

66

all else, did not hide.

At 6:45 PM, I stood outside her door. I was wearing the armor of my world — a black tuxedo, sapphires at my wrists, my hair slicked back with ruthless precision. I looked like a prince. I felt like a man walking toward a firing squad.

I knocked.

The door opened, and whatever I had been preparing to say dissolved completely.

The emerald green dress should have been illegal. It was off-the-shoulder, exposing the elegant line of her neck — the same neck I had felt pulsing with terror and defiance beneath my hand only days ago. The silk clung to her curves and pooled at her feet like a forest of shadows. She had done something simple with her hair, a few dark strands left loose to frame her face, and she wore no expression I could easily read. She looked composed. She looked furious beneath that composure. She looked like she could walk into that gala and own every room she passed through.

She looked like she belonged to the night. She looked like she could ruin me without even trying.

"You're staring," she said. Her voice was flat, controlled, but her pupils were blown wide.

"The car is waiting," I rasped, my voice sounding like it had been dragged over gravel. I caught her wrist as she stepped forward — barely a touch, a ghost of a contact — and felt the electric spike of her pulse jump against my fingertips. I made myself release her. "You look beautiful, Dakota. Whatever you feel about tonight, whatever you feel about me, set it aside. Don't flinch. Don't pull away. My father is watching. The entire city is watching. Tonight, you are mine."

She looked up at me, and something moved behind her eyes — not submission, never submission, but calculation.

"I am a prisoner," she whispered.

I leaned in, close enough that my breath grazed her ear, close enough that I could feel the warmth radiating off her skin. "Tonight," I said quietly, "you are a queen. Act like it."

*

The gala at the Palazzo Borghese was a blur of flashbulbs and predatory smiles, of champagne flutes catching chandelier light and old money pretending it had never had blood on its hands. I kept my hand anchored to the small of her back all evening, my fingers splayed over the silk of her dress. It was a claim. A warning broadcast to every man in that room. She belonged to me, or so the story went. She played her part with a precision that impressed and unnerved me in equal measure, laughing at the right moments, tilting her chin at exactly the correct angle when the cameras turned our way.

I was starting to think I had underestimated her entirely.

And then Demitry appeared.

"Lorenzo." My cousin materialized from the crowd with a champagne flute in hand and a smirk that made my knuckles ache. "And the enchanting Dakota."

His eyes didn't simply look at her. They mapped her, slow and deliberate, the way a man surveys something he intends to acquire. He reached out and let his fingers graze her arm, a touch that lasted two seconds too long, casual enough to be dismissed, deliberate enough that I felt my vision narrow.

"That dress," Demitry said softly, "is a sin. It almost makes me wish I'd bid higher for your father's debt."

The world went red.

I took his wrist. My grip was tight enough to feel the small bones shift beneath my fingers, tight enough to watch the color drain from his face even as his smile held. "Don't touch her," I said. Very quietly. "Don't look at her. Don't breathe near her again."

"Possessive," Demitry chuckled, though his eyes had gone careful. "Careful, cousin. People are starting to notice you've lost your cool."

He was right. I could feel my father's gaze from across the room — cold, dispassionate, cataloguing the scene with the detached interest of a man watching an experiment go wrong. I released Demitry's wrist and turned to Dakota, my pulse loud in my own ears.

"We're leaving."

*

The cool night air hit us like a slap. The moment the car door closed and the city noise fell away, Dakota pulled her arm from my grip and turned on me, her eyes lit with something beyond anger.

"What was that?" she demanded. "You acted like a maniac."

"He touched you." The words came out stripped of everything I usually kept carefully in place. "I've spent five nights trying not to think about you, trying not to cross a hall I have every right to cross, and he simply puts his hand on you as though you're—"

"Property?" She threw the word like a stone. "I *am* property, Lorenzo. You bought me."

"I didn't buy you." I leaned across the seat before I could stop myself, one hand braced against the leather beside her head, the space between us shrinking to something dangerous. The scent of her perfume and the heat radiating from her skin made clear thinking nearly impossible. "I am trying to keep you alive. I am trying to keep my father from breaking you in ways I cannot undo. And I am trying — God help me — to keep myself from doing exactly what I'm doing right now."

She held my gaze. Didn't flinch. "Which is what?"

"This," I said, and I held still. I didn't close the distance. I couldn't — not yet, maybe not ever, with nine days left before a wedding I hadn't wanted and was now beginning to want desperately and for entirely the wrong reasons. But I stayed there, close enough to feel her breathe, close enough to watch her pupils swallow the green of her eyes and the hard line of her defiance soften into something that looked terrifyingly like hunger.

"Lock your door tonight, Dakota," I said quietly. My voice broke slightly on her name. "Because if I hear that lock turn, I won't walk away again. And we are only nine days from a wedding neither of us chose."

I pulled back. Told Marco to drive. Kept my eyes on the city lights sliding past the window.

I was completely, utterly finished.

11

Chapter Eleven: Dakota

I didn't sleep.

Every time I closed my eyes, I saw Lorenzo's face when Demitry touched my hand. The way his jaw had locked into a jagged line, the sudden, ink-black eclipse that had swallowed the warmth in his eyes. He hadn't just been angry; he'd looked like a man watching someone try to steal the air from his lungs. I could still feel the phantom vibration of the air around him—that static charge of a predator about to strike—when he'd snapped his hand around Demitry's wrist.

His voice outside my door: *"I hate that I want—"*

And me, pressed against the heavy oak of Alonzo's study, breathing in the scent of old paper and expensive cigars, hearing things meant to stay in the shadows.

The way you look at her. Remove the temptation entirely. You're obsessed with this girl.

The words looped in my mind, a scratched record skipping on the most dangerous notes.

Around six a.m., I gave up. I kicked off the silk covers and stared at the ceiling, at the frescoes that likely cost more than the house I grew up in.

Lorenzo was jealous. Not the petty, "who-are-you-texting" kind of jealous. This was something primitive. Primal.

And the worst part? I'd liked it.

70

God, what is wrong with me? I hated him. I hated the digital eyes of the cameras that followed me, the way he'd rewritten the map of my life without a single "please." He'd moved me like a chess piece across a board I didn't even know we were playing on.

But last night, seeing that crack in his armor… feeling his hand clamp onto my lower back, staking a claim that felt both possessive and desperately fragile…

I'd felt a spark of power. For the first time since I stepped foot in this villa, I had something he couldn't hack, buy, or intimidate.

He wanted me.

The realization was a cocktail of sickness and exhilaration. Because wanting him back—even a flicker, even a heartbeat of it, felt like a betrayal of the girl I used to be.

By eight, I was showered and dressed, staring at my phone as if it were a ticking bomb.

Mom had texted again.

Sweetheart, I miss you. Can we talk soon? Your father says you're adjusting well. I hope that's true. I worry about you all alone in Italy. Please call when you can. Love you. - Mom

I drafted a reply five times. Deleted it five times.

What was I supposed to say? *Hey Mom, I'm great. I'm being held captive by a man who looks at me like I'm a religious experience he's trying to debunk. I'm surrounded by marble and murderers, and I'm pretty sure I'm losing my mind. How's the weather in the States?*

I threw the phone onto the bed. It bounced on the duvet, silent and useless.

A knock made me jump, my heart hammering against my ribs.

"Signorina?" Maria's voice was a soft anchor. "Signora Bianca asked me to remind you about lunch. She's waiting in the east sitting room."

I'd completely forgotten the gala invitation. "Give me five minutes."

Bianca was a vision in cream linen and pearls, looking like the human embodiment of "old money." She had Lorenzo's eyes, but where his were cold obsidian, hers were dark coffee—deep, but capable of warmth.

She stood as I entered, a mischievous glint in her gaze. "Dakota. I was worried Lorenzo might try to lock the doors today."

"Does he know?"

"That we have lunch? Yes." She adjusted her leather clutch. "That I'm taking you out of the villa and into the city? He'll find out when he checks his GPS. Which should make for a very loud evening."

"Should I be worried?"

"About my son's temper?" She smiled, though it didn't quite reach her eyes. "Always. But today, we are ghosts. He can't catch what he can't see."

We left through a side service entrance, slipping into a sleek Mercedes driven by an older man named Giorgio. As the villa shrank into a cream-colored speck on the Roman hillside, I felt a physical weight lift off my chest.

"You're not what I expected," Bianca noted, her eyes scanning my face with surgical precision.

"What did you expect? Someone more… broken?"

"Broken. Defeated. A girl who has cried herself into a shadow." She tilted her head. "But you aren't a shadow, are you? You're a fire. You're angry."

I didn't have a word for what I was. *Angry* felt too small.

"Good," she said, her voice turning to steel. "Broken women are consumed by this family. Angry ones survive. Angry ones learn to bite back."

"Is that what you are? Angry?"

Her smile turned wistful, distant. "I was. Once. A long time ago." She watched the ancient Roman ruins blur past the window. "Now I've just… adapted. I've made peace with the geometry of my cage."

"How long have you been married to Alonzo?"

"Twenty-eight years. I was nineteen. My father had a gambling debt that outpaced his soul, so I became the currency."

My stomach curdled. "Just like me."

"Just like you." She reached over, her hand cool and steady on mine. "But I am still here, Dakota. I am still myself. I have simply learned which battles are worth the blood, and which are just noise."

"Does it get easier?"

"No. But you find the cracks in the walls. You find the things they can't touch." She paused, her voice dropping an octave. "Lorenzo is not his father. I need you to hear that."

"He's still my jailer."

"He is. But Alonzo sees you as a ledger entry. A transaction. Lorenzo sees you as…" She trailed off, a pained look crossing her face. "I don't think he knows yet. Which makes him dangerous. Men like him—men who have been taught that control is the only safety—they don't handle the 'unknown' well. And you, cara, are a vast, terrifying unknown."

Lunch was in Trastevere, at a place so tucked away it felt like a secret. Three other women were already there—Gabriella, Francesca, Isabella. They were polished to a high shine, their diamonds catching the light, but there was a common thread in their eyes: a hollow, haunted stillness.

The wine was poured, the questions asked. *How did you meet? Is he treating you well?*

They spoke in a coded language of sighs and knowing glances. When I told them it was a "business arrangement," the tension in the air shifted from curiosity to a heavy, shared grief.

"Find something that is yours," Francesca whispered halfway through the meal. "Something he cannot reach. I paint. It's terrible, but it's mine. Isabella has her garden. Bianca has her charities."

"What about your husbands?" I asked, the red wine making my tongue reckless. "Don't you have them?"

The silence that followed was a physical thing.

"We have marriages," Isabella said, her voice like cracking glass. "We have partnerships. But *have* them? No, Dakota. We survive them."

"And if fighting doesn't work?" I pressed.

"Then you get smarter," Gabriella said, her smile as sharp as a razor. "You find their soft spots. You make yourself the only thing that soothes their demons. You make them need you more than they need the control."

I felt a chill. They weren't talking about love; they were talking about psychological warfare.

The drive back was quieter. Bianca bought me gifts along the way—a silk scarf, a book of poetry, a bracelet that felt like a set of golden handcuffs, however beautiful.

"Lorenzo has spent his life trying to be the perfect weapon for his father," Bianca said as we climbed back toward the villa. "He was taught that softness is a death sentence. And then you walked in and broke his rhythm."

"I'm not trying to break him. I just want my life back."

"I know. But freedom and whatever is growing between you… they might not be able to live in the same room."

We pulled up to the main entrance. Lorenzo was there.

He wasn't pacing. He was perfectly still, a stone statue against the sunset. But his shoulders were drawn tight, and his hands were curled into white-knuckled fists at his sides.

"Looks like someone missed you," Bianca murmured. "Go easy on him. He's not as strong as he looks when it comes to you."

I stepped out, my shopping bags feeling like lead.

"You left," he said. His voice was a low, vibrating hum—not quite a shout, but the sound of a storm held back by a crumbling dam.

"Your mother invited me."

"You should have told me."

"She did tell you."

"You should have asked." He stepped down, his eyes like scorched earth.

"Asked permission?" I climbed the steps, meeting him halfway until we were chest-to-chest. "I'm not a dog you leave in a kennel, Lorenzo. I don't need a leash."

"You were out of my sight for five hours."

"I was with your mother. You were tracking my phone anyway. You knew exactly where I was. Don't pretend this is about safety."

His jaw worked, a muscle jumping in his cheek. "You don't understand the risks—"

"I understand that you panicked," I snapped. "Because for five hours, you couldn't dictate the air I breathed. You hate that you can't control my every heartbeat."

He didn't move. He didn't blink. He just stared at me with a look so raw it made my skin itch. I pushed past him, heading for my wing, but his footsteps trailed me—heavy, rhythmic, relentless.

"Dakota, wait."

"No!" I spun around. "I'm done. I'm tired of being a prisoner and I'm tired of your 'protection' being a cage."

He grabbed my wrist, not to hurt, but to anchor me. He spun me toward the wall, caging me between his arms. His breathing was jagged, his eyes wide and frantic.

"I thought you'd gone," he whispered, the words sounding like they were being torn out of his throat. "I checked the cameras and the room was empty. I thought you'd finally found a way out and you were just... gone."

The vulnerability in his voice was a physical blow.

"Would you have let me go?"

"No." No hesitation. "I would have hunted you to the ends of the earth."

"Then you're the problem, Lorenzo. You can't claim you're worried about me when you're the one holding the keys."

"It's about control," I whispered, my face inches from his. "Admit it."

"Fine," he rasped, his eyes dropping to my lips before snapping back to mine. "It's about control. Because control is the only thing that keeps the world from falling apart. And without you in this house, the world feels like it's ending."

He slammed his hand against the wall beside my head, the sound echoing through the hall. He was caging me in, but he was the one who looked trapped.

"I hate you," I breathed.

"I know."

"This is never going to work."

"I know that, too." His gaze was a fire, hot enough to burn. "We are completely, irreversibly fucked."

He looked like he was going to kiss me—or break. Instead, he ripped himself away, his shadow retreating down the hall like a wounded animal.

I collapsed against my door, sliding down until I hit the floor.

I'd wanted perspective today. I'd wanted a way out. Instead, I'd realized that the women in Rome weren't just survivors—they were prisoners who had learned to love the bars.

And Lorenzo? He wasn't just my captor. He was a man drowning in an obsession he didn't have the tools to survive.

Something was going to break soon. I just didn't know if it would be the cage, or us.

12

Chapter Twelve: Lorenzo

I watched her sleep.

I wasn't in the room, I hadn't crossed that final threshold into total madness yet, but the line between "security" and "stalking" was a blurred smear on the horizon.

I sat in my office at 2:00 a.m., the amber glow of expensive whiskey my only company. On my laptop screen, Dakota was a study in silver and shadow. This was the feed from the camera she didn't know existed. I'd installed it myself, a secondary eye hidden in the molding of her ceiling. The standard security feeds weren't enough. I needed to see the rise and fall of her chest. I needed to see the way she looked when the armor of her anger finally cracked.

She'd cried.

It lasted five minutes. I'd watched her sink to the floor, her knees pulled to her chest, her small frame shaking with silent, jagged sobs. She'd wiped the tears away with a ferocity that made my own chest ache—furious at her own heart for leaking.

Then she'd washed her face, climbed into bed, and stared at the ceiling until sleep claimed her.

She'd broken my heart without even knowing I was watching.

I replayed the footage of her crying three times. Was it the lunch? Was it the poisonous things the other wives had whispered over wine? Or was it me?

"I don't know how to let you go."

I shouldn't have said it. I'd handed her a live grenade with the pin pulled. I'd let her see the rot underneath my control, the way she had dismantled twenty-six years of Marchetti discipline with nothing but a defiant look and a camera bag.

My phone buzzed. A text from Marco: *Everything okay? Need anything for morning security?*

All fine, I typed back. *Standard protocols.*

Liar. Nothing was fine. I was unravelling. I'd missed three payment deadlines for the Calabrian contract because I'd been busy zooming in on the way the sunlight hit the back of Dakota's neck in the garden. I was a liability. A "compromised man," as my father liked to say.

And my father didn't keep liabilities around for long.

"Close the door," Alonzo Marchetti said.

His study was a tomb of dark wood and the smell of ancient sins. Even at 2:17 a.m., he looked as though he'd just stepped out of a board meeting. He didn't have circles under his eyes. He didn't have a cracked laptop screen. He had only a cold, predatory focus.

"The Calabrians called," he began, his voice like dry leaves. "They're concerned about your focus, Lorenzo. They say you're... distracted."

"I'm handling it."

"Are you?" He leaned into the light. "Because you've tracked that girl's phone seventeen times in twenty-four hours. You've installed unauthorized cameras. You've threatened Demitry in public." He stood, his shadow stretching across the floor like a shroud. "Dakota Phillips was a business transaction. A tool to leverage her father. But you've turned her into a weakness."

"She's my responsibility."

"She's my asset. One you are currently mismanaging." He walked to the window. "I'm giving you a choice. Either you regain your composure immediately, or I find a Marchetti who can."

My blood turned to slush. "What does that mean?"

"Demitry called me. He thinks the girl is… spirited. He's offered to take the engagement off your hands. He believes he can provide the 'stability' you're currently lacking."

The world tilted. The thought of Demitry's hands on Dakota—the thought of him in her room, in her bed, breaking that fire until only ash remained— triggered a roar of violence in my gut so loud I thought the windows might shatter.

"Dakota is engaged to me," I said, my voice a lethal whisper.

"She is engaged to whoever I designate. Two weeks, Lorenzo." My father's eyes were flat, merciless. "Two weeks to prove you can lead this family without being led by your dick. Two weeks to show me you aren't compromised. If you fail, the contract transfers to Demitry. And you get to watch him have what you were too weak to keep."

I stood in the hallway after the door clicked shut, my hands shaking so violently I had to shove them into my pockets.

Two weeks.

I went back to my office and checked my second phone. A message from Demitry was already waiting.

Heard about the ultimatum, cugino. Two weeks is generous. She's beautiful when she's angry, isn't she? Such a waste of fire. I look forward to the wedding.

I threw the phone. It hit the wall and died.

On the screen, Dakota shifted in her sleep. Peaceful. Untouched.

I reached for the laptop, my finger hovering over the "Disable" button for her bedroom camera. My father was right. This was pathetic. This was the behavior of a man who had already lost. I should turn it off. I should prove I could function without seeing her.

I hit the button. The screen went black.

I lasted four hours.

At dawn, with the sun bleeding rose-gold over Rome, I turned the feed back on.

She was sitting up, staring at her phone with an expression of such profound longing it made my throat tighten. She was looking at a world that didn't include me.

I can't let him have her.

The realization wasn't a romance; it was a war cry. I didn't care if it made me a monster. I didn't care if I was proving my father right.

I pulled out my spare phone and messaged Marco: *Change of plans. Dakota doesn't leave the villa. No visitors. Increase surveillance on all exits. And I want to know the second Demitry tries to contact her.*

I paused, my heart drumming a frantic, possessive rhythm.

Also, install more cameras. Library. Dining room. The gym. I want every angle covered. I don't want her out of my sight for a single second.

Dakota would hate me for this. She would rage, she would fight, she would call me a tyrant.

But she would be safe. She would be *mine.*

Fourteen days.

I'd burn the world down before I let the clock hit zero.

13

Chapter Thirteen: Dakota

I knew the world had shrunk the moment I tasted the air.

It felt heavy. Stagnant. Like the villa had exhaled and forgotten to breathe back in. My breakfast tray sat on the floor outside my door, cold coffee, eggs congealing under a silver dome. No Maria. No polite morning chatter. Just a silent, silver "stay put."

I grabbed my phone. A text from Bianca: *Lunch this week? Thursday?*

Relief surged—a temporary exit visa. I typed back: *Yes! Where?*

The three dots appeared. Vanished. Appeared again, like a stuttering heartbeat.

Finally: *I will check with Lorenzo. He has... updated the protocols.*

The phone nearly slipped from my hand. *Updated the protocols.* That was Mafia-speak for "the cage just got smaller."

I threw on jeans and a t-shirt, yanking my hair into a ponytail with enough force to make my scalp sting. I didn't bother with makeup. I didn't need a mask; I needed a weapon.

I met Marco at the base of the grand staircase. He didn't look at me. His hand hovered near his holster, his posture rigid with an apology he wasn't allowed to voice.

"I'm going to the garden, Marco."

"Mr. Marchetti has requested you remain indoors, Signorina."

"Requested?" I stepped down to the final marble tier. "Then I'm declining the request."

I marched to the front doors—the massive, iron-reinforced oak portals that represented my only view of the world. I grabbed the handle and hauled.

Metal groaned against metal. The bolt didn't budge.

"It's deadbolted," Marco said softly. "Electronic override. From the office."

I spun around, my blood turning to liquid fire. "He locked me in. Like an animal."

"For your safety—"

"Where is he?"

"He's not to be disturbed—"

I didn't hear the rest. I was already a blur of movement, my sneakers squeaking against the polished floors. I didn't knock. I hit the door to Lorenzo's office with my shoulder, the wood slamming against the stopper with a crack that sounded like a bone breaking.

Lorenzo looked up. For a split second, the mask was off. He looked haggard—his tie loosened, his hair a chaotic mess of dark strands where he'd clearly been clawing at it. He looked like a man who had spent the night wrestling ghosts.

Then, the shutter clicked. His face went flat. Obsidian. "Dakota."

"Unlock the doors."

"No."

"You locked me inside a fucking house, Lorenzo!" I slammed my palms onto his desk, scattering a neat pile of dossiers. "What changed? What did I do?"

"You did nothing." He stood slowly, the movement graceful and deadly. "The world outside changed. I am simply adjusting the perimeter."

"Don't give me that corporate-killer bullshit. Yesterday I was in Rome. Today I'm in solitary confinement. Tell me why."

He walked to the window, his back to me. His silhouette was a sharp, dark blade against the morning sun. "There are threats. I am handling them."

"Is the threat Demitry?"

The silence that followed was heavy enough to crush lungs. I saw his shoulders lock.

"He wants you," Lorenzo said, his voice a low, gravelly rasp. "He's made his intentions clear to my father. And I will not have him near you."

"So you turn me into a ghost? You hide me away so you don't have to deal with him?"

"I hide you away so he can't *touch* you!" He spun around, the raw violence in his eyes making me flinch. "He's a scavenger, Dakota. He sees something I value, and he wants to take it to prove he can."

"Value?" I echoed, stepping closer. "You value me like a vintage car or a piece of land. This isn't about me. This is about your ego."

"You think this is ego?" He laughed, a hollow, jagged sound. "My father gave me an ultimatum last night. Two weeks. Fourteen days to prove I'm not 'compromised' by you. Fourteen days to show him I can manage this 'asset' with cold, Marchetti precision."

He moved around the desk, stalking toward me until I was backed against the leather chair.

"And if I fail? If I stay 'distracted'?" His voice dropped to a terrifying whisper. "He transfers the engagement. He gives you to Demitry. He lets my cousin break you just to teach me a lesson in focus."

The air left the room. I felt the floor tilt. "He'd... he'd give me to him?"

"To prove he can. To show me that nothing belongs to me unless he allows it." Lorenzo's hand came up, hovering inches from my face, trembling with a restrained urge to touch. "So yes. I locked the doors. I've doubled the cameras. I've turned this villa into a fortress. Because I would rather you hate me from inside these walls than have you smile at him from inside his."

"You're sick," I breathed, though my heart was traitorously thudding against my ribs.

"I'm compromised," he corrected, his gaze dropping to my mouth. "I can't sleep. I can't work. I spend my nights watching the feed of you sleeping because it's the only time you aren't looking at me like I'm a monster."

The confession felt like an execution.

"I'm not going back to my room," I said, my voice shaking but firm.

"Dakota—"

"You want to prove you aren't distracted? Fine." I dropped into the chair across from his desk, crossing my arms. "I'm staying right here. Every time you look up from your laptop, you're going to see exactly what you're trying to control. You want to manage the asset? Manage it. But don't think for a second that locking the door makes me yours."

Lorenzo stared at me, a flicker of something—admiration, terror, desire—passing through his dark eyes.

"You're going to make these two weeks hell, aren't you?"

"I'm going to make you regret every lock you turned."

A ghost of a smile touched his lips—sharp and sad. "Good. I'd be disappointed if you didn't."

He sat back down and opened his laptop. I pulled out my phone and stared at the blank screen.

The silence between us wasn't quiet. It was a countdown.

Fourteen days. The cage wasn't the villa anymore. It was the air between us, vibrating with the terrifying realization that we were both losing a war we hadn't even realized we were fighting.

14

Chapter Fourteen: Lorenzo

She stayed for three hours.

Dakota planted herself in the leather wingback chair like she was staging a sit-in, watching me with the detached curiosity of a scientist observing a dying nerve. I tried to work. I pulled up the Calabrian contracts, but the legalese looked like a foreign language. I missed half of two conference calls because I was too busy rhythmically counting her respirations.

The way her teeth caught her bottom lip. The way she smirked when she caught me staring. She was winning, and she was enjoying the spoils of war.

"You're on the same paragraph, Lorenzo," she said, not looking up from her phone. "Twenty-two minutes. I've been timing you."

I slammed the laptop shut. The sound echoed like a gunshot. "Are you enjoying this?"

"Watching you realize that 'locking the door' doesn't actually give you control? Immensely." She leaned back, her eyes sparking. "Is this the part where you tell me how focused you are?"

My phone buzzed. My father: *Status on the Calabrian revisions? I'm watching.*

"Daddy's checking in?" Dakota's voice dripped with a sarcasm that didn't quite hide the edge of anxiety underneath. "You have a look. Like a kid waiting to be hit."

The accuracy of it stung more than her anger ever had.

"Can I ask you something?" she continued, her voice dropping its shield. "What does the 'transfer' actually look like? Am I traded like a horse? Is there a ceremony, or do I just get loaded into a different car?"

The bitterness in her tone was a physical weight.

"There's a contract," I said, my voice tight. "Between our fathers. It specifies a Marchetti heir. It doesn't specify which one."

"So I'm debt repayment with a pulse." She laughed—a sharp, ugly sound. "And Demitry wants me because stealing me from you is the ultimate trophy."

"It's not a game, Dakota."

"No? Then why are you so terrified of him?"

I moved to the window, unable to look at her. I didn't want to give the monster a name, but she deserved to know what lay outside the walls.

"When we were kids, Demitry was the golden boy. Magnetic. I worshipped him." I looked out at the Roman hillside. "Then I saw what happened to the people he 'loved.' There was a girl… the daughter of an associate. After three months with Demitry, she stopped eating. She stopped speaking. I heard her through the walls of his villa once, begging her mother to take her away. She looked like a ghost with the skin still on."

I turned to find Dakota pale, her eyes wide.

"My father knows," I said. "Everyone knows. But Demitry is useful, so they look away. If I fail this ultimatum, my father will hand you to him without a second thought. He'll sign the papers, and you'll be Demitry's wife within the week."

The silence that followed was suffocating.

"So the locks," Dakota whispered. "The cameras. You're actually trying to protect me."

"Yes."

"That doesn't make it okay," she said, stepping closer until I could smell the floral scent of her hair. "But it makes it less simple."

"I don't know how to do this," I admitted, the truth bleeding out of me. "Keep you safe without caging you. Stop wanting you when wanting you is what makes me weak."

"Then let's call a truce," she said. "Stop trying to control my every breath, and I'll stop making your life a living hell. We survive the next twelve days. Then we figure out the rest."

I looked at my phone. My father's looming shadow. The ticking clock.

"Truce," I agreed. I pulled up the security app and, with a hand that wasn't quite steady, deleted the bedroom feed. "The bedroom camera is gone. Permanently."

She stared at the screen, then at me. "Surprisingly honest of you."

"I'm tired of lying to myself about what this is, Dakota. It's an obsession. I'm leaning into it."

Dinner was a masterclass in tension. We sat at opposite ends of the table, civil and silent, while my mother watched us with the eyes of a hawk.

"You're both very well-behaved," she noted. "Should I be calling a priest or a lawyer?"

"We're trying a new strategy," Dakota said. "It's called 'not committing murder.'"

After dinner, the summons came. My father's study.

"The Calabrian revisions were perfect," Alonzo said, not looking up from his desk. "Thorough. No errors. It seems you had a very… focused afternoon."

"I'm back on track."

"Are you?" He slid a black folder across the desk. "Milan. Tomorrow morning. Three days. You're handling the Rossi shipping contracts personally."

The trap snapped shut around my ankles.

"Three days away from the villa?"

"A test, Lorenzo. No contact with the girl. No texts. No calls. Prove you can function without her. Prove you aren't so addicted to her presence that you're useless in a boardroom." He smiled, and it was the coldest thing I'd ever seen. "If you can't handle seventy-two hours of separation, you've already lost her."

"I'll be on the 6:00 a.m. flight."

"Good. Because Demitry is already asking if he should start choosing a florist."

I walked out of the office on numb legs. Three days. Seventy-two hours without seeing her. Without knowing she was safe.

I stood in the hallway, looking toward her wing. I should tell her. I should say goodbye.

Instead, I went to my room and packed. I couldn't risk seeing her. If I looked into her eyes now, I wouldn't leave. I'd stay, I'd fail, and Demitry would win.

I pulled out my phone. I went to the hallway camera outside her door.

I watched the sliver of light beneath her frame and waited. I was supposed to be proving I wasn't obsessed.

I was failing before the flight even took off.

15

Chapter Fifteen: Dakota

He didn't even say goodbye.

I woke up to a villa that felt like an abandoned museum. The breakfast tray was there at 8:00 a.m., cold and clinical, but the air across the hallway was empty. No heavy footsteps. No scent of espresso and expensive tobacco. Just a hollow, pressurized silence that made my ears ring.

"Milan," Maria told me, her eyes fixed on a bouquet of white roses as though they might bloom into an explanation. "Mr. Marchetti left at six. He'll be away for three days."

Three days. Seventy-two hours of "freedom" that felt suspiciously like being forgotten. I checked my phone. Nothing. Not a text, not a warning, not even a set of instructions about what I was and wasn't allowed to touch.

I sent a text. *Three days in Milan and you couldn't mention it at dinner?* Read. 9:14 a.m. No reply.

The anger was immediate — a hot, white flash in my gut. But beneath it, a cold, oily slick of abandonment started to spread. It was a test. Alonzo was holding a stopwatch, and Lorenzo was proving he could stop breathing my air.

Day One was a fever dream of petty rebellions. I sat in his study with my feet on his mahogany desk. I used up all the hot water. I left my camera lying in places it didn't belong. Marco shadowed me like a silent, grieving ghost, but he didn't stop me.

"He's concerned about your safety while he's away," Marco said when I caught him watching me in the library.

"He has a funny way of showing it," I snapped. "Silence isn't protection. It's a vacuum."

Day Two was when the silence started to scream.

I woke before dawn without knowing why — some animal instinct reaching for a presence that wasn't there. The villa was too still. Too obedient. Even the light felt muted, coming through the curtains in flat, grey panels rather than the sharp gold I'd grown used to. I lay there for a long time, staring at the ceiling, telling myself the tightness in my chest was irritation. Just irritation.

It wasn't irritation.

I scrolled through our old texts with the dim screen pressed close to my face in the dark. Mostly commands. Snarky retorts. A handful of exchanges that had started as sparring and sharpened into something else — something I couldn't name without my pulse doing something stupid. I looked for a pulse in those messages and found only the ghost of one. Something that had been alive in the spaces between the words.

I got up. I made my own coffee badly, burning the milk because I'd never had to learn, and drank it standing at the kitchen window watching the garden go pale with morning. The roses were very white and very still. I thought about nothing. I was getting good at that.

Then Bianca arrived at noon with a bottle of prosecco and the eyes of a woman who knew exactly how much I was hurting.

She didn't say anything at first. She just set the bottle on the table, sat down across from me, and looked at me with that particular kind of patience that felt almost unbearable — the kind that said *I already know, you don't have to perform for me.*

"He's texted me twelve times," she said finally, sliding her phone across the table.

I looked down at the screen.

Is she eating?

Marco says she stayed in the library until 3 a.m. Why?

If Demitry calls, tell me immediately. I don't care what my father said.

My heart did a slow, painful roll in my chest. I pushed the phone back across the table like it had burned me. I didn't want to feel what I was feeling. It was too much like softening, and softening felt like losing something I needed to survive him.

"He's failing the test," I whispered.

"Spectacularly," Bianca agreed. She poured two glasses and pushed one toward me. "He doesn't know how to care about someone without trying to grip them until they bruise, Dakota. He's fighting his father, and he's fighting his own nature. And he's losing both because of you."

"I didn't ask for this."

"No one asks to be the sun," she said gently. "But everything else starts to orbit you regardless."

I stared at my glass. The prosecco caught the light and held it, and I thought about how exhausting it was to be wanted like this — wanted in the desperate, white-knuckled way Lorenzo wanted, like I was something he'd found after years of looking and couldn't bring himself to set down even when his arms were shaking. I thought about how it should have felt like power. How it didn't. How it felt more like responsibility, which was so much heavier.

"What does he think is going to happen?" I said. "He goes away, I wait quietly, he comes back and everything is the same?"

Bianca was quiet for a moment. "I think," she said carefully, "that he doesn't know what he thinks. He's never done this before. Any of it." She looked at me. "That doesn't excuse it. But it might explain it."

I didn't answer. I drank my prosecco and watched the garden and tried very hard not to count the hours.

Day Three was the breaking point.

I was in the garden, the sun hot on my neck, when my phone rang. An unknown number.

"Dakota." The voice was honey and broken glass. Demitry. "I heard the keeper is away. Must be lonely in that gilded cage."

My skin crawled. "How did you get this number?"

"I have my ways. I'm calling to remind you that there are other cages, bellissima. Ones with prettier views. Lorenzo is a man who thinks love is a deadbolt. I could offer you air. I could offer you a choice."

"You offer nothing but a different set of bars, Demitry."

"Do I? Think about it. When he comes back and locks that door again, remember my voice. Remember that I'm the one who didn't leave you behind to prove a point to a cold old man."

I hung up. My hands were shaking. Marco appeared at my elbow before I'd even drawn breath, his phone already raised to his ear. He didn't ask; he reported. His voice was low and clipped, and I watched the roses sway in the breeze while he spoke, counting the petals to keep myself from falling apart.

Five minutes later, my phone shrieked. Lorenzo.

"Are you okay?" His voice was stripped raw — no edges, no control, nothing between his fear and my ear. "Tell me exactly what he said. Every word."

I told him. I heard his breathing change as I spoke. Heavier. Slower. The deliberate, practiced restraint of a man crushing something with his bare hands.

"I'm coming back," he rasped. "Tonight. Fuck the meetings. Fuck my father."

"No." The word came out harder than I expected. I stood up straighter, looking at the high stone walls of the villa, the carved statues guarding the gate. "If you come back now, you lose. He'll see that I'm your weakness, and he'll give me to Demitry just to amputate the limb. You stay in Milan. You finish the test."

"Dakota, I can't — knowing he's circling you —"

"I'm safe. Marco is here. The doors are locked." My voice cracked somewhere in the middle and I pressed through it. "You're the one who told me those things matter, remember? So let them matter. Don't let him win because you couldn't stay away for one more day."

The silence on the line was a physical thing. I could feel him through it — leaning against a hotel window somewhere in Milan, eyes closed, jaw tight, fighting himself harder than he'd ever fought anyone else.

"You called me your captor," he said softly. The words sounded like they cost him blood.

"What else are you?"

"I don't know." A long pause. "But you're the only person who doesn't flinch when they see the monster. You're the only one who tells me the truth." His voice dropped lower. "One more day, Dakota. And then we talk. About the cameras. The rules. Everything."

I closed my eyes. The sun was still hot on my face. "I still hate you, Lorenzo."

"I know," he whispered. "I'm counting on it."

He hung up.

I sat in the garden until the shadows swallowed the roses whole. The sky went from gold to bruised violet to the deep, starless black of a night that felt sealed. Final. Like the end of something I couldn't name.

I missed him. It moved through me slow and shameful, this admission — a fever I hadn't consented to. A betrayal of everything I'd held onto to stay sane in this place. I missed the weight of him, the specific gravity of a man who took up space like the room owed him something. I missed the way he looked at me like I was a prayer he didn't know how to say. Like I was the answer to a question he'd never dared ask out loud.

It terrified me more than Demitry's voice ever could.

Tomorrow he'd be back. He'd walk through that door and the air would change again — thicken, charge, rearrange itself around him. And I would feel it. I would feel it in the way I always felt it, somewhere below the breastbone, like a key turning in a lock I hadn't known was there.

The truth settled over me quietly, the way the dark had settled over the garden. I wasn't just his prisoner anymore. I hadn't been for a while. We were both locked inside something of our own making now, something that had grown up around us while we were busy fighting, and I stood at the threshold of it and looked in and thought:

I wasn't sure I wanted the key.

16

Chapter Sixteen: Lorenzo

I failed.

The Rossi meeting wasn't just a setback; it was an execution. I'd sat in that mahogany-lined conference room in Milan, surrounded by men whose respect I'd spent a decade earning, and I couldn't remember a single goddamn number.

It wasn't nerves. I didn't get nervous. I'd closed deals in rooms that smelled like blood and old money, with men who'd put knives in backs they'd just finished patting — and I'd never once lost the thread. Numbers were the one language I'd always trusted. Immovable. Honest. Indifferent to feeling. I'd built my entire professional self on the fact that when everything else went sideways, I could still read a room, read a contract, and cut exactly where it needed cutting.

Milan took that from me in seventy-two hours.

Every time Giovanni Rossi spoke about shipping lanes, I heard Demitry's voice. Low and deliberate and aimed, like a man who knew exactly where the soft tissue was. Every time I looked at a contract, I saw the curve of Dakota's neck. The way she'd looked in the garden that last morning before I left — not watching me go, which would have meant something, but looking at the roses instead, with that particular kind of stillness that meant she was working very hard at feeling nothing.

I'd been doing the same thing across a conference table in Milan. Working

94

very hard at feeling nothing. Failing.

I agreed to lopsided terms just to end the meetings faster. I came across as a man with a ghost in the room — distracted, hollow, performing competence rather than embodying it. The Rossis are old enough and sharp enough to know the difference. I watched it register on Giovanni's face around the second afternoon: a slight recalibration, the way a predator adjusts its assessment of prey. He'd come in expecting Lorenzo Marchetti the machine. He left with the knowledge that Lorenzo Marchetti was a man with a leash, and that somewhere at the other end of it, a girl was pulling.

My father had a word for it. *Compromised.* He used it the way a surgeon uses a diagnosis — clean, clinical, without cruelty, which somehow made it worse. There was no anger in it. Just the flat arithmetic of a man calculating losses.

I'd spent the entire flight back to Rome confirming every calculation he'd ever made about me.

The drive from the airport was a blur of Roman outskirts and self-loathing.

I watched the city give way to stone walls and cypress trees and said nothing. The evening light was going amber and long, the kind of light that made everything look deliberate, like a painting of itself. I found it intolerable. I didn't want beauty right now. Beauty required a kind of openness I couldn't afford.

"She's in the garden," Marco said. His eyes found mine in the rearview mirror for just a moment — careful, measuring. "She's been there all afternoon. Watching the gate."

I looked out the window. "Did she speak to my father?"

"No. But she spoke to Demitry. And your mother." A pause. The kind Marco used when he was deciding how much to give me. "She's different, Lorenzo. Quieter. Like she's stopped fighting the house and started fighting herself."

I didn't answer. I pressed two fingers to the bridge of my nose and breathed out slowly through my teeth and told myself that the sensation moving through my chest was not relief. It was not the loosening of something that had been wound too tight for three days. It was nothing. It was tiredness.

It was the reasonable physiological response of a man who hadn't slept properly since Monday.

I didn't wait for Marco to kill the engine.

The villa rose up ahead of me and I was already moving, door open before we'd fully stopped, gravel crunching under my shoes. I went through the front entrance and didn't stop — past Maria, who said something I didn't catch, past the hallway table with its weekly flowers still fresh, past the study where I could see the light on my desk still burning the way I'd left it. Three days ago. Another life.

The French doors to the garden were ahead of me.

I stopped with my hand on the handle.

It was the first time I'd hesitated since I'd stepped off the plane. I stood there for a moment that felt longer than it was, looking through the glass at the garden going gold in the fading light, at the fountain, at the stone bench beside it. At her.

She was small inside an oversized sweater, the sleeves pulled down over her hands. Her camera sat in her lap but she wasn't shooting. She was just sitting, very still, looking at the gate — the same gate I'd just come through. Her face in profile was unguarded in a way I rarely got to see. No performance. No sharpness assembled for my benefit. Just Dakota, tired and pale and real.

I pushed through the door.

The gravel shifted under my step and she turned. Something moved across her face that she pulled back almost immediately — fast enough that I might have missed it if I hadn't been watching for exactly that. I had been watching for exactly that. I hated that I had been watching for exactly that.

I stopped ten feet away. It felt like miles. It felt, absurdly, like the only place in three days that had felt like standing still.

"Hi," she said. Her voice was a fragile thread pulled too thin.

"Hi."

The word came out softer than I intended. I let it. I was too tired to recalibrate.

I'd missed her. The acknowledgment moved through me like something breaking — clean, irrevocable, the specific crack of a thing that had been holding weight for too long. Three days. Three days of the most important meetings of the last fiscal year, and I had spent every second of them starving for the sight of a woman I had no business wanting the way I wanted her. I hated it. I hated what she'd made of me without even trying — without even *wanting* to. That was the part that made it so much worse. She hadn't done this deliberately. It had just happened, the way damage happens. The way weather happens.

The way I apparently happened to her, whether either of us chose it or not.

"Milan was a disaster," I said. My voice came out harsh. I didn't soften it. Harsh was honest. "I spent three days thinking about you instead of my work. I made mistakes that will cost millions. I proved my father right."

"Your mother showed me your texts," she said. Her fingers moved along the lens of her camera. "You were breaking the rules every hour to check on me."

"Because Demitry was circling." The words came out tighter than I intended, pressure behind them I hadn't fully accounted for. "Because you were here and I was there and I couldn't—" I stopped. The word I'd been about to say lodged in my throat like something foreign. *Protect.* I choked it off.

"You couldn't control me," she finished softly.

"Yes. No." I paced the gravel, the movement automatic — the body doing what the mind had always done when it ran out of clean answers. "I hated that when Marco called about Demitry, I wanted to burn down the city just to get back to you. I wanted to kill him for even having your number. I wanted to touch what's mine."

Her eyes flashed. The old fire, returning like a signal through static. She stood up and closed the distance between us until we were inches apart, and I felt the specific quality of her fury the way you feel weather changing — a shift in pressure, something that prickles along the skin.

"I am not yours, Lorenzo."

"Your father sold you. You live in my house. You eat my food. By every law in our world, Dakota, you belong to me."

"You're a bastard," she hissed.

"Yes," I said. "I know."

It wasn't a deflection. It wasn't performance. It was the flattest, most honest thing I'd said in three days, and something about saying it out loud in her presence — in front of the one person who already knew it and hadn't looked away — felt like setting down a weight I hadn't realized I was still carrying.

"I hate that you control my life," she said. Her voice had shifted. The fury was still there but underneath it something else had cracked open, something rawer and harder to look at. "I hate that you watch me. And I really, really hate that I spent three days missing you."

The world stopped. "What?"

"The house was too quiet," she whispered. "I thought I'd feel free, but I just felt empty. I hated that when Demitry called, my first thought was *I wish Lorenzo were here.* I hate that I'm standing here telling you this. And I hate that I can't make myself want to leave anymore."

The confession hung between us, jagged and honest and impossible to put back.

"We're fucked," I managed.

"Completely."

"I don't know how to care about you without owning you," I said. My hand hovered inches from her cheek, trembling with the effort of not closing the gap. "It's the only way I was taught to keep things safe. To grip them until they can't move."

"That's not enough," she said.

"I know. But I'm willing to try. Less cameras. More truth. A truce that actually means something." I looked into her dark eyes. "I'd rather have you here hating me than not have you at all."

A tear escaped. She didn't wipe it away. "Honest disasters," she said quietly. "That's what we are. Toxic, messy, and completely real. You're the only person who doesn't lie to me, even when the truth is that you're a bastard."

"It's a low bar."

"It's the only one I have."

I didn't touch her. I couldn't. If I crossed that line, the asset would be gone forever, replaced by something I couldn't control even if I tried — something I wasn't sure I deserved to have.

My phone buzzed. My father. The reckoning for the Rossi disaster, arriving exactly on schedule.

"I have to go," I said, stepping back into the cold.

"Lorenzo."

I stopped.

"I'm glad you came back."

I didn't look back. I couldn't. "I was always coming back, Dakota. I'm an addict, and you're the only thing that makes the world stop spinning."

I walked toward the house, leaving her in the darkening garden. My father would scream. There would be blood, or money lost, or both. But I heard the quiet click of her camera shutter behind me — small and deliberate, the sound of someone choosing to preserve a moment — and I knew the truth of it.

I'd lost the war against my father. I'd lost the Rossi deal. I'd lost three days of careful, constructed distance in seventy-two hours of proving I couldn't maintain it.

For the first time in my life, I didn't care.

17

Chapter Seventeen: Dakota

I woke up with the phantom heat of him still hovering over my skin and the immediate, sickening urge to take it all back.

I missed you.

The words tasted like ash in the 3:00 a.m. darkness. I'd handed him the one weapon I swore he'd never have: proof that he'd gotten under my skin. I'd looked at my captor—the man who bought me, the man who watches me sleep on high-definition feeds—and admitted that the world felt wrong without him in it.

I wasn't just a prisoner anymore. I was a volunteer. And that was a thousand times more dangerous.

By dawn, I'd rebuilt my walls. I wrapped myself in white-hot fury, using the cameras as a reminder of why I should want him dead. When he texted me at 8:00 a.m. saying *We need to talk*, I shut it down.

It was a mistake, I replied. *Forget it happened.*

But the villa didn't forget. The air was heavy with the scent of a brewing storm.

I found Lorenzo in the library at noon. He looked like he'd been pulled through a meat grinder—yesterday's suit wrinkled, his eyes bloodshot, his jaw a jagged line of tension.

"My father happened," he said, his voice a dead, flat rasp. "He saw the garden. He heard every word. He saw me tell you I was falling for you and decided I was a liability that needed to be liquidated."

My heart hammered against my ribs. "What did he do?"

"He moved the wedding. It's not three weeks away anymore, Dakota. It's seven days."

The floor seemed to tilt. "He can't—"

"He can. He finalized it with your father this morning." Lorenzo stepped closer, his presence suffocating. "He said if I'm this 'compromised,' we might as well lock the cage now. One week, and you're my wife."

"This is exactly why yesterday was a mistake!" I shouted, the panic finally breaking through. "You stood there and told me those things, and now we're trapped even deeper."

"*I* told you?" He laughed, a sharp, unhinged sound. "You told me you missed me. You admitted you couldn't breathe without the surveillance. Don't you dare put this all on my lack of control."

"I was confused!" I lied, the words feeling like knives in my throat. "I was lonely and you were there. But today? Today I remember that you're just the man who bought me. You're exactly what Demitry said—a man who thinks love is just a different word for ownership."

Lorenzo went stone-cold. The mask slid back into place, erasing the man who had looked at me with such longing in the garden.

"Fine," he whispered. "If that's the truth you want, then we're done. No more honest conversations. No more standing too close. We'll have the wedding, we'll sign the papers, and I'll be the bastard you clearly want me to be."

He walked out, and the click of the door sounded like a cell finality.

Dinner was a funeral.

Alonzo sat at the head of the table, looking like a man who had just won a grand slam. Bianca was pale, her eyes darting between Lorenzo and me with a mother's desperate intuition. Lorenzo sat across from me, a statue of ice.

"Seven days," Alonzo mused, swirling a vintage Barolo. "A small ceremony here at the villa. Dakota, you'll call your parents tomorrow. Maria will supervise. Tell them you're happy. Tell them the debt is settled."

"I won't do it," I said, my voice shaking.

"You will," Alonzo replied, not even looking at me. "Or your father goes to prison for the embezzlement I've been sitting on for six months. Choose your martyrdom, Dakota. But the wedding happens regardless."

I looked at Lorenzo. My last hope. "You're not going to say anything?"

He looked up, his eyes empty pits of darkness. "What would you like me to say? You made it clear this morning that I'm your jailer. Jailers don't argue with the warden. They just lock the doors."

He stood and walked away, leaving me alone with the monster at the head of the table.

Alonzo leaned forward, a predator sensing a kill. "You care about him, don't you? That's why you're so angry. Because you're realizing that the cage is comfortable."

"I hate him."

"Then you have a choice." Alonzo set his glass down. "Seven days. If you decide you'd rather have a different cage—one where you can actually run—tell me. I can arrange for Demitry to take you tonight. Lorenzo would never have to know."

My blood turned to ice. "You'd betray your own son?"

"I'm protecting my legacy. Lorenzo is weak for you. Demitry is strong for himself. I'll keep the heir that functions." He smiled. "Think about it, Dakota. Seven days is a long time to decide which man you want to be destroyed by."

He left me alone in the dining room.

I looked at the cameras. I looked at the empty chair where Lorenzo had sat. I was seven days away from a wedding I feared, with a man I loved-hated, being offered a "rescue" by a man who wanted me to disappear.

I didn't call my mother. I didn't cry.

I just sat there and realized that in a world of monsters, I had to decide which one I was willing to bleed for.

18

Chapter Eighteen: Lorenzo

I'd built an empire on people's hatred.

It was a clean, predictable currency. You knew exactly where you stood with a man who wanted you dead — his moves were logical, his motives legible, his hatred a thing you could map and plan around. Hatred, in my world, was almost a form of respect. It meant you mattered enough to destroy.

But Dakota's hate was different. It wasn't professional. It wasn't the cold, calculated variety I'd grown up reading like a second language. It was personal in the way only truth can be personal — specific, aimed, impossible to deflect with money or distance or the particular brand of silence I'd spent years perfecting. It was jagged glass shards in my lungs every time she looked at me with that clinical disgust, the kind that said *I see exactly what you are and I'm not impressed.*

Most people, when they looked at me that way, were performing. Dakota wasn't performing. That was the problem.

"You're exactly what Demitry said you were," she'd hissed.

That was the one that stuck. Lodged itself somewhere between the ribs and refused to move. Because I didn't have a counter-argument — not a real one. I was a man who'd spent twenty-six years learning that to care was to be compromised, and to be compromised was to be dead. My father had taught me that when I was eight years old, calmly and without malice, by giving away my dog the morning after he'd caught me crying over a scraped knee. Attachment was a luxury the Marchetti heir couldn't afford. He'd said it the way you'd explain the weather. Factual. Inarguable. And I had believed him, because what else do you do at eight years old when the only person you're supposed to trust hands you that particular lesson?

I believed him for twenty years. I built the machine. I became the machine.

And then Dakota looked at me like I was Demitry, and the machine stopped working.

"You look like someone shot your dog," my mother said.

She slid a cup of espresso across her vanity at 7:00 a.m. without looking up from her mirror, which meant she'd been watching me in the reflection since I walked in. She missed nothing. It was the one Marchetti trait I'd inherited that I actually respected.

"She told me the garden was a mistake," I rasped. I sat down on the edge of the chaise and held the espresso without drinking it. "She thinks I'm manipulating her. She thinks I'm him."

My mother set down her brush. That was how I knew it was serious — Bianca Marchetti did not set down her brush mid-routine for anything less than a genuine crisis.

"And are you?" She turned to look at me directly, her eyes doing the thing they'd always done — that particular searching quality, like she was reading something written underneath the surface of my face. "Are you the man who locks the cage? Or the man who built it because he doesn't know how else to keep her close?"

The question sat in the room between us. I turned the espresso cup in my hands.

"I don't know the difference anymore."

She was quiet for a moment. Outside the window, the garden was pale with early light. Somewhere out there, Dakota was probably already awake, already holding her camera like a shield, already deciding how much of herself to withhold today.

"Then find it," my mother said. Firm. Final. The voice she used when she was done being gentle. "Before the wedding in seven days turns into a life sentence for both of you."

The Cake Tasting. 2:00 PM.

The formal dining room smelled like sugar and the particular kind of despair that settles into rooms where important decisions are being made badly.

Six cakes sat on the marble table. They had been arranged with architectural precision by Francesca — our wedding planner, a woman of terrifying competence and an apparent immunity to tension — each one accompanied by a small placard naming its flavor profile as though we were at an exhibition rather than a negotiation dressed up as a party. I stood in the doorway for a moment before entering, taking stock the way I always took stock of rooms before walking into them. Exits. Atmospherics. Threat level.

Dakota was already there.

She stood by the window with her back to the door, one hand braced lightly on the sill. She wore a simple sundress, her hair in a knot that was losing its battle with gravity, a few dark strands coming loose around her neck. She looked exhausted in the specific way of someone who had slept but not rested. She looked like the only thing I wanted in a world made entirely of things I owned, which was a fact I noted with the cold, precise self-awareness of a man cataloguing his own pathologies.

I was bitter enough to recognize the irony. I had everything. I wanted the one thing that didn't want me back.

"Lorenzo," she said, without turning around.

She'd heard my footsteps. She always heard my footsteps — I'd noticed that weeks ago, the way her shoulders made a small, involuntary adjustment whenever I entered a room, a recalibration she probably wasn't even aware of. It could have been fear. I'd spent a long time telling myself it was just fear.

"Dakota."

We sat at opposite ends of the thirty-foot table like diplomats from countries that had been at war so long neither side remembered the original cause. Francesca moved between us with practiced brightness, narrating each cake with the enthusiasm of a woman being paid extremely well to pretend the atmosphere was normal. Tahitian vanilla. Raspberry coulis. Dark chocolate with a salted caramel layer that she described as *deeply romantic*, apparently without irony.

I ate what was placed in front of me and tasted none of it.

"It's fine," I said to the third plate.

"Just *fine*?" Francesca's smile developed a hairline fracture. She looked between us — really looked, the way people did when they'd finally run out of ways to pretend not to notice. "You two look like you're sampling poison."

"It's cake, Francesca," Dakota snapped. "It doesn't change the fact that I'm being traded like a commodity."

The planner set down her clipboard. It was a small gesture but it had the quality of a door closing — the moment a professional decides that professionalism has its limits.

"I've planned weddings for couples who were actively suing each other," she said, with the measured calm of someone choosing their words very carefully. "I've planned weddings where the groom didn't speak the bride's language — literally, not figuratively. I've planned a wedding where the best man was also the other man." She paused. "But this? This is worse. You look at her like you're drowning, Lorenzo. And you look at him like he's the one holding your head under, Dakota. I'm giving you thirty minutes. Figure out how to be in the same room without vibrating with misery, or I'm quitting."

She walked out. The door didn't slam — Francesca was too composed for that — but the silence she left behind was loud enough to compensate.

I looked at the cakes. Six of them, perfectly constructed, completely untouched by anything resembling joy. A neat little metaphor, if I were the kind of man who went in for metaphors.

"Do you honestly think I hate you?" Dakota asked suddenly.

The question hit me with the specific force of something I hadn't braced for. "You've said it enough times."

"I do hate you." She finally turned to look at me, her eyes bright with something she hadn't decided to let fall yet. "I hate that you took my life. I hate the cameras. I hate that I had to negotiate for basic dignity like it was a business term." She stopped. Drew a breath. "But then you defend me to your father. You text your mother at midnight to make sure I'm eating. And I don't know how to hate a man who does that. I don't know how to hold both things at once."

I stood up, the chair scraping. "I'm trying, Dakota. I'm trying to give you space, to be what you need. But I'm a *too much* kind of man. I don't know how to exist in the middle."

"Then don't," she whispered, standing too. "Just be honest. No more cold masks. No more pretending this is just a contract."

"Another truce?"

"An honest disaster," she corrected, with the ghost of a smile. "No cameras in my room. More freedom to leave the villa. And you stop comparing yourself to Demitry."

"And you?" I asked, stepping closer. "What do you give?"

"Patience. Because I know you're going to mess this up. You're going to be too controlling, and I'm going to be too stubborn."

We stood over the half-eaten cakes, two people trying to negotiate a peace treaty in a war neither of us could win.

"The vanilla raspberry," I said, looking at the table.

"Yeah," she agreed. "It was the best of a bad lot."

We'd picked a cake. A small, ordinary, almost laughable detail for an impossible life.

"Dakota." She was already moving toward the door. "I meant what I said in the garden. Every word."

She didn't look back. "I know, Lorenzo. That's why I'm still here."

She left. I stood alone with the sugar and the silence and the six cakes and the ghost of a smile she'd almost given me, and I did the accounting the way I always did the accounting — clear-eyed, unsentimental, bitter enough to be honest.

Seven days until the wedding. Seven days to find out whether a truce built on honest disasters could survive a father who wanted us broken and a cousin who wanted us dead.

I wasn't optimistic. Optimism had never been a Marchetti trait.

But when I walked back toward my office, something in my chest had shifted a fraction — loosened, like a knot that hadn't been touched in years and had finally been given the slightest amount of slack.

We weren't fine. We weren't even close to fine.

But for the first time since Milan, I could breathe.

19

Chapter Nineteen: Dakota

The camera felt like a lead weight.

It wasn't the weight of professional glass anymore. It was the weight of a leash, the particular heaviness of something that had once been mine and had quietly become part of the architecture of my captivity. I carried it anyway. It was the last thing in this place that still felt like it belonged to me.

Three days since the cake tasting. Three days of Lorenzo and me circling each other like wounded wolves, all polite distance and careful words. I was "free" to walk the coastal path, provided Marco and another shadow in a black suit stayed exactly six feet behind me. I'd counted. Six feet. Close enough to intervene. Far enough to feel like a courtesy.

My phone buzzed. An unknown number.

Relax. I'm not stalking you. Much. Coffee? Two blocks east.

Demitry.

I should have told Marco. I should have turned around, handed the phone over, and been the obedient investment Lorenzo needed me to be. I knew that. I knew it the way you know a stove is hot — not as a theory but as a felt thing, somewhere below conscious thought.

I went anyway. Because I was so tired of being managed. Because I wanted, just once, to prove that my life was still mine to risk.

The café was tucked into a corner of the village that felt too quiet. Not peaceful-quiet. The other kind — the kind where sound seemed to have been deliberately removed, like a room someone had just left. Demitry sat outside at a small iron table, looking like he'd been placed there by a photographer. Easy smile. Easy posture. The particular relaxation of a man who had never once worried about who might be watching.

"Dakota." He said my name like he'd won something. "You came."

He didn't ask what I wanted. He ordered two cappuccinos with a small flick of his wrist and settled back in his chair, watching me sit down with an expression that was almost warm. Almost. There was something underneath it that I couldn't name yet — something that made the back of my neck prickle faintly, the way it did before a storm.

"You look tense," he said. "Lorenzo suffocating you?"

"What do you want, Demitry?"

"To offer you a choice." He leaned forward, dropping his voice to something more intimate. Conspiratorial. "Lorenzo is going to turn you into his mother — a ghost in a silk dress, decorative and contained. He thinks owning you is the same as protecting you. He always has."

"And you're different?"

"I'm honest." His smile didn't waver. "I want things. I take them. At least you'd know where you stood."

I watched him over my cup. The dread was still quiet then — a low frequency, more feeling than thought. Something my body had registered before my mind caught up. The charm was very good. Practiced and layered and convincing enough that I could see exactly how it would work on someone who didn't know to look underneath it.

I was looking underneath it.

"When I'm talking to you," he said, his hand moving across the table, "I expect you to be present." He reached over and covered my hand with his. "Put the phone away."

The shift was so fast I almost didn't catch it. One moment warmth, the next — something else entirely. His hand didn't just cover mine. It pinned it. Flat against the table, deliberate and immovable, the grip calibrated with a precision that told me this was not the first time he'd done this. Not even close.

The dread sharpened into something with edges.

I kept my face neutral. I was good at neutral — I'd had practice. But underneath the neutral, something cold was spreading through my chest, moving outward from the place where his hand pressed down on mine. My bones felt the pressure. Not enough to be undeniable yet. Enough to be a message.

My phone buzzed against the table.

Lorenzo: *Where are you?*

I moved to reach for it. Demitry's grip tightened.

"He can wait," he said softly. His voice hadn't changed — still low, still smooth, still wearing the costume of intimacy. But his eyes had gone flat. "I'll decide when we're done."

And there it was. The thing underneath the charm, finally surfaced. Not desire. Not even possessiveness in the way I'd come to understand it. Something colder than either. Something that looked at another person and saw an object that had not yet learned its place.

Everything Lorenzo had warned me about crystallized in a single moment of clarity so sharp it almost hurt.

Lorenzo controlled my movements. He tracked me, managed me, kept me within walls I hadn't chosen. I'd hated him for it.

Demitry wanted to control my will. He wanted to reach inside and rearrange what I wanted until it matched what he wanted, and call it a relationship.

The difference wasn't small. It wasn't a matter of degree. It was the difference between a cage and something that had no name because the people inside it didn't survive long enough to give it one.

I yanked my hand back. The table rocked, cappuccino sloshing onto the iron surface, and I was on my feet before he could recalibrate.

"I'm leaving."

"Run to Lorenzo, then." The warmth was completely gone now, his face rearranging itself into something uglier and more honest. "But remember — I don't like being ignored. And in four days, when he gets bored of his new toy, I'll still be here."

I didn't answer. I walked away with my camera clutched against my chest and the feeling of his grip still printed on my bones.

Lorenzo was waiting in the villa's courtyard.

He didn't look angry. Anger I could have handled — anger had shape and edges and followed predictable patterns. This was something else. He was very still in the way that pressure is still, the way a thing is still right before it gives. His eyes found me the moment I came through the gate and didn't move.

"Inside," he said. "Now."

His office. The door locked behind us with a sound like a period at the end of a sentence. He stood with his back to it for a moment, looking at me — taking inventory, I realized. Checking for damage with the systematic focus of someone running through a list.

"Did he touch you?" His voice was stripped of everything except the question. No performance. No control. Just the raw, unguarded thing underneath. "Dakota. Look at me. Did he lay a hand on you?"

I told him. I told him all of it — the hand over mine, the pressure, the way the warmth had switched off like a light, the text Lorenzo had sent arriving at exactly the wrong moment. I told him about the grip tightening. The words *I'll decide when we're done.* The way Demitry's face had changed when I stood up.

With every word, I watched Lorenzo's face do something I hadn't seen it do before. It didn't harden. It went pale — slowly, progressively, the color leaving like water draining — and his eyes shifted into something so cold and so absolute that for a moment I forgot which one of them I was supposed to be afraid of.

He picked up his phone.

"Shut down his accounts." His voice was very quiet. That was worse than shouting would have been. "Every credit line. Every business tie. And find out who gave him her number. I want a name by sunset."

He set the phone down and turned back to me. His hands, I noticed, were not entirely steady. He pressed them flat against the edge of his desk and I watched him breathe — once, twice — rebuilding the architecture of his control from the inside out.

"He put his last girlfriend in a hospital," he said. "Broken ribs. A fractured jaw. She was too frightened to name him." He stopped. "I didn't tell you the details because I thought 'dangerous' was enough. I thought you'd trust me."

The air went out of the room. My lungs forgot their job for a moment.

A hospital. Not a bad ending. Not a cautionary tale. A hospital, with specific injuries, from a man who'd just had my hand pinned to a café table while he told me he'd decide when we were done.

"I'm sorry," I whispered.

He flinched. Like the words had made contact with something unguarded. "For what?"

"For being stupid. For thinking I was proving something."

"Don't apologize for wanting to be free." He closed the distance between us — not touching, but close enough that I could feel the heat radiating off him, the barely-contained enormity of what he was holding back. "Apologize for the secrets. I don't want you obedient. I just want you alive."

I looked at him. My captor. My future husband. The man who had put cameras in my hallway and a shadow six feet behind me on every walk. And I looked at him clearly, maybe for the first time — without the scrim of resentment I'd been looking through since the beginning.

Lorenzo was a cage. Heavy and gold-plated and suffocating in ways I hadn't finished cataloguing.

Demitry was a grave.

"The wedding is in four days," I said.

"I know."

"No more secrets."

He searched my face for the defiance. The familiar resistance he'd learned to brace for. He found only something quieter and grimmer — a mutual understanding that had come at a cost neither of us had expected to pay.

"Go rest," he said finally. "We have a rehearsal tomorrow."

That night I lay in my bed with the door locked, staring at the ceiling in the dark, turning it over.

I'd spent weeks fearing the man I was being forced to marry. Cataloguing his controls, his silences, his particular brand of possession. I'd been so focused on the cage that I hadn't looked carefully enough at what was outside it.

In four days I'd be Lorenzo's wife. His responsibility. His, in all the ways that word had terrified me.

And as I drifted toward sleep, I found the most unsettling truth of all settling quietly over me like a weight I hadn't consented to but couldn't shake off:

I was no longer afraid of the wedding.

I was afraid of what would happen if the gates ever opened — and Lorenzo wasn't there to close them.

20

Chapter Twenty: Lorenzo

I didn't sleep.

I spent the night rebuilding the walls.

Not the ones around the villa, those were Marco's territory, and by midnight he'd already doubled the perimeter staff and pulled the security logs from the previous seventy-two hours. I meant the other walls. The internal architecture I'd been constructing since I was eight years old, the ones that kept the noise out and the machinery running. The ones Dakota had been quietly dismantling for weeks without either of us fully acknowledging it.

I rebuilt them the only way I knew how. I worked. I pulled every financial record connected to Demitry's recent movements, every call log, every transaction that had touched anyone inside this household in the past month. I was methodical about it. Methodical was the one thing I could always be, regardless of what else was happening underneath.

*

By 8:00 a.m., I had identified the leak.

Sophia Greco. A household staffer with a forgettable face, four years of unremarkable service, and a fifteen-thousand-euro deposit in her personal account made eleven days ago from a shell company I recognized as Demitry's third layer of financial insulation. It wasn't sophisticated. It didn't need to be. Fifteen thousand euros was enough to make someone

115

with a forgettable face decide that loyalty was a flexible concept.

I had her brought to my office at eight-fifteen.

She came in already knowing. I could see it in the set of her shoulders — that particular brace of someone who has spent the night preparing for a conversation they cannot avoid. She sat down across from my desk and folded her hands and looked at the middle distance, and I looked at her for a long moment before I spoke.

I didn't shout. I never shouted in situations like this. Shouting was for men who needed volume to feel powerful, and I had never needed volume.

"You sold her out for the price of a used car," I said. My voice came out flat and dead and very quiet. I watched her hands begin to shake. "Be grateful I'm only taking your career and not your life. If I ever see you near Dakota again, that trade-off changes."

She signed the NDA without speaking. I watched her do it and felt nothing in particular — only the clean, administrative satisfaction of a problem being correctly resolved. That was the part I noted with cold precision. Not anger. Not even contempt. Just the mechanical click of a variable being removed from the equation.

That was what I was good at. Removing variables.

The question I didn't examine too closely was what it meant that I'd spent an entire sleepless night doing it for her.

By noon, my father was in my office, smelling of expensive tobacco and the specific brand of indifference he'd perfected over forty years of treating people as instruments.

He didn't knock. He never knocked. He moved through spaces as though the concept of permission had been designed for lesser men and he had simply opted out of it. I watched him settle into the chair across from my desk with the ease of a man who had never once doubted his right to be wherever he was, and I thought — not for the first time — that this was what I looked like to Dakota. This exact quality. This assumption of access.

The thought was not comfortable. I set it aside.

"You're overreacting," Alonzo said. He crossed one leg over the other and looked at me with the patient, faintly disappointed expression of a man reviewing a subordinate's error. "Demitry is a brat, not a strategist. He likes to play with his food. That's all."

"He put his last girlfriend in a hospital with three broken ribs." I kept my voice level. "That's not playing, Father. That's a signature."

"And you are surprised by this?" He tilted his head slightly. "You knew what he was when you agreed to the arrangement. The question was never whether Demitry was dangerous. The question was whether you could manage the asset without becoming compromised by it."

The asset. He said it without any particular emphasis. Just a word. Just the correct word for the thing we were discussing.

I looked at my father and performed, as I often did in these conversations, a kind of internal audit. I catalogued what I saw: a man of sixty-one who had built an empire by understanding exactly what everything was worth and never once making the mistake of valuing anything above its market rate. A man who had loved his wife, in his way, by ensuring she never wanted for anything except the things money couldn't purchase. A man who had raised me to be useful.

He had succeeded completely. That was the uncomfortable part.

"You're attached," he said, his voice dropping into something almost gentle — the gentleness of a surgeon, not a father. "It makes you predictable, Lorenzo. And in this family, being predictable is a death sentence. For both of you."

He let the silence hold the weight of that. Then he stood, adjusted his jacket, and left me with it — a gift of pure, unadulterated poison, delivered with the impeccable timing of a man who had never once needed to raise his voice.

I sat with it for a long moment after the door closed.

The worst part was not that he was wrong. The worst part was the specific, surgical accuracy of a man who knew exactly where to cut.

*

The Fitting. 2:00 PM.

I wasn't supposed to see the dress. Wedding superstition — not that either of us had approached this marriage with anything resembling sentiment

— but I stood in the hallway outside the fitting room anyway, my hand flat against the wall, listening.

I told myself I was there for security reasons. A cursory check of the corridor, a confirmation that Marco's people were positioned correctly. I was good at telling myself things.

What I was actually doing was listening for her.

Dakota fought me. That was the constant, the given, the thing I had built my understanding of her around. She argued and snarked and radiated a defiance that had gotten under my skin in ways I was still mapping. Even in the moments of fragile truce, even in the garden and over the cake tasting and in my office after Demitry, there had always been the sense of a person pushing back against the shape of her circumstances. Refusing to simply fit.

From inside the fitting room, I heard the seamstress murmur a direction.

And then Dakota's voice, hollow and perfectly flat: "Whatever you think is best."

I stood very still in the hallway.

Whatever you think is best. Four words. The most frightening thing she'd said to me since the day she arrived.

I caught her in the library afterward. She was standing by the window with her arms wrapped around herself, not looking at anything in particular — the posture of someone who has stopped expecting the view to offer anything useful. She looked smaller. Not physically, but in the way a person looks smaller when they've stopped occupying their full dimensions. When they've started editing themselves down to fit a space that was never built for them.

It hit me harder than her hatred ever had. Her hatred, at least, had been alive.

"We need to talk about security," I started.

"Why?" Her voice was flat. Not angry. Just flat, which was so much worse. "You've already changed my phone. You've added more shadows. You've fired the staff. What else is there to say?" She turned from the window. Her eyes were clear and exhausted and utterly without their usual fire. "I'll go where you tell me. I'll marry you in three days. I'll be the perfect, compliant asset."

"I don't want you compliant, Dakota."

"Yes, you do." She stepped closer, arms still wrapped around herself. "You want me safe, and in your world, safety and control are the same word. So congratulations, Lorenzo. You won. You broke the one part of me that still thought I had a choice."

I could have argued. I had the counter-arguments assembled — I'd been building them for weeks, the careful case for why what I did was different, why the cameras and the shadows and the locked doors were protection rather than possession. I knew the argument well. I'd been making it to myself since she arrived.

Standing in that library, looking at her hollowed-out eyes, I couldn't make it.

Because the argument required believing that the outcome justified the method. And the outcome was standing in front of me with her arms around herself like the only protection she had left, telling me in a dead voice that she'd show up at the altar on schedule.

I had wanted her contained. I had achieved it.

"I'm tired, Lorenzo." She said it quietly. Not a complaint. Just a fact, stated with the precision of someone who has run the numbers and arrived at a clear conclusion. "Tired of fighting a man who owns the air I breathe. Just tell me what time to show up at the altar."

She walked past me. And for the first time, I didn't reach out to stop her.

I stood in the library after she'd gone and looked at the space she'd left and did what I always did — I assessed it clearly, without flinching, with the cold self-awareness of a man who had learned that honesty about one's own nature was the only remaining form of integrity available to him.

I had done this. Not Demitry. Not my father. Me.

I had taken something that burned and I had methodically, systematically put it out. And I had called it keeping her safe.

That night I watched her from my office window.

She was on the terrace below, her camera raised toward the sunset. From this distance she looked like a photograph of herself — composed, still, beautiful in the specific way of things that have been reduced to their essential lines. Up close, I knew she was a ruin I had helped to make.

My phone buzzed. Antonio: *Marchetti made three more attempts to contact her. All blocked. He's poking around the wedding venue.*

Double the perimeter, I typed. *If he breathes near the gates, end him.*

I set the phone down and pressed my forehead against the cool glass and looked at her below, this woman I had purchased and surveilled and protected and hollowed out, and I thought about an eight-year-old boy standing in a doorway holding a dog collar with nothing in it. Learning, from the man who was supposed to teach him everything worth knowing, that love was a liability and attachment was a weapon your enemies would use against you.

I had learned the lesson perfectly. I had never once questioned the curriculum.

Three days until the wedding. Three days until she was mine in every legal and social sense the word could carry. Three days until I officially became the thing she'd always accused me of being.

Below me, she packed up her camera and disappeared into the shadows of the villa. I watched her go.

I should have felt like a man who had secured what he needed. Instead I felt like a man standing with both fists clenched, watching sand fall between his fingers — knowing that the tighter he squeezed, the faster it went.

I didn't open my hands.

I didn't know how.

21

Chapter Twenty-One: Dakota

Two days.

Forty-eight hours until Dakota Phillips ceased to exist and a polished, silent version of me took her place. I sat in the morning room, staring at a wedding checklist that felt like a set of instructions for my own taxidermy.

"You look like you're preparing for an execution," Bianca said, appearing in the doorway. She didn't offer comfort. She offered a glass of wine. It was 10:00 a.m.

"I'm marrying a Marchetti," I said, taking the glass. "Isn't that the same thing?"

"It doesn't have to be." She sat across from me, her silk suit perfectly pressed, her expression unreadable. "I hated Alonzo when I married him. I tried to run twice. He caught me both times and locked me in this very house."

"And you just... stayed?"

"I stopped fighting the walls and started looking for the doors," she said, her voice dropping. "Surrender is for the weak, Dakota. Strategy is for the survivors. Lorenzo is his father's son, but he isn't a carbon copy. Find the cracks in his armor. Use them to carve out a life. Otherwise, you'll end up like me—a ghost who still breathes."

I spent the afternoon in the library, the "strategic" advice rattling in my brain like a loose marble. Then, my new phone—the one Lorenzo had encrypted—buzzed.

An unknown caller.

"Hello?"

"Dakota Phillips?" The voice was a frantic whisper, echoing with distance. "My name is Elena. I was engaged to Demitry Marchesi two years ago."

My blood turned to ice. "The woman in Switzerland."

"He doesn't let go," she rasped. "He's asking about the wedding venue. He's planning something. I know Lorenzo Marchetti is a cage, Dakota. I know he's possessive. But Demitry is a coffin. Lorenzo wants to own you; Demitry wants to *break* you. Don't let him get close."

She hung up before I could ask how she found me.

Lorenzo is a cage. Demitry is a coffin. The words felt like a physical weight. I'd spent weeks trying to pick the lock on the cage, never realizing that the predator was waiting just outside the bars.

Dinner was a slow-motion car crash. Alonzo sat at the head of the table, radiating a smug, predatory satisfaction.

"I trust there will be no more… *unauthorized* excursions before the ceremony?" Alonzo asked, his eyes tracking me like a hawk. "We wouldn't want another display of poor judgment."

The insult hung in the air, thick and oily.

"Dakota understands," Lorenzo said, his voice coming out like a low growl.

"I'm sure she does," Alonzo sneered. "Two days. Try to act like a woman worth the Marchetti name."

I felt the heat rise in my neck, the urge to throw my wine in his face clawing at my throat. But then I looked at Lorenzo. His jaw was so tight I thought it might shatter. He wasn't looking at me with judgment; he was looking at his father with a pure, murderous loathing.

He came to my room an hour later. He didn't barge in. He knocked.

"My father was out of line," he said, leaning against the doorframe. He'd ditched his jacket, his tie hanging loose. He looked human. He looked exhausted.

"He's right, though," I said, leaning against my bedpost. "I proved I can't be trusted. I proved I need a leash."

"No." Lorenzo stepped into the room, his eyes fixed on mine. "You proved you're desperate for a life you're allowed to lead. I'm the one who put you in a position where Demitry looked like an escape."

I blinked. "Is that an apology?"

"It's an admission." He ran a hand through his hair. "Demitry is poking at the venue security. Elena called you, didn't she? My team flagged the patch through the encryption."

"She said you were a cage and he was a coffin."

Lorenzo flinched. The honesty of it seemed to hurt him more than any insult I'd thrown. "She's right. I know what I'm doing to you, Dakota. I know I'm taking your life and replacing it with mine."

"Then why do it?"

"Because I can't let you go into a world where men like him are waiting." He stepped closer, stopping just short of touching me. "I don't want you broken. I don't want you to become a ghost like my mother. I just... I need you to survive the next forty-eight hours."

"And then?"

"And then you're a Marchetti. And God help anyone who tries to touch what belongs to me."

He left before I could tell him that "belonging" to him didn't feel like the death sentence it used to. It felt like a bunker.

I pulled out my camera and looked at the last photo I'd taken of him through the office window. He looked trapped. Just like me.

Two days. I wasn't looking for freedom anymore. I was looking for the strongest lock in the world. And as I looked at the closed door, I realized I'd already found it.

22

Chapter Twenty-Two: Lorenzo

One day.

Twenty-four hours until Dakota Phillips becomes the property of the Marchetti estate. I spent the predawn hours staring at security feeds, watching the perimeter guards pace like restless ghosts. Demitry was still out there, a shadow in the static, but he wasn't my primary concern anymore.

My primary concern was the woman in the east wing who hadn't turned her light off since yesterday.

"Attachment makes you weak," my father's voice echoed in the hollows of my chest.

He was right. I was compromised. I was a man who could dismantle a rival family's shipping empire by noon but couldn't figure out how to walk across a hallway and talk to a twenty-three-year-old girl without feeling like I was stepping onto a landmine.

At 2:00 p.m., I found myself standing outside her door. I didn't have a report. I didn't have a command. I just had a hollow ache where my certainty used to be.

I knocked.

"Go away, Lorenzo," her voice muffled through the wood.

"Open the door, Dakota."

When she finally did, the sight of her nearly broke me. She looked exhausted. The wedding dress was hanging on the wardrobe, a white, silk shroud waiting for its occupant. Her camera was buried under a pile of lace.

"I'm sorry," I said. The words felt clumsy, unpracticed.

She stilled, her hand gripping the doorknob. "For which part? The kidnapping? The forced marriage? Or the part where you're currently tracking my heart rate through my phone?"

"All of it. For being exactly the man you think I am." I leaned against the doorframe, my composure fraying. "I'm sorry you're the price I had to pay to keep a throne I'm not even sure I want."

Dakota looked at me then, really looked at me, and the ice in her eyes softened into something far more dangerous: empathy.

"Your mother told me to be strategic," she whispered. "She told me to find the cracks in you and use them to survive."

"Did you find any?"

"A few." She stepped back, inviting me into the chaos of her room. "I don't despise you, Lorenzo. I want to. It would be so much cleaner if I did. But I just feel… tired. I'm tired of us being enemies when we're both just breathing the same poisoned air."

"A truce, then?" I asked. "A real one. No more fighting the inevitable."

"A truce," she agreed. "But don't expect me to smile when the priest asks if I take you. I'm a good photographer, Lorenzo, but I'm a terrible actress."

3:00 AM — The Night Before

I stood at my window, watching the moonlight hit the Mediterranean. My phone buzzed.

Dakota: *You awake?*

Lorenzo: *Yes.*

Dakota: *I keep looking at the dress. It looks like a ghost.*

Lorenzo: *It's just fabric, Dakota. It doesn't have power over you.*

Dakota: *Liar. It has all the power. Tomorrow, I disappear.*

I stared at the screen, my heart hammering against my ribs.

Lorenzo: *I won't let you disappear. I'll make sure there's always space for the girl with the camera. I promise.*

Dakota: *Promises are dangerous in this house, Lorenzo.*

Lorenzo: *Then call it a contract. I always honor my contracts.*

A long silence followed. Then, the light in her room finally flickered out.

One day. In twenty-four hours, the world would see a powerful union. They would see a Marchetti heir claiming his prize.

They wouldn't see the two prisoners holding onto a digital thread in the dark, terrified of the morning, yet somehow, for the first time, not terrified of each other.

I closed my eyes and prayed that the "cage" I'd built would be strong enough to hold us both. Because tomorrow, the door was locking. And I was the one holding the key, wishing I could throw it into the sea.

23

Chapter Twenty-Three: Dakota

Three weeks after I signed the contract, I stood in a white dress that didn't feel like mine.

The mirror didn't lie, but it didn't tell the whole truth either. It showed a bride in ivory silk, a masterpiece of lace and structure that cost more than my father's first house. It showed a woman who looked composed, radiant, and expensive. It didn't show the way my lungs felt like they were being squeezed by a pair of iron hands.

"Ms. Phillips, you have a visitor."

Maria's voice was the only thing keeping me from ripping the veil off and climbing out the window. When my mother stepped into the room, the "Dakota" I had been pretending to be for three weeks shattered.

"Mother—"

The sob was out before I could choke it back. She smelled like home—lavender and laundry detergent—not the cold, metallic scent of the Marchetti villa.

"Sweetheart, you look like a dream," she whispered, holding me so tight I could feel her heart racing. Then, she pulled back, her eyes flicking to the door. "Your father... he's outside. He's terrified you won't speak to him."

The anger was there, simmering, but today it was drowned out by a cold, hollow exhaustion. "Let him in."

Robert Phillips entered like a man walking toward a firing squad. He looked aged. The guilt had carved deep lines into his face. When he took my hand, his fingers were trembling.

"I am so sorry, baby girl," he whispered, his voice thick. "I never meant for it to go this far."

"But it did, Dad," I said, my voice eerily calm as I adjusted my bouquet. "It went exactly this far. Let's go."

The walk to the chapel was a blur of marble corridors and silent security guards. But the moment the double doors opened, the world narrowed to a single point: **The Altar.**

The Marchetti chapel was a monument to old-world power—stained glass that turned the afternoon sun into pools of blood on the floor, and three hundred guests who looked like they'd stepped out of a high-fashion funeral.

Then I saw him.

Lorenzo stood at the end of the aisle, a silhouette of sharp black tailoring against a wall of white peonies. *Peonies.* My favorite. My stomach did a slow, sickening roll. Had he done that to be kind, or to show me that even my smallest preferences were documented in a file somewhere?

As I reached him, my father placed my hand in Lorenzo's. The contact was electric. His skin was warm, his grip firm—a silent command to stay still.

"You look beautiful," he murmured, his voice a low vibration that seemed to settle right under my skin.

"And you look stupid," I whispered back, my eyes stinging.

A tiny, almost imperceptible scoff escaped him. His jaw tightened, but he didn't let go of my hand.

The ceremony was a haze. I listened to the Latin, the vows of *richer or poorer, sickness and health*, feeling like I was signing a confession. When the priest asked for objections, I looked at the exit. I looked at the snipers I knew were on the roof. I stayed silent.

"I do," Lorenzo said. He sounded like a man closing a billion-dollar deal.

"I do," I whispered. I sounded like a ghost.

Then came the rings. They were heavy, cold gold. When I slid the band onto his finger, I felt the calluses on his palm—the hands of a man who knew how to use a weapon as well as a pen. His thumb traced a slow, deliberate circle against my palm as he took my hand. It was a secret language, a claim whispered in front of God and three hundred witnesses.

"You may kiss the bride."

Lorenzo didn't hesitate. He stepped into my space, his scent—dark cedar and expensive whiskey—overwhelming the flowers. His hand cupped my jaw, his thumb brushing my cheekbone with an aching gentleness that felt like a trick.

"Relax," he breathed against my lips, so low only I could hear. "It's just a kiss, Dakota."

But when his mouth met mine, it wasn't "just" anything. It was soft, then deep, then demanding. My hands found the lapels of his tuxedo, intending to push, but my fingers curled into the fabric instead. For a heartbeat, the performance ended and something raw and terrifyingly real took its place. Heat bloomed in my chest—treacherous, unwanted, and undeniable.

When he pulled away, he lingered for a second, his forehead against mine. I saw something in his eyes—a flicker of hunger, of something almost like relief—before the mask of the Marchetti heir slammed back into place.

The reception was a masterclass in atmospheric dread. The grand hall was a sea of crystal chandeliers and whispered alliances. I stood by the bar, my third glass of champagne trembling in my hand.

"Two weeks in Bora Bora," my mother gushed, appearing at my side. "Lorenzo's mother said it's a surprise!"

The champagne nearly went down the wrong way. *Bora Bora.* An island. Total isolation. No cameras, no parents, just Lorenzo and the weight of that ring.

I turned and found him across the room, leaning against a pillar while a circle of men in dark suits hung on his every word. He wasn't looking at them, though. He was staring at me. His whiskey glass was poised halfway to his lips, his gaze tracking the curve of my neck as I talked to his aunt.

I set my glass down and walked toward him, my silk train hissing against the marble like a snake. The men parted for me like the Red Sea.

"Is there a reason you've been staring at me for twenty minutes?" I asked, my voice sharp enough to draw blood.

Lorenzo didn't look away. He took a slow, methodical sip of his drink, his eyes darkening. "You're my wife, Dakota. I'm allowed to look at what belongs to me."

"It's creepy," I snapped, though my pulse was hammering against my throat. "Stop it."

"No." A ghost of a smile—predatory and beautiful—tugged at the corner of his mouth. "I don't think I will."

He stepped closer, his shadow falling over me. "The dance is starting. And we have a very long night ahead of us, Mrs. Marchetti."

The way he said my new name made the "Truce" from the night before feel like a lie. The cage hadn't just locked; the walls were starting to move inward.

24

Chapter Twenty-Four: Lorenzo

The penthouse was a cage made of glass and cold ambition.

I flicked the lights on, watching Dakota flinch at the starkness of the space. No frescoes here. No history. Just charcoal silk, polished concrete, and a view of the city that made everything below look like ants.

"The villa was for my father," I said, dropping my keys. They hit the marble with a sharp *crack*. "This is for us. Or whatever 'us' is going to be."

"You didn't think to mention we were moving?" she asked, her voice tight. She was still clutching her bouquet, the white petals bruised and wilting.

"I'm mentioning it now." I stripped off my tuxedo jacket and tossed it onto the sofa. "The bedroom is at the end of the hall. I sleep on the left."

The silence that followed was heavy enough to drown in.

"The left side," she repeated, her eyes widening. "As in... one bed?"

"You're a Marchetti now, Dakota. People talk. My staff talks. A 'happy' couple doesn't have a guest wing." I poured two fingers of scotch, the amber liquid glowing under the recessed lighting. "Don't look at me like that. I told you I wouldn't touch you. I keep my word. But you *will* be in that bed."

"Everything is a command with you," she whispered, but she followed me. She always followed, even when her eyes were screaming *murder*.

The Master Suite

The bed was a black-on-black king, positioned so the city lights felt like they were inside the room. It was an intimidating piece of furniture.

131

"Ensuite is through there," I said, gesturing to the frosted glass door. "Change. Get comfortable. Or as comfortable as you can be while hating me."

She disappeared into the bathroom, slamming the door hard enough to vibrate the floor. I stripped down to my sleep pants, feeling the sudden, jarring silence of the apartment. For years, this place had been my sanctuary—the one spot where no one expected anything from me. Now, there was a woman in the next room who viewed me as a terminal illness.

When she finally emerged, she was wearing an oversized t-shirt that made her look painfully young and impossibly fragile. Her hair was down, a dark silk curtain that hid her face.

"I'm not doing this," she said, standing by the edge of the rug.

"Then sleep on the floor," I said, pulling back the duvet. "But when you wake up with a sore back, don't come to my side for sympathy."

She glared at me, a sparks of pure defiance in her eyes, before stalking to the right side of the bed. She climbed in like she was entering a cage of lions, staying so close to the edge I thought she might roll off.

I turned out the light.

"Goodnight, wife," I said.

"Go to hell, husband," she snapped.

2:14 AM

I woke up to a sudden, biting chill.

I reached out, expecting the heavy weight of the duvet, only to find nothing but the fitted sheet and cold air. I cracked an eye open.

Dakota had transitioned from a terrified bride to a professional thief. She was a human burrito, wrapped in three layers of Egyptian cotton, huddled on the far edge of the mattress.

"Dakota," I rasped.

Silence. Her breathing was too shallow. She was awake.

"Give me the covers."

"I'm asleep," she muffled into the fabric.

"Liars don't talk in their sleep with that much clarity. Give them back."

"No. You said the bed was non-negotiable. You didn't say I had to share the heat."

I didn't argue. I reached across the expanse of the bed and grabbed the edge of the duvet. I gave it a sharp tug. She yelped, rolling toward the center as the momentum took her.

"Stop it!" she hissed, grabbing for the fabric.

"It's my bed, my blanket, and currently, my frostbite," I said, pulling harder.

She lunged for it, and suddenly we were tangled in the middle of the mattress. In the struggle, her leg brushed mine—warm skin against cold— and we both froze.

In the dim glow of the city lights, her eyes were huge, dark pools of gold and shadow. Her lips were parted, her chest rising and falling against the duvet trapped between us. I could smell her now—not the wedding perfume, but her. Vanilla and soap and something that smelled like a problem I couldn't solve.

I should have let go. I should have moved back to my "left side" and re-established the DMZ.

Instead, I gripped the blanket tighter, pulling her an inch closer.

"Equal distribution," I said, my voice dropping an octave. "That's the deal."

She let go of the fabric, her hands hovering nervously near my chest. "Fine. Take them. Just… stay on your side."

I straightened the covers, laying back down and pulling my half over my shoulders. She scrambled back to her edge, but the "canyon" between us had shrunk. The air in the room felt different now—thicker, charged with a static that had nothing to do with the air conditioning.

I closed my eyes, but I didn't sleep. I listened to her breath hitch, then smooth out as exhaustion finally won.

She was mine. Legally. Socially. But as I felt her foot accidentally brush mine under the covers in her sleep, I realized the "transaction" was becoming a lot more complicated than a debt on a ledger.

I didn't move my foot away.

25

Chapter Twenty-Five: Dakota

I woke up in a furnace.

My first thought was that the penthouse was on fire. My second was that the fire had a heartbeat. I was tangled—limbs, hair, and breath—against the solid, radiating heat of Lorenzo's chest.

I was the one who had migrated. I was tucked into his side, my arm draped across his stomach like I belonged there. His hand was heavy on the small of my back, his fingers splayed possessively even in sleep.

I froze, my heart hammering against his ribs. I tried to pull away, a millimeter at a time.

"Where are you going?" his voice rasped, vibrating through his chest and into my skull. It was deep, rough with sleep, and far too intimate for a Tuesday morning.

"Back to my side," I whispered, my face burning.

"You sleep like an octopus," he murmured, his thumb tracing a lazy, maddening circle on my spine. "I woke up an hour ago and you were using me as a life raft."

"I was not."

"You were." He opened his eyes, dark and heavy-lidded, looking entirely too smug. "But I don't mind. You're a lot warmer than the silk sheets."

He let me go, and I scrambled to the edge of the mattress, clutching the duvet like a shield. "We leave for the airport at noon," he said, stretching with a predatory grace that I pointedly ignored. "Pack light. Bora Bora doesn't require much besides a swimsuit and a lack of inhibitions."

The Packing War

The closet was a battlefield. I was shoving sundresses into a suitcase with the coordination of a panicked squirrel when Lorenzo appeared in the doorway, wearing nothing but a low-slung towel and a look of mild judgment.

"You're going to wrinkle the silk," he said, stepping into my space. He began folding my clothes with a terrifying, military precision.

"I can pack my own things, Lorenzo."

"You pack like you're fleeing a crime scene, *moglie*," he said, his hands lingering on a lace slip. "The crime is already over. We're married. Stop running."

He reached for my swimsuits, and I snatched them away. "I'll handle those."

His lips twitched. "The red bikini? The one with the strings?"

My heart stopped. "How do you—"

"I bought it, Dakota. I bought everything in this closet. I know exactly what's in your armor rack." He stepped closer, the scent of his shower—sandalwood and citrus—filling my lungs. "In Bora Bora, there are no cameras. No Alonzo. No Maria. Just us. You can drop the act."

"And what if the 'act' is the only thing keeping me sane?"

He looked at me then, the smugness fading into something harder, more intense. "Then find a new way to stay sane. Because for the next fourteen days, I'm the only person you'll see."

The Flight

The private jet was a flying palace of leather and hushed tones. As we leveled out over the Mediterranean, Lorenzo retreated to the small mahogany desk at the front of the cabin, immersed in his phone.

"I need to finish some correspondence before we lose signal over the Pacific," he said, not looking up.

I wandered the cabin, restless. I went to the galley to find a coffee, but on my way back, a gust of turbulence shook the plane. I stumbled, catching myself on the edge of his desk. A heavy leather folio slid off the surface, spilling papers across the plush carpet.

"Sorry, I—"

I stopped.

My father's name was at the top of the first page. *Robert Phillips: Asset Analysis.*

I knelt to pick it up, my eyes scanning the text before I could stop myself. It wasn't a debt ledger. It was a timeline.

Project 'Vines': Phase One. Initial contact with R. Phillips regarding the construction bids. Phase Two. Targeted market manipulation to induce liquidity crisis.

My breath hitched. My hands started to shake.

Phase Three. Proposal of 'Alternative Debt Resolution' (D. Phillips).

It wasn't a gamble my father lost. It wasn't a mistake. It was a hunt. Lorenzo hadn't saved me from a debt; the Marchettis had manufactured the debt to put me in that villa.

I looked up. Lorenzo was standing now, his expression unreadable, his eyes fixed on the paper in my hand.

"Dakota," he said, his voice dangerously soft. "Put the file down."

"You trapped him," I whispered, the realization cutting through me like a blade. "You didn't marry me to help him. You broke him so you could buy me."

The plane dipped again, but this time, the turbulence was all inside my chest.

26

Chapter Twenty-Six: Lorenzo

The flight was a silver needle threading through the dark.

I'd expected Dakota to stay awake out of sheer spite—to vibrate with the same restless energy she'd had in the penthouse. But forty minutes into the Pacific crossing, the adrenaline that had fueled her since the wedding finally burned out.

She fell asleep with her head tilted against the porthole, her dark hair fanned out against the cream leather. In the dim cabin lights, she looked fragile. It was a lie, of course. I knew the steel that lived under that skin, but seeing her like this—defenseless—made my chest tighten in a way that had nothing to do with the altitude.

I took a sip of whiskey and tried to focus on the shipping manifests Matteo had sent. But my eyes kept drifting to her.

Business, I reminded myself. *This is a merger. A debt collection.*

But debt collections didn't involve memorizing the way a woman's pulse thrummed in her throat. They didn't involve wanting to reach out and smooth the tiny, stressed furrow between her brows.

14 Hours Later — The Arrival

The transition from the private jet to the puddle-jumper was a test of nerves. Dakota gripped the armrests as the small plane bucked through the tropical thermals.

"Breathe, Dakota," I said, reaching over to cover her hand with mine.

She was rigid, her knuckles white. "I am breathing."

"You're vibrating. Look out the window."

She did, and I saw the exact second the "Marchetti Iron" cracked. Below us, the lagoon was a hallucinogenic shade of blue—electric turquoise bleeding into deep sapphire. Mount Otemanu rose out of the center like a jagged emerald.

"Oh," she breathed. It was the first sound of genuine wonder I'd heard from her since I'd entered her life.

"Beautiful, isn't it?" I didn't let go of her hand.

"It's… it doesn't look real."

"Nothing in my world is quite what it seems," I murmured.

The Bungalow

The resort was a string of pearls draped across the water. Ours was the last one on the pontoon—the most expensive, the most isolated. Total privacy. Total silence.

I led her inside, watching her take in the thatched ceilings, the glass floor panels showing the reef below, and finally, the bed. It was a massive king-sized altar of white linen, positioned perfectly to face the sunset.

One bed.

Dakota walked to the edge of the glass floor, watching a stingray glide beneath her feet. "It's a cage," she said quietly, her back to me. "A gorgeous, five-star cage, but there's nowhere to run, is there?"

"I don't want you to run, Dakota." I moved toward her, stopping just close enough to catch the scent of the sea air on her skin. "I want you to be here. With me."

"What am I supposed to do with that?" she asked, turning to face me. Her eyes were raw, the frustration finally boiling over. "You kidnap me, you force me into your bed, you buy my father… and then you're *nice* to me. You hold my hand on the plane. You fold my clothes. What kind of monster does that?"

"The kind who knows that fear only gets you so far," I said, tilting her chin up with one finger. Her skin was electric. "Fear is for my enemies, Dakota. You're my wife."

"Those aren't mutually exclusive in your family, Lorenzo."

"They are in my house." I stepped back, giving her space before the tension snapped. "You have an hour to unpack. We'll have dinner on the deck. No family. No phones. Just us."

"Just us," she repeated, looking at the bed.

"Just us," I confirmed.

I walked toward the bathroom, but I could feel her gaze on my back. She was off-balance, terrified of the kindness more than the cruelty.

Good.

Because for the next fourteen days, there were no walls to hide behind. No parents to perform for. Just the water, the sun, and the slow, inevitable erosion of the woman she used to be.

27

Chapter Twenty-Seven: Dakota

The dinner was a masterpiece of psychological warfare.

Lorenzo had traded his Roman armor for white linen and rolled sleeves, looking like a man who belonged in the sun. He sat across from me on the private deck, the silver domes of our plates reflecting the bruised purple of the Tahitian sunset.

"You're not eating," he observed, his voice competing with the rhythmic *slap-hush* of the waves against the pylons.

"I'm waiting for the catch," I said, picking up my fork. The fish was local, caught that morning, seasoned with lime and ginger. It tasted like everything I didn't deserve.

"There is no catch, Dakota. It's just dinner."

"Nothing with a Marchetti is 'just' anything." I looked at him, the candlelight flickering in the dark depths of his eyes. "Why did you really bring me here? And don't give me the PR answer. There are no photographers on this reef."

Lorenzo set his wine glass down. The stem looked fragile between his scarred fingers. "I wanted the noise to stop."

"The noise?"

"The family. The business. The constant performance of being the man they expect me to be." He leaned forward, his knees nearly brushing mine under the small table. "I wanted to see who you are when you aren't looking

140

for an exit sign."

"I am the exit sign, Lorenzo. That's all I've been since the day I met you."

He didn't flinch. "Then let's walk. Maybe the air will help you find a different perspective."

The Shoreline

The sand was like powdered sugar, still radiating the day's heat. Lorenzo didn't ask; he simply took my hand as we stepped off the deck. His palm was a solid, grounding weight. For a moment, with the stars starting to puncture the velvet sky, it felt like a real honeymoon.

And that was the danger.

"It's quiet," I whispered.

"No distractions," he agreed.

"No escape routes."

His grip tightened, just for a second, before he let go entirely. He stopped walking and turned to face the black expanse of the ocean. "Is that all I am to you? A warden in a tailored suit?"

"You bought me, Lorenzo. You can dress it up in five-star resorts and private jets, but at the end of the day, my father's life was the price tag, and I was the currency."

He spun around, his face illuminated by the rising moon. The "gentleman" was gone. The predator was back. "Your father would be in a shallow grave in the Roman countryside if I hadn't stepped in! I didn't buy you, Dakota. I *saved* you."

"By putting me in a different cage? By forcing me into your bed? You gave me an ultimatum, not a choice." I stepped into his space, my heart thundering. "Don't pretend this is romance. This is a transaction. You're just frustrated because your 'property' isn't grateful."

"Grateful?" He laughed, a harsh, jagged sound. "I don't want your gratitude. I wanted—" He cut himself off, his jaw working.

"What? What did you want?"

"I wanted to be wrong," he said, his voice dropping to a low, dangerous vibration. "I wanted to believe that if I took you away from the madness, you'd see the man, not the name. But you're right. I'm the monster. And you're the martyr."

He turned and began walking back toward the bungalow, his strides long and furious.

"Lorenzo!"

He didn't stop. He didn't look back. By the time I reached the deck, he was already inside, throwing a spare blanket onto the small, stiff sofa in the corner of the living area.

"What are you doing?" I asked, breathless.

"Giving you what you want," he said, his voice cold and flat. "Space. Safety from the monster. Take the bed, Dakota. It's big enough for your ego and your resentment."

"You don't have to sleep on the couch. You're too tall for it."

"I've slept in worse places," he snapped, turning his back to me. "Go to sleep. We have thirteen days left of this 'prison sentence.' Let's try to survive them without drawing blood."

I stood in the doorway, the warm tropical breeze mocking the ice in the room. I looked at the massive, empty bed, then at the man crumpled onto a sofa designed for decoration, not rest.

I'd won the argument. I'd asserted my truth.

So why did it feel like I was the one who had just lost everything?

28

Chapter Twenty-Eight: Lorenzo

I woke up with a crick in my neck and the grim realization that nobility was a painful, poorly designed virtue.

The sofa was a designer masterpiece of leather and sharp angles—perfect for an architectural digest shoot, miserable for a six-foot-two man. My spine felt like it had been reassembled by an amateur, and my ego wasn't faring much better.

You're a monster.

The accusation from the beach still echoed in the quiet of the morning. I made espresso with aggressive precision, the steam hissing as I watched the dawn light hit the lagoon. I'd spent my life being the hunter. I'd manufactured a debt, manipulated a crisis, and secured a prize.

But looking at the closed bedroom door, I felt less like a conqueror and more like a fool who had bought a bird and was surprised it didn't want to sing.

I took my coffee to the deck, my laptop open to a sea of territorial disputes and shipping manifests. I needed the cold comfort of logic. I needed to remember that this was a transaction.

Then the sliding glass door drifted open.

I didn't look up. I focused on a spreadsheet regarding the Calabrese port fees. I was a professional. I was a Marchetti. I was—

Splash.

The sound of her hitting the water broke my concentration like a gunshot. I lasted exactly twelve seconds before my gaze betrayed me.

Dakota was in the infinity pool, and she was wearing the red bikini.

It wasn't just a swimsuit; it was a provocation. It was held together by strings that looked as fragile as our truce, a vibrant, violent crimson against the turquoise water. She was floating on her back, her hair a dark halo around her head, her skin glistening with salt and sun.

I slammed my laptop shut. The sound was sharp, desperate.

She didn't look at me. She drifted to the edge of the pool, resting her chin on her crossed arms, staring out at the ocean. The water lapped at the small of her back—at the delicate bow of the strings that held the bottom in place.

One tug. That was all it would take to unravel the whole thing.

"Do you need something, Lorenzo?"

Her voice was cool, bordering on bored. She hadn't moved, but I could see the slight curve of her lips in profile. She knew. She knew the spreadsheets were a lie. She knew the espresso was cold. She knew exactly what she was doing to the "monster."

"No," I rasped, my throat suddenly as dry as the sand.

"You're staring," she said, finally turning her head. She pushed her sunglasses down her nose, her eyes mocking and golden in the light. "Is there a problem with my 'armor'?"

"The problem, Dakota, is that you're playing a game you aren't prepared to finish."

She stood up then, water sluicing off her in a way that made my vision blur. She didn't scramble for a towel. She walked to the lounge chair with a slow, deliberate grace, every movement a calculated strike against my sanity.

"I'm not playing a game," she said, picking up her book. "I'm just living in my cage. Isn't that what you wanted?"

She laid back, exposing herself to the sun and my helpless gaze.

I went back inside. I poured a whiskey I didn't need and stared at the wall. I'd spent millions to bring her here. I'd moved mountains to make her mine. And now, as I listened to her humming softly on the deck, I realized the terrifying truth.

I wasn't the warden anymore.

I was the one behind bars, and she held the key in the palm of her hand.

145

29

Chapter Twenty-Nine: Dakota

I had intended to be a ghost today.

After the silent war on the deck—after I'd used that red bikini to dismantle his composure—the satisfaction had soured into a restless, hollow ache. I needed to do something that didn't involve staring at the man who had bought my life. I needed to be Dakota Phillips again, the girl who cooked her own meals and didn't live in a gilded cage.

I found the kitchen stocked with terrifyingly perfect ingredients. I grabbed a chef's knife, a heavy, German-engineered blade that felt like a weapon. I started on the tomatoes, my movements frantic, my mind miles away in a kitchen in Ohio that smelled like home, not expensive sea salt.

Slice. Slice.

My eyes drifted to the window. Lorenzo was a dark silhouette against the twilight, his voice a low, melodic rumble as he spoke Italian into his phone. He looked like a king surveying a conquered territory.

"Dammit," I hissed.

The knife slipped. The steel bit into my index finger before I could blink.

The pain was a bright, hot flash. Blood bloomed instantly, a vivid, startling red against the white marble counter. I grabbed a dish towel, wrapping it tight, my breath hitching.

The sliding door didn't just open; it hit the frame with a crack.

"Dakota?" Lorenzo was across the room before I could even formulate a lie. His phone was gone, his focus narrowed down to the red stain spreading on the towel. "Let me see."

"It's fine, I'm just clumsy—"

"Let. Me. See." It wasn't a request. He took my wrist, his grip firm but careful, and led me to the sink.

He ran the cool water over the cut, his other hand splayed across my lower back to steady me. The contrast was dizzying—the cold water, his burning skin, and the silver flash of the knife still lying on the counter.

"It's deep," he murmured, his brow furrowing. He looked more concerned about a half-inch cut than I'd seen him look about a multi-million dollar shipping dispute.

He guided me to a stool and retrieved a first-aid kit from a drawer he hadn't even opened yet. He knelt between my knees, a position so intimate it made my lungs seize.

"This will sting," he warned.

He cleaned the wound with a steady hand. I winced, my fingers twitching in his grasp, and instinctively, his free hand landed on my thigh—a grounding, possessive weight that told me to stay still.

"Why are you doing this?" I whispered, watching him apply a butterfly bandage with clinical precision. "You could just call the resort staff. You could just let me bleed."

Lorenzo looked up. Our faces were inches apart. I could see the dark rings around his pupils, the scent of expensive tobacco and cedar wood wrapping around me like a shroud.

"I don't want anyone else touching you," he said, his voice dropping to a rough, private register. "Even to heal you."

"That's… that's not normal, Lorenzo."

"Nothing about us is normal, Dakota." He smoothed the edges of the bandage, his thumb lingering on my palm. "But I'm not a monster. I'm just a man who takes care of what belongs to him."

He didn't wait for my rebuttal. He stood, picked up the knife, and began dicing the tomatoes I'd abandoned. He moved with a practiced, lethal grace.

"What are you doing?"

"Making dinner. My mother's recipe." He didn't look back, but the tension in his shoulders had eased. "And tomorrow, you're going to wear a different swimsuit. The red one is… distracting."

"Distracting? Or did you just realize you aren't as in control as you thought?"

He paused, the knife poised over an onion. He turned his head just enough for me to see the predatory tilt of his mouth. "I am in total control, Dakota. I'm just choosing to be merciful tonight."

He finished the sauce in silence, the air filling with the scent of garlic and basil. When he finally set a plate in front of me, he didn't return to the couch. He sat across from me, watching me eat.

"Lorenzo," I said, my voice small. "Take the bed tonight."

He paused, a fork halfway to his mouth. "The couch is fine."

"The couch is a lie. You're too tall, and you're in pain." I looked down at my bandaged finger. "We can share. No touching. No… whatever this is. Just sleep."

He studied me for a long time, the silence stretching until it felt like a physical weight.

"Just sleep," he repeated, his voice like velvet over gravel. "Fine. But don't complain when you wake up wrapped around me again, octopus."

I felt the blush heat my cheeks, but I didn't look away. For the first time, the "cage" felt less like a prison and more like a sanctuary. And that was the most terrifying realization of all.

30

Chapter Thirty: Lorenzo

Sharing a bed with Dakota and not touching her was a slow-motion execution.

I lay in the dark, staring at the thatched ceiling, cataloguing every crack and weave in the pale fibers above me like a man with nothing left to count on. Four inches. Maybe five. The Egyptian cotton between us might as well have been the Atlantic — cold, vast, and full of the kind of pressure that could crush a man without warning. I'd slept in stranger places. On cots aboard cargo ships that smelled of diesel and brine. On the floor of a Lisbon holding cell once, for six hours, waiting for Marco to sort out a misunderstanding with a port authority officer who had very expensive tastes. I had never once lain somewhere and felt this particular brand of awake — the kind that lives behind the sternum, electric and insistent.

I could hear the catch in her throat. The rhythmic slap-hush of the tide beneath the floorboards. The maddening scent of her skin — something like sea salt and expensive soap and something else beneath it that was purely her, something I hadn't been able to name in three weeks of trying.

Outside, the palms shifted against each other in the rising wind.

"You can breathe, Dakota," I said. My voice cut through the humid air more roughly than I intended. "I'm not going to lunge at you."

A pause. Then: "I know." Her voice was barely above a whisper. "I'm just… thinking."

"About how much you want to be back in Ohio?"

"No." She shifted, and the mattress dipped — a small gravitational adjustment, barely a degree, but I felt it in my spine like a compass needle swinging. "About why you bandaged my finger today. You didn't have to be gentle. You could have been the man everyone thinks you are."

I turned my head. In the moonlight filtering through the palm fronds and the thin muslin curtain, her eyes were huge and dark and searching — the way they got when she was trying to solve something she didn't have all the pieces for. I'd noticed that about her early on. Dakota Hale did not accept incomplete information. She picked at it, quietly, relentlessly, until it gave.

"And who is that?" I asked. "The monster? The debt collector?"

"Yes."

One word, no hesitation, no cruelty in it. Just honesty. I'd hired men who couldn't do that.

I looked back up at the ceiling. "I was gentle," I said slowly, "because it matters to me." The admission felt strange in my mouth — too light for something that cost me this much to say. "Because from the moment I saw you at your father's house, standing in that hallway with your arms crossed like you were bracing for a hurricane, I couldn't breathe. Because I've spent three weeks watching you hate me while I lost my goddamn mind wanting to know what you were thinking."

She said nothing. I pressed on, because I was already past the point of careful.

"Every time you looked out at the water with that expression you get — like you're calculating the exact distance to the nearest exit — I wanted to ask you where you'd go. What you'd do. Whether it would be enough." I exhaled through my nose. "I've spent a great deal of time trying not to want things I can't earn. I'm not particularly good at it."

The silence that followed was taut, a wire stretched to the breaking point. I could hear the sea working at the stilts beneath us, patient and indifferent.

"You've been thinking about me?" she asked. Her voice was trembling now, in a register I hadn't heard from her before — not afraid, not angry, but close to something softer and more unguarded than either.

"Every second." The words came out without ceremony. "Even when I'm yelling at Marco about port fees. Even when I'm reviewing contracts at two in the morning. Even when I was sleeping on that miserable couch with my feet hanging off the armrest, which I will point out is a structural defect and not a personal failing." I reached out — my hand moving on its own — hovering near her cheek before discipline reasserted itself and I pulled back. My arm fell between us on the mattress, inches from her hand. I stared at the space. "I forced this on you, Dakota. I know that. There's no version of this situation where I didn't put you in a position you never asked for, and I've — I've thought about that, too. But I can't stop wanting you to look at me without that wall in your eyes. Just once. Without the wall."

The wind pushed against the roof. Something small and wooden knocked against the outside of the bungalow — a loose shutter, maybe, or a branch surrendering.

Then she did something that destroyed my last shred of discipline.

She reached out and placed her hand over my heart.

It wasn't demanding. It wasn't seductive. It was just — a hand, laid flat against my chest, as if she needed to confirm something empirical. As if the only data she trusted was the kind she could feel.

"It's beating so fast," she breathed.

"Because you're touching me."

I don't know how long we stayed like that. Long enough for the wind to find a higher pitch. Long enough for my entire nervous system to reorganize itself around the pressure of her palm.

I didn't think. I couldn't. I turned toward her and closed the distance.

The kiss wasn't like the one at the altar. There had been an audience then, and champagne, and the performance of it — the production of two strangers making it look like something it wasn't yet. This was none of that. This was slow at first, almost questioning, my hand coming up to her face as if she might change her mind, as if I needed to leave her the exit. Then it became something else entirely — hungry and desperate, tasting of all the things we hadn't said in three weeks of careful distance.

I tasted the salt on her skin. The gasp in her lungs.

"Tell me to stop," I groaned against her mouth. My hand had found her hair, tangling in it gently, tilting her head back. "Tell me right now and I'll walk out that door and sleep on the sand. I mean it. But if you don't say it—"

She pulled me closer. Her fingers dug into my shoulders like she'd made a decision and intended to keep it. "Don't stop," she whispered. Her voice had lost every careful construction I'd ever heard in it — all the composure, the wariness, the exquisite self-containment. Just her, underneath. "I'm tired of fighting this. I'm tired of fighting you. Just — don't stop."

So I didn't.

The night dissolved into silver light and warm skin and the particular silence of a storm gathering offshore but not yet arrived. I took my time — something I hadn't expected to feel, this patience, this need to go slowly. I'd spent too long watching her from the wrong side of a wall to rush through being allowed past it. I found the exact curve of her shoulder. The precise place on her neck that made her breath catch against my collarbone. Every sound she made — every hitch and sigh — felt like a language I was learning in real time, one I hadn't known I was hungry for until I was already fluent in it.

When I finally pulled her against my chest, her head resting in the crook of my arm, the storm had found the windows. Rain ticked against the glass in fitful bursts. The bungalow creaked and settled around us.

Her breathing slowed. I watched the ceiling, tracing the weave in the thatch, which looked different now than it had an hour ago. Or maybe I was the thing that was different.

"Lorenzo?"

"Hmm."

A pause. I could feel her working up to it — the particular stillness of someone choosing words.

"Does this change things?"

I pressed my lips to the top of her head. Her hair smelled like the sea. Outside, the palms moved and the tide kept its count, and somewhere in the dark, Marco was almost certainly asleep on a boat that needed repainting, blissfully ignorant of the fact that his employer had just lost the last argument he'd been having with himself for three weeks.

"Everything," I said.

And I kept my eyes on the dark horizon, and I knew — with the same bone-deep certainty I usually reserved for contracts and coordinates and the weight of a man's word — that I meant it completely.

Chapter Thirty-One: Dakota

We didn't get two weeks.

We barely got a handful of days before reality came crashing back in.

The call changed everything.

It always does.

The storm didn't just arrive. It attacked.

I woke to the bungalow shuddering on its stilts, the thatched roof groaning under a deluge that sounded less like rain and more like gravel being hurled from a great height. For a disoriented moment — that strange, cotton-headed gap between sleep and sense — I thought I was back in Ohio, eleven years old, crouched in the cellar with my mother while a tornado warning droned on the battery radio. The darkness was the same quality. The feeling of smallness was identical.

Then the lightning flashed, and the room strobed silver, and I saw him.

Lorenzo was already awake. He was sitting up at the edge of the bed, the sheet pooled at his waist, his back to me. In the flickering light I could trace the map of him — the tension across his shoulder blades, the old scars I'd noticed last night without asking about, the rigid line of his spine that told me whatever he was looking at had his full and terrible attention. He wasn't watching the storm through the window. He was staring at a satellite phone in his hand, its blue screen casting his features in a cold, skeletal glow.

"Lorenzo?" My voice came out sleep-thick, tentative. Almost a question about whether he was still the same man.

He didn't turn. "The line to the mainland is down," he said. His voice was flat and precise, stripped of everything from a few hours ago. "The cellular towers on the north side of the island are gone."

I sat up slowly, pulling the duvet to my chest. The warmth of the night — the silver light, his hand in my hair, the way he'd said *everything* like he was signing something in blood — was evaporating in real time, replaced by the chill of the open window and the sound of the sea doing damage somewhere beneath us.

"It's just a storm," I said. The words sounded foolish as soon as they left my mouth.

"It's not the storm." He turned then, and the look in his eyes stopped whatever else I'd been about to say. It wasn't cold, exactly. It was worse than cold — it was evacuated. Cleared out. This wasn't the man who had sat at the edge of my bed to wrap my finger with the concentration of someone defusing something fragile. This wasn't the man who had pressed his lips to my hair and stared at the dark horizon like a person making a private accounting of his life. This was the other one — the one the newspapers photographed leaving courthouses, the one Marco deferred to with a particular kind of careful stillness. The man who ran things. "Marco got a burst transmission through before the satellite link went down. There's been a hit."

The word landed like a stone dropping into still water. "A hit. On who?"

"My father." He stood, and his nakedness was entirely unselfconscious now — not intimate, just irrelevant. He moved toward the closet with a focused, economical energy, like a machine that had been switched back on. "The Calabrese didn't wait for the honeymoon to end. They hit the villa two hours ago. My father is in surgery." He pulled a dark shirt from a hanger, shoved his arms in. "Matteo is missing."

I sat with that for a moment. Matteo — the younger brother, the one Lorenzo had mentioned exactly once in three weeks, briefly and with the careful neutrality of someone who had practiced not showing what something cost him.

The bungalow walls flexed inward in a gust. Outside, the lagoon that had spent two weeks being turquoise and docile was doing something else entirely.

"What does that mean for us?" I asked. My heart was making itself known in a way hearts usually have the decency not to.

"It means the performance is over, Dakota." He buttoned the shirt without looking down at his hands. "We're leaving. Now. I don't care what the pilots say about the crosswinds. We are going back."

He stopped at the edge of the bed and looked down at me. Whatever tenderness had lived in him last night — and I had felt it, I knew I hadn't imagined it, I'd had my hand on his chest and felt what it cost him to be honest — was buried now under something dense and cold and very old. He had a look I recognized from my father's worst years: the look of a man who has sealed a room inside himself and swallowed the key.

"Pack your things," he said. "The red bikini stays here. You won't be needing it where we're going."

The transition from paradise to purgatory took less than twenty minutes.

Lorenzo didn't help me pack this time. He was already on the deck before I'd found my second shoe, his voice carrying through the storm in sharp, jagged Italian — the kind that doesn't leave room for responses. I moved through the bungalow in a kind of daze, shoving things into the suitcase without folding them, without caring. The white sundress I'd worn to dinner two nights ago. A damp swimsuit. The book I hadn't opened since the first day, spine unbroken, still optimistic. I kicked it into the corner and didn't go back for it.

By the time I dragged my bag to the door, the boat was already idling at the private dock below us. It wasn't the sleek, quiet craft from our arrival — the one with the white cushions and the crew member who'd handed me a cold drink before I'd even stepped aboard. This was something rawer. Rugged and fast and stripped of any pretense of leisure. The man at the helm had the particular stillness of someone who had been in situations that didn't allow for fidgeting.

"Get in," Lorenzo said. His hand closed around my arm — not rough, but absolute, the way a current is absolute.

The wind hit us the moment we stepped onto the dock. It was a physical thing, salt-laden and aggressive, and the rain had the stinging quality of something with a point to prove. I gripped the railing as we cleared the dock and hit the first open-water swell. The boat launched upward, hung for a nauseating half-second, and slammed back down. My teeth knocked together. Lorenzo, at the center of the boat with his feet braced wide and his dark hair plastered flat, seemed to absorb the impact through sheer refusal to acknowledge it. He was staring toward the horizon. Toward the airstrip.

"We won't make it!" I shouted over the roar of the gale. "The plane can't take off in this!"

"It has to." He didn't look at me. The wind took the words and shredded them but I heard them anyway. "The Calabrese think I'm trapped here. They think they have two weeks to dismantle everything I've built while I sit on an island drinking from a coconut. I am going to show them exactly how badly they've miscalculated."

Another wave took the hull broadside. I pressed myself against the railing and said nothing else.

We reached the airstrip just as the second band of the storm swept in from the south. The hangars were lit a sickly yellow under the emergency lights, and our pilot was waiting on the tarmac with the expression of a man who had recently done the math and not liked the answer.

"Signore, the crosswinds are at forty knots. The runway—"

Lorenzo didn't let him finish. He crossed the tarmac in four strides and took hold of the pilot's flight suit in one fist, not violently, but with a controlled force that made the point more clearly than violence would have. He said something in Italian too low for me to hear over the engines and the rain. The pilot nodded once, with the resignation of someone who has decided that their employer is the more immediate threat.

Lorenzo released him and turned. The rain was sheeting off his hair, his face expressionless in the amber light. For a moment he just looked at me, the way you look at something you're committing to memory.

"Dakota. Go inside. Strap yourself in. Don't come out until we're at thirty thousand feet."

"Lorenzo—"

"Go." Not a shout. Something quieter than a shout, and harder.

I went.

I climbed the stairs to the cabin and sat down in a leather seat that felt obscene in its softness, and I pressed my back against it and listened to the engines begin to wind up while the fuselage shook in the gusts. Through the oval window the tarmac was slick and silver and empty except for Lorenzo, who was still outside. I watched him speak briefly to the boat pilot — a clipped exchange, one hand reaching to the small of his back in a movement that was so automatic, so unconscious, that it took me a full second to understand what I was seeing. The handgun holstered there. The weight of it checked without ceremony, the way another person might check their watch.

I looked away.

The engines screamed up to pitch. The plane began to move, shaking in a way that commercial aircraft are specifically engineered not to shake, every rivet announcing its presence. I pressed my palm flat on the armrest. Then, without quite deciding to, I lifted my hand and touched my index finger — the bandaged one, the one he had wrapped with such focused, unnecessary care while the afternoon light came through the slats and neither of us said what we were thinking.

The bandage was still there. A little loose from the water and the rain. Still there.

The plane tilted sharply, angling up into the gray, and the lagoon fell away beneath us — all that ruined turquoise, all that warm and temporary water — and we climbed hard into the belly of the storm, rattling and straining, until the turbulence cracked once like a whip and then smoothed, and outside the window there was only the dark above the clouds.

I didn't move for a long time.

We were going back to Rome. Back to the blood, back to the debts, back to a house where a man I'd never met was on a surgical table and a boy I knew almost nothing about was simply *missing*, which in the vocabulary of this world meant something specific and terrible.

And sitting in that ridiculous leather seat with the cashmere blanket folded untouched beside me, I turned over the most frightening realization I'd had since my father had first said Lorenzo 's name in a voice stripped of all options.

I wasn't only afraid for myself anymore.

I was afraid for the man in the cockpit — the one currently forcing an aircraft through forty-knot crosswinds by the sheer pressure of his own will, who had said *everything* in the dark like a person surrendering something they'd guarded a long time.

The man who, despite everything, I was no longer sure I wanted to survive this without.

32

Chapter Thirty-Two: Lorenzo

The hum of the jet's engines usually acted as a sedative, but tonight it sounded like a countdown.

I'd collapsed into the captain's chair four hours ago, my body demanding a debt of sleep I couldn't afford to pay. Behind my closed eyelids, the world was a jagged montage of the storm in Bora Bora and the blood on the stones of the villa in Rome. But even in the shallowest depths of sleep, my mind was anchored to the woman sitting ten feet away.

I felt the shift in the cabin before I heard it. A change in the air, the soft *scuff* of a footstep that didn't belong to the flight crew.

I opened my eyes slowly, not moving a muscle.

Dakota was standing by my desk. The amber floor lights caught the gold in her hair, casting her silhouette against the dark abyss of the window. I watched, frozen in a state between exhaustion and instinct, as the plane hit a pocket of turbulence. My laptop slid. She caught it.

I should have moved then. I should have snapped at her to step away. But I was curious. I wanted to see if she would close it or if the curiosity that made her so captivating would finally be her undoing.

She sat in my chair. She clicked a file. And I watched the light of the screen drain the color from her face.

"Dakota."

My voice was a low rumble, cutting through the silence of the cabin. She spun around, her eyes wide and glassy with a shock that quickly sharpened into a jagged, visceral hatred.

"You've been stalking me," she whispered. Her voice was thin, brittle enough to snap. "For years. Before the debt. Before the wedding. You were watching me when I didn't even know you existed."

I stood up, the movement fluid and predatory despite the ache in my bones. I didn't deny it. Lies were for men who feared the truth; I simply owned it. I walked toward her, my shadow stretching over the desk until it eclipsed the screen—eclipsed the photos of her in Ohio, the records of her art classes, the timeline of her father's ruin.

"I wasn't stalking you," I said, my voice cold, shedding the warmth of the island like a discarded skin. "I was protecting an investment."

"An investment?" She stood up, shoving the laptop toward me as if it were a physical weapon. "I'm a person, Lorenzo! I thought… last night, I thought you actually cared. That the 'Monster' was just a mask. But this? This is calculated. You didn't marry me to save my father. You broke him so you could have me."

I reached out, my hand slamming onto the marble desk, pinning her between the chair and the heat of my body. I leaned in, the scent of her fear mixing with the cedar and rain on my skin.

"I didn't break him, Dakota. Your father broke himself through greed and incompetence. I just ensured that when the floor fell out from under him, I was the only one standing there to catch you."

"Why?" she screamed. The sound was raw, echoing off the luxury wood paneling. "Why me? Why go to all this trouble for a girl from Ohio?"

I caught her chin, my grip firm, forcing her to look into the darkness I'd lived in my entire life.

"Because I saw you once," I whispered, the memory hitting me with the force of a blow. "At a gala in New York. You were wearing a dress the color of woodsmoke, looking at a painting like it was the only real thing in a room full of ghosts. And I decided right then that I didn't want the painting. I wanted the girl."

She sobbed, a broken, jagged sound that made something in my chest tighten—a phantom pain I didn't have time for.

"You bought me," she choked out. "Every touch, every 'kind' word on this trip… it was just part of the plan, wasn't it? To make the prisoner love her jailer?"

My expression flickered. For a heartbeat, the mask of the Capo cracked. Last night hadn't been a plan. Last night had been the first time in my life I'd felt truly alive, and now, I'd turned that life into a weapon she would use against me forever.

"Last night wasn't part of a plan," I said roughly. "Last night was a mistake. One I clearly shouldn't have made."

The plane dropped sharply in a pocket of air. We swayed, but I didn't let go of her. I couldn't.

"We land in Rome in six hours," I said, my voice turning to iron. "My father is dying. My family is at war. You will play your part, Dakota. You will be the devoted wife, and you will stay behind the walls I built for you. Because now, more than ever, you are the only thing in this world I refuse to lose."

I released her and walked toward the cockpit. I didn't look back at her. I couldn't bear to see the girl from Ohio looking at me like I was the devil, because I knew that today, I finally was.

The red bikini was in Bora Bora. And the man who had loved her there was dead.

33

Chapter Thirty-Three: Dakota

The Safe Room wasn't a room. It was a vault.

The walls were thick limestone, the kind that had been here long before the house above it, probably long before the family that built the house. They sweated faintly in the cold — damp with the smell of aging grapes and turned earth and something older underneath, something that had nothing to do with wine. The ceiling was low enough that the single emergency light mounted above the door cast more shadow than illumination, painting the corners in a deep amber dark that my eyes kept trying to resolve into shapes.

Marco's footsteps retreated up the stone passage, steady and purposeful, and then the heavy door swung to with a sound like a period at the end of a sentence. The silence that followed was so complete it made my ears ring. Not quiet — *silent*, the specific silence of a space built to keep the outside world outside. I could feel it pressing against my eardrums.

I stood in the middle of the room and breathed.

Against the far wall, beneath a mounted rack of dusty bottles that no one had touched in years, sat a steel-reinforced tunnel door. Brushed metal. A keypad with a small green ready light that pulsed once every few seconds, patient and indifferent. Marco had given me the code. Four digits, easy to remember. He'd said it twice, his eyes steady on mine, making sure I had it.

The American Embassy. Freedom.

I stared at it for a long moment.

I could leave. The math was simple enough — four digits, a tunnel, however many meters of dark passageway, and then daylight on the other side of the estate wall. I knew roughly where it came out; Marco had told me that too, with the particular efficiency of a man briefing someone he doesn't expect to see again. A side street. A consular car, if the timing held. By sunrise I could be in a building with a flag outside it, sitting in a fluorescent-lit room drinking bad coffee while someone in a suit explained my options in careful, bureaucratic English.

I thought about my father's voice on the phone three weeks ago — that particular hollowness, the sound of a man who has run out of road. I thought about the files on the laptop. Years of my life reduced to a spreadsheet, annotated and cross-referenced and archived by a man who had decided that wanting something was the same as being entitled to it. The surveillance reports. The photographs. The fact that he had known the brand of coffee I ordered before I'd ever said his name.

I thought about the man who had kissed my forehead twenty minutes ago — deliberate, soft, final — and told me to run.

I didn't move toward the tunnel.

I moved toward the grate in the door.

It was a small thing — a ventilation grille set into the steel at eye height, just wide enough to press your face against and see the passage beyond. I pressed mine against it and saw nothing useful: the dim stone corridor, the bottom step of the staircase that curved up and out of view, the edge of something dark on the floor that might have been a shadow or might have been Marco's jacket. I couldn't hear anything from up there. The walls were doing their job.

Don't do anything stupid, I'd told him. An almost laughable thing to say to Lorenzo Marchetti, who had built his entire adult life on the principle that if a thing was worth doing, it was worth doing with a complete disregard for personal cost. He had engineered a marriage out of nothing because he couldn't manage the ordinary vocabulary of wanting something. He had built a cage around me and called it protection and meant both things simultaneously, and somehow that was more frightening than if he'd only meant one.

But upstairs, in the thirty seconds before Marco had taken my arm and moved me toward the passage — Lorenzo had looked at me differently. Not like a man managing an asset. Not like the version of him that appeared in news photographs, face composed into something that disclosed nothing. He'd looked at me like a person who had done a final accounting and made his peace with the result, as long as one particular variable survived the equation.

I understood, standing in the vault with my forehead against a ventilation grate, that I did not want to be the variable that survived while everything else burned.

I stepped back from the door.

Against the wall beside the decorative fireplace — cold, ornamental, the kind that exists in old stone rooms purely to suggest comfort rather than provide it — a heavy iron fire poker leaned in its stand. I reached for it. The weight of it was immediate and serious, soot-dark and real in my grip. I wrapped both hands around the shaft and felt something that wasn't quite calm settle over me. Not bravery. Something more pragmatic. The kind of clarity that arrives when the number of available options gets small enough to count on one hand.

"I'm not leaving," I whispered. The shadows absorbed it without comment.

I positioned myself to the left of the door — not in front of it, not visible through the grate, but close. I stood with my back against the cool limestone and the poker held low against my leg and I waited. The emergency light pulsed its amber rhythm. The wine bottles held their long patience on the rack.

I waited for the sound of Lorenzo's boots on the stone. For Marco's precise, unhurried knock — three, then two, the pattern he'd told me to listen for. I waited for some signal that the men upstairs had done what men like them were built to do, and that the world above was returning to whatever passed for its baseline.

Instead, I heard a body hit the floor.

It was close — just beyond the vault door, in the passage. A heavy, definitive sound, the kind that has no ambiguity to it. Not a stumble. Not a man going down to one knee. The particular finality of dead weight meeting stone.

Then: a key at the lock. Frantic. Scratching at the housing, missing, finding it, missing again. Not Marco's steady hand — Marco, who had moved through three weeks of controlled crisis with the unhurried precision of someone who had agreed long ago not to be rattled by anything. This was someone else's hand. Someone working fast and slightly wrong, breathing audible through the door, scraping at the steel.

The bolt slid back with a sound like a blade being drawn.

The door swung inward.

For one suspended moment I saw only a silhouette: a man in a dark tactical vest, compact and deliberate in his dimensions, a submachine gun slung across his chest on a single-point mount. His face was masked — not the improvised kind, but the fitted black balaclava of someone who had come prepared to be unidentifiable. His head moved in a single practiced sweep of the room, the habitual threat-assessment of a person who does this professionally. Left wall. Right wall. Center.

He wasn't looking for a wife.

He was looking for a target. He had a picture of one somewhere — in a briefing, on a phone screen, in his head — and he was comparing it against the contents of the room.

His weapon came up.

And I understood, with a jolt of cold clarity that traveled from my sternum out to my fingertips, what Lorenzo had actually built down here.

Not just a cage. Not just a place to keep me safe from the world above. He had built a room with one door and one way out and stone walls too thick to breach and an exit only I knew the code to — which meant that anyone who came through the door while I was still here had made a fatal miscalculation about the room's contents.

He had built me a vault.

And I was the only one in it who knew where the exit wasn't.

The man in the vest took one step across the threshold, adjusting his angle, and I moved — not toward the tunnel, not toward freedom, but toward the door, swinging the poker in a short, hard arc toward the hand that held the weapon, everything in me committed to the single brutal geometry of making him drop it before he had time to understand that he'd walked into the wrong room.

The vault had been built to keep things out.

Tonight, it was going to keep something in.

34

Chapter Thirty-Four: Lorenzo

The smell of gunpowder and expensive wine shouldn't mix. They belong to different worlds, different vocabularies, different versions of what a life can look like. But in the cellar of Villa Marchetti, with the emergency lighting casting everything in the color of old amber, they were the only two scents left — sharp and acrid cutting through something soft and aged, neither one winning.

I kicked the vault door open with my shoulder, my Beretta raised in both hands, my heart hammering out a rhythm of pure, unadulterated terror. Not for my life. That had been forfeit the moment I took the name Marchetti — not as a burden but as a declaration, understanding what it cost and paying it anyway, every year, with interest. No. The fear threading through my chest as I cleared the doorframe had a specific shape and a specific name, and she was somewhere in the dark ahead of me.

I saw her.

She wasn't cowering. She wasn't pressed into the corner with her arms over her head the way every sane person would have been. She was standing in the center of the vault — feet planted, spine straight — with an iron fire poker gripped in both hands, her knuckles white against the soot-dark shaft, her eyes blazing with a feral and focused light I hadn't known she possessed. A Calabrese soldier was on the floor at her feet, groaning, one hand pressed to a wrist that was bent at a persuasive angle. He wasn't getting up. She had made certain of that.

She looked at me. I looked at her.

The vault smelled of cold stone and dust and something metallic that I didn't examine too closely. The emergency light pulsed. Outside and above us, the villa made a sound like a body settling into something permanent.

My mind, with spectacular and treacherous timing, chose that moment to abandon the present entirely.

The sunlight in Bora Bora had been a different substance than sunlight anywhere else. I had noticed it on the first morning, standing on the deck with an espresso going cold in my hand, watching the lagoon make its slow transition from pre-dawn silver to the particular layered turquoise that looked like something a painter had invented rather than a body of water. I had stood there calculating the angle and thinking, distantly, that light this quality should be protected from men like me. That it was wasted on someone who spent it cataloguing threat vectors and checking the satellite phone every twenty minutes.

Dakota had appeared in the doorway wearing nothing but my t-shirt, her hair wrecked by sleep, squinting against the brightness.

"You're up early," she'd said.

I remembered the weight of her against me when she'd come to stand beside me at the railing. The way she'd taken the espresso from my hand without asking and tried it and handed it back without comment. We had been learning each other in those weeks in a way that felt provisional and terrifying — every moment of ease undermined by the knowledge of what waited at home, every laugh carrying the faint echo of everything I hadn't told her yet.

We had developed a language for it, the way people develop languages for things too fragile to address directly. *Excessive togetherness. Annoying amounts of presence.* Small jokes that were also something else, something larger and more serious that neither of us had the vocabulary for yet.

I had promised her things on that deck. The Pantheon at sunset — the specific hour when the light comes through the oculus at an angle that makes even the most resolutely unromantic person stand still for a moment.

Cornetti from the place on the Via della Croce, the ones that were better than anything in any other city. A version of Rome that was mine to give and not a trap to be navigated. I had made these promises the way a man makes promises when he is standing in borrowed sunlight and trying to extend it by will alone.

"I'm not going to run the first time I see you be cold," she had told me in the tangled sheets of our last afternoon, the ceiling fan moving the heavy air above us, the lagoon outside turning gold with the late hour. Her voice had been steady in that particular way of hers — not the steadiness of someone performing courage, but the quieter steadiness of someone who has simply already made their decision. "I'm already in. I already care."

I had not said the equivalent back. I had done what I always did with things that mattered too much: filed it, held it at a precise internal distance, told myself there would be time.

The flight back had been its own particular punishment. I had sat across the aisle from her while she slept against the window, and I had spent four hours conducting a silent argument with myself about how to do this correctly — how to bring her into my world without the world consuming her, how to let her close without making her a target, how to be both honest and protective when those two things had spent my entire adult life pulling in opposite directions. I had felt, more than once in those hours, like a man trying to carry water in his hands across a great distance, watching it disappear between his fingers and unable to move faster.

And then she had found the files.

The spreadsheets. The surveillance notes. Three years of compiled information about a woman who had no idea she was being compiled. I had watched her face change in the study — the specific quality of that change, the way it moved through confusion and into something colder and more considered — and I had understood that I had confirmed every worst assumption she'd arrived with. That I had handed her the evidence myself.

The present rushed back in a cold and violent wave.

The villa groaned above us — structural, deep, the sound of a building absorbing something it wasn't designed to absorb. A second explosion, farther away than the last but significant. Dust sifted from the vault ceiling in a fine curtain that caught the amber light and hung there for a moment before settling.

Dakota didn't drop the poker. She didn't move toward me with relief or away from me with fear. She stood exactly where she was and held my gaze, her breathing audible and uneven, her eyes doing that thing I'd spent three weeks trying to decode — the rapid internal assessment, the weighing, the decision being reached in real time. She looked at me not as her captor. Not as the monster from the laptop files. Not even as the man who had kissed her forehead in the dark and told her to run.

She looked at me as her partner.

In a war she had never agreed to enter, in a house she'd had no reason to defend, with a fire poker she'd picked up on her own, for reasons that had nothing to do with obligation and everything to do with a choice she had made somewhere in the silence of the vault while I was fighting my way down the stairs.

"You didn't go to the embassy," I said. My voice sounded foreign to me — too rough, scraped clean of its usual register by the last forty minutes of things I was not going to recount in detail. "The tunnel was right there, Dakota. Marco gave you the code. You could have been out."

"I told you in Bora Bora," she said. Her voice was trembling — fine, visible tremor, completely unashamed — but it didn't break. It held the sentence to its end. "I'm not going to run just because things got complicated." A beat. Something that was almost dry moved through her eyes, brief and startling. "But you owe me considerably more than a sunset at the Pantheon for this."

The laugh that came out of me was brief and involuntary and tasted like blood and relief in approximately equal measure. It surprised us both.

"I'll give you the whole city," I said, stepping over the groaning Calabrese soldier without looking down. "If we make it through the night, I will burn Rome to the ground and rebuild it in whatever configuration you find acceptable."

I crossed the vault to her. My hand came up toward her face — and then stopped, hovering. My knuckles were dark with something I hadn't had time to think about. My shirt was ruined. I was, in any objective assessment, not something clean to touch. But Dakota looked at my hand, hanging there in the cold air between us, and she leaned forward. Pressed her cheek into my palm. The cold of the cellar was in her skin, and I felt it through every line of my hand.

"The *together* part of the deal starts now," she said quietly. "No more sending me to the vault and handling it alone."

"Together," I said. The word felt different in the vault than it had on the deck in Bora Bora. Heavier. More load-bearing.

I took the fire poker from her hand and set it against the wall. Then I reached to my waistband and drew the spare Beretta — smaller than mine, better for her grip — and held it out to her flat across my palm. I watched her look at it. Watched the flinch move through her, quick and honest, the entirely reasonable response of a person who was raised in Ohio and not in rooms like this one. And then I watched her take it.

Her fingers curled around the grip with more steadiness than she probably felt.

"Safety is already off," I said. My voice had shifted into the register I used for things that needed to land clearly and stay. "Point. Squeeze. Don't think. Don't look at their faces." I kept my eyes on hers. "You will not have to. I intend to make sure of that. But if you do—"

"I know," she said.

I believed her.

I believed her in a way I hadn't believed anything in a long time — not because she had proven herself in any of the ways I'd spent years cataloguing and measuring, but because she was still standing in this vault when she didn't have to be. Because she had chosen, in the silence and the dark, to stay.

The last day in Bora Bora felt like a photograph in a language I no longer spoke. The girl in the honey-gold light, the borrowed t-shirt, the espresso and the promises about cornetti — that version of us had been real, and it had been good, and it was gone. Replaced by something that had been tested by the specific gravity of an actual disaster and had not collapsed.

I did not want the girl in the sun anymore.

I wanted the woman standing in the dark with a Beretta she'd never fired, choosing the stairs.

I moved to the door, checked the passage. Turned back once.

"Stay close," I said. "Exactly one step behind my left shoulder. When I stop, you stop."

She nodded once. Precise. Ready.

We went up.

35

Chapter Thirty-Five: Dakota

The doorbell chimed exactly thirty minutes after Bianca hung up.

I'd scrambled into a pair of tailored black trousers and a silk cream blouse—the "Marchetti Uniform" I'd instinctively reached for. I checked my reflection one last time. I looked like a wife. I felt like an imposter.

I opened the door to find Bianca Marchetti standing there with a silver-foiled box of pastries and an expression that could peel paint off a wall. She didn't wait for an invitation; she stepped inside, her scent of jasmine and expensive leather filling the foyer.

"You look tired, Dakota," she said, handing me the box. "And the espresso you made smells burnt. Throw it out. We will start over."

"Lorenzo said—"

"Lorenzo says many things when he is trying to be a husband," Bianca interrupted, heading straight for the kitchen as if she owned the building. Maybe she did. "But he is a Marchetti man. They are excellent at starting fires, but they are terrible at tending the hearth."

I followed her, watching as she effortlessly navigated the chrome machine that had baffled me earlier.

"He told me he loves me," I said, the words slipping out before I could stop them. I needed to say it out loud to see if the air would reject it.

Bianca froze, her hand on the steam wand. She turned slowly, her dark eyes searching mine with a terrifying intensity.

"He said those words? To you? This morning?"

"Yes. Before he left."

Bianca turned back to the machine, her shoulders dropping an inch. "Then God help us all. A Marchetti who loves is a Marchetti who takes risks. And right now, with the Calabrese scratching at the gates, risks are a luxury we cannot afford."

"What is he actually doing, Bianca? He said a shipment… a leak."

She set two tiny porcelain cups on the counter and poured the dark, oily liquid. "He is hunting, Dakota. Someone in our inner circle sold the coordinates of the Sicilian docks. If Lorenzo doesn't find them by noon, the police will find the crates. And if the police find the crates, the Marchetti name becomes a liability to the Board."

The "Board." The nebulous group of shadows that actually ran the city.

"He told me he'd be back by lunch," I whispered, my hand trembling as I reached for my cup.

"Lorenzo lives in a world of 'mights' and 'maybes,'" Bianca said, sitting across from me. She pushed a cannoli toward me. "Eat. You will need your strength. Because while my son is out hunting the fox, you and I are going to discuss the reality of your new position."

She leaned in, the softness of her voice belying the steel in her words.

"You are no longer just a girl from Ohio with a debt. You are the heartbeat of this family. If you fail to be strong, Lorenzo will stumble trying to carry you. Do you understand?"

I looked at the window, at the Roman skyline that Lorenzo had promised to show me. The "I love you" felt less like a gift now and more like a heavy, golden collar.

"I'm trying, Bianca."

"Don't try," she snapped, though not unkindly. "Be. Now, tell me… what did you see on his laptop before we left Bora Bora? Don't lie to me, child. I saw the look on your face when you got off that plane."

The room went cold. She knew.

36

Chapter Thirty-Six: Lorenzo

The air in the warehouse was stagnant, thick with the scent of rusted iron and the cold, sharp tang of fear. It was a smell I'd known since I was fifteen, a scent that signaled the shift from man to monster.

I watched Paolo being dragged away, his pleas for his daughter's future echoing off the corrugated steel walls. My face remained a mask of marble, but inside, a jagged crack was forming.

I love you.

I'd said those words to Dakota this morning. I'd tasted her skin, felt the pulse in her neck, and whispered the truth like a prayer. Now, three hours later, I was ordering a man's ruin. The transition should have been seamless—it always had been before. But today, the shadow of the girl from Ohio was standing in the corner of the warehouse, watching me with invisible, judgmental eyes.

"Lorenzo." Marco's voice broke through my thoughts. He was wiping grease from his hands, his expression unreadable. "You did the right thing. Loyalty is the only currency we have left. If the Calabrese think we're bleeding from the inside, they'll stop scratching at the gates and start kicking them down."

"I know," I said, my voice like gravel. "Just find out who paid him. I want a name, Marco. Not a shell company. A name."

I walked out into the blinding Roman sun, the heat pressing against my

176

black button-down. I felt filthy. Not with blood—I hadn't touched Paolo—but with the reality of the life I was asking Dakota to share.

I stopped at Bellini's on the way back. The contrast was almost laughable.

"Peonies," I told the florist, my hand resting near the holster concealed by my leather jacket. "The large arrangement. And the card… just write *'I meant it.'*"

The florist smiled, a soft, civilian smile that made me want to flinch. She saw a husband buying flowers for his wife. She didn't see the man who had just sentenced a father to a basement interrogation.

The Penthouse — 12:45 PM

When I entered the penthouse, the scent of jasmine and expensive leather hit me first. My mother was here.

I found them on the couch, the delicate clink of china a stark contrast to the heavy *thud* of boots I'd heard all morning. Dakota looked small next to my mother—vulnerable, yet she was holding her teacup with a steady hand.

"Be nice to her," I'd texted my mother. Looking at them now, I realized I should have been more worried about Dakota being nice to *me*.

After my mother left, the silence in the room became a living thing. Dakota stood by the window, the Roman skyline framing her like a Renaissance portrait.

"How did it go?" she asked. "The situation?"

"Handled," I said. I moved behind her, wrapping my arms around her waist, burying my face in the crook of her neck. I wanted to wash the warehouse out of my lungs with the scent of her hair.

"You left this morning looking like you might not come back," she whispered.

"I always come back."

"Don't do that, Lorenzo. Don't say you love me and then walk into a fire. It makes me…" She turned in my arms, her eyes searching mine, looking for the man who had whispered to her in Bora Bora. "It makes me care. And I didn't want to care."

I tipped her chin up, the weight of the peonies on the table behind us a silent witness to my desperation. "I'm not asking you to be ready to say it back. I'm just asking you to stay. To let me show you the city. The real Rome."

"The one that demands blood?" she asked, her voice trembling.

"And the one that offers everything else," I promised.

I saw the internal battle in her eyes—the girl who wanted to run back to Ohio vs. the woman who had already begun to weave her soul into mine.

"Okay," she said finally. "Show me."

I grabbed my keys, but as we walked toward the door, my phone vibrated in my pocket. A burst transmission from Marco.

Paolo talked. It wasn't just the Calabrese. It's an uprising. They're moving on the Villa tonight.

I looked at Dakota, her hand already reaching for mine, her face full of a tentative, beautiful hope. The Situation wasn't handled. It was just beginning.

"Ready?" I asked, my grip on her hand tightening until it was almost painful.

"No," she said, leaning into me. "But let's go anyway."

37

Chapter Thirty-Seven: Dakota

The sugar from the cornetto was still sweet on my tongue when the air in the Trastevere street turned to ice.

Lorenzo had been different at Nonna Rosa's. He'd been the boy who hid in bookstores and failed at his first kiss. But as we stepped out into the golden afternoon light, the man who had ordered an interrogation three hours ago returned with a vengeance.

"Lorenzo? Lorenzo Marchetti?"

The voice was like a blade sliding across silk. Antonio Calabrese stood from a nearby bistro table, his tailored suit the color of a bruise.

I felt Lorenzo's grip on my hand tighten—not in affection, but in a warning. He was anchoring me, or perhaps anchoring himself.

"Signor Calabrese," Lorenzo said, his voice dropping an octave into that dangerous, neutral territory.

I watched the older man's eyes. They didn't just look at me; they appraised me, calculating my worth in blood and leverage. When he took my hand, his skin was unnervingly cold. He didn't kiss my knuckles; he lingered, his eyes locked on Lorenzo's, watching for the twitch in my husband's jaw that would signal a weakness.

"You're even lovelier than the wedding photos suggested," Calabrese murmured.

"Tomorrow night," Lorenzo cut in, his voice like a slamming door. "My office. Seven o'clock."

"Of course." Calabrese's smile was a jagged line. "I look forward to it. And perhaps your lovely wife can join us for drinks afterward? My wife would love to meet her."

"We'll see."

Lorenzo pulled me away so sharply I nearly stumbled. He didn't speak until we were three blocks away, tucked into the shadow of an ancient stone archway. He slammed his hand against the wall, the sound echoing in the narrow alley.

"He was testing me," Lorenzo hissed, his eyes dark with a feral, protective rage. "He touched you to see if I'd burn the street down. He wanted to see if I've gone soft."

"Have you?" I whispered, my heart hammering.

"No," he rasped, cupping my face with hands that were shaking. "It's made me worse. Because now, Dakota, I have a soul. And a man with a soul is a man who can be broken."

The romantic afternoon was dead. The "real Rome" Lorenzo wanted to show me wasn't the fountains or the hidden cafes; it was this—the constant, suffocating weight of being a target.

"Tomorrow night, you stay in the penthouse," he commanded. "Lock the doors. Don't answer for anyone. Marco will have four men on the landing."

"Lorenzo, you can't keep me in a cage."

"Better a cage than a coffin!" he snapped. The bluntness of it stole my breath. He saw the shock on my face and immediately pulled me into his chest, burying his face in my hair. "I'm sorry. I'm sorry, *amore*. But he saw you. He saw that I love you. And in my world, that's a death warrant if I'm not careful."

As we walked back to the car, the city looked different. The terracotta roofs looked like dried blood; the shadows between the buildings looked like places for men with guns to hide.

I'd thought I was ready to be a Marchetti wife. I'd thought I understood the "business."

But as Lorenzo checked the locks on the penthouse door three times, his eyes darting to the windows, I realized the truth. The honeymoon wasn't just over.

The war had found us.

38

Chapter Thirty-Eight: Lorenzo

The drive back to the penthouse was a blur of neon lights and adrenaline. Tony was pushing the armored sedan through Roman traffic like a getaway driver, but to me, we were moving through molasses.

"The view from the street is quite good," the voice had said.

That sentence was a physical blow. It meant they had been positioned. They had been watching her move, perhaps watching her drink her tea, watching her wait for a husband who was busy trading percentages of blood and oil.

I burst through the door, my lungs burning, my hand already on the grip of my sidearm.

"Dakota!"

She emerged from the bedroom, her face a pale mask of confusion. I didn't speak; I just hauled her into my arms. I needed to feel the steady thrum of her heart to silence the roar in my ears.

"Lorenzo, you're hurting me," she whispered, though she didn't pull away.

"He was watching you," I rasped into her hair. "The penthouse… it's a glass box, Dakota. I thought the height made us safe. I thought the security at the door was enough. But Calabrese… he didn't want to kill you tonight. He wanted to show me that he *could*."

I pulled back, searching her eyes. She was terrified, yes, but there was a flicker of that same iron I'd seen in Bora Bora. She wasn't breaking.

"What does this mean?" she asked. "What happens now?"

"We can't stay here," I said, already turning to the closet to grab an emergency bag. "The penthouse is compromised. If he can see in, he can put a red dot on your chest from a kilometer away. We're moving."

"Moving where? My mother's? A hotel?"

"No." I stopped, the weight of the decision settling in my gut like lead. "The Villa. My father's estate. It's a fortress. Triple-reinforced stone, private grounds, a full garrison of men who've been with us for twenty years. It's the only place in Italy where I can put a wall between you and the world that actually holds."

I didn't tell her that the Villa was also a lightning rod. That by moving there, I was consolidating all my targets in one place. My dying father, my brother Matteo, and the woman who had become my soul.

"Lorenzo," she said, catching my wrist. "Is this about safety, or is this about you wanting to hide me away again?"

"It's about survival," I snapped, then softened as I saw her flinch. I cupped her face, my thumb tracing the line of her jaw. "I meant what I said. I love you. And I will not let you become a footnote in a war over shipping lanes. We go to the Villa tonight. We lock the gates. And we wait for the 48 hours to expire."

I checked my watch. 11:45 PM.

"Tony!" I roared toward the door. "Bring the lead car around. Tell Marco we're moving the 'Investment.' Full convoy. Blackout protocols."

Dakota looked at the suitcase, then back at me. "The 'Investment'?"

"A habit," I lied, my heart aching. "You're my wife, Dakota. But to the men outside, you're the crown jewels. We're going to treat you like it."

As we descended to the garage, I felt a prickle on the back of my neck. The city felt predatory. Every shadow in the parking structure looked like a hitman; every distant siren sounded like a funeral dirge.

I tucked Dakota into the back of the reinforced SUV, shielding her body with mine until the door hissed shut.

"We'll be at the Villa by dawn," I promised as the convoy pulled out into the rainy Roman night.

I didn't know then that the "fortress" was already breached. I didn't know that by taking her to the Villa, I was handing Calabrese exactly what he wanted:

All of us, in one cage, waiting for the match to be struck.

39

Chapter Thirty-Nine: Dakota

The penthouse didn't feel like a home anymore. It felt like a high-end aquarium where the glass was slowly cracking.

Lorenzo was a whirlwind of controlled violence and logistics. He stood at the dining table with Marco and Tony, maps of the building spread out next to half-eaten pastries from Nonna Rosa's. The contrast was sickening—the sweetness of the morning replaced by the metallic tang of gun oil as Marco cleaned his sidearm.

"I want sensors on the service elevator," Lorenzo barked. "And I want a drone in the air. If a bird flies too close to the balcony, I want to know its heartbeat."

"Lorenzo," I said, stepping into the room. The three men went silent instantly. It was a terrifying kind of respect. "You're turning this place into a tomb."

"I'm turning it into a stronghold," he countered, his eyes dark with exhaustion.

"You're turning it into a target," I said, walking to the window. I reached for the heavy velvet curtain, but Lorenzo was there in a heartbeat, his hand clamping over mine.

"Don't," he hissed. "He told me the view from the street was good, Dakota. Don't give him a front-row seat."

I looked at his hand—scarred, powerful, and trembling. That was the moment it hit me. He wasn't just being a "Capo" or a "Monster." He was a man who was terrified of losing the only thing that made him feel human.

I led him to the bedroom, closing the door on the war room outside.

"I'll learn to shoot," I whispered, watching the relief flood his face. "But Lorenzo… you have to understand. If we stay here, trapped behind these curtains, we've already lost. We're just waiting for him to find a bigger hammer to break the glass."

"Then we leave," he said, his voice dropping. "Not to a hotel. Not to your mother's. We go to the Villa. My father's estate. It's a fortress of stone, not glass. There are tunnels, a garrison, and walls that have held off better men than Antonio Calabrese for three hundred years."

I sat on the edge of the bed, the reality of it sinking in. Moving to the Villa meant entering the heart of the Marchetti power. It meant meeting his dying father. It meant the honeymoon was officially, bloodily over.

"Okay," I said. "The Villa."

He sat beside me, taking my hand. "Dakota, why are you doing this? You could have demanded a flight back to the States. You could have used that laptop file to bury me. Why stay?"

I looked at him—really looked at him. I saw the man who bandaged my finger in Bora Bora and the man who ordered a traitor's ruin in a warehouse. They were the same person. And God help me, I loved both of them.

"Because I'm a Marchetti now," I said, the lie tasting like truth. "And we don't run."

He kissed me then, a desperate, hungry thing that tasted of espresso and fear. He still didn't know I loved him, but as he pulled me against his chest, I realized I was staying for the man, not the protection.

"Tomorrow," he whispered against my lips. "We start your training. And then, we move to the Villa."

I nodded, watching the shadows dance on the ceiling. I didn't know then that the "fortress" was already being mapped by the enemy. I didn't know that by choosing the Villa, we were choosing the battlefield where everything would end.

I just knew that for the first time in my life, I wasn't afraid of the monster under the bed. I was married to him.

40

Chapter Forty: Lorenzo

It had been weeks since I arrived in Italy.

Days since Bora Bora.

And everything that had felt soft and distant there had sharpened into something real again.

Dakota stared at the gun in my hand like it might bite her.

"It's not loaded," I said, holding it out. "Just feel the weight first."

We were in one of our private ranges—a converted warehouse in an industrial district that asked no questions. Soundproofed, secure, and far enough from the penthouse that I could breathe slightly easier knowing she was here, protected, learning.

Marco stood near the door, giving us space but present. Tony was outside. Three other guards were stationed around the perimeter.

Excessive, maybe. But after last night, I wasn't taking chances.

"It's heavier than I expected," Dakota said, finally taking the gun from me. A Glock 19—standard, reliable, not too much recoil for a beginner.

"That's good. Means you'll respect it." I moved behind her, adjusting her grip. "Fingers here, thumb here. Support hand wraps around like this."

She tensed when I touched her, and I realized how close I was standing. Close enough to smell her shampoo, to feel the warmth of her body.

Focus. This was about safety, not—

"Like this?" she asked, and I forced my attention back to her hands.

"Almost. Rotate your support hand slightly. There." I stepped back before I could do something stupid like kiss her neck. "How does it feel?"

"Weird. Heavy. Dangerous."

"It is dangerous. Which is why you need to know how to use it properly." I handed her safety glasses and ear protection. "Put these on."

She complied, looking adorably serious with the oversized glasses perched on her nose. I had to suppress a smile.

"Okay." I loaded the magazine, chambered a round, and handed it back to her. "It's live now. See that target?"

She looked downrange at the paper silhouette twenty feet away. "Yes."

"That's what you're aiming for. Center mass—the chest area. Biggest target, easiest to hit." I moved behind her again, guiding her arms up. "Stance is important. Feet shoulder-width apart. Lean forward slightly. You want to be stable."

"Stable. Right." She adjusted her feet, and I could feel the nervous energy radiating off her. "Lorenzo, what if I miss?"

"Then you miss. That's what practice is for." I checked her grip again. "But Dakota, if you ever have to use this for real—if someone is threatening you—you aim for center mass and you keep shooting until the threat stops. Understood?"

"That's... intense."

"That's reality." I softened my voice. "But we're not there yet. Right now, we're just learning. No pressure."

She nodded, took a breath, and raised the gun.

"When you're ready," I said quietly. "Gentle squeeze on the trigger. Don't jerk it."

She squeezed.

The gun fired, the recoil making her stumble back slightly. I caught her shoulders, steadying her.

"Good," I said. "That was good."

"I missed by like three feet."

"You hit the wall behind the target. For a first shot, that's not bad." I guided her arms back up. "Try again. This time, don't flinch when you pull the trigger."

She fired again. Then again. By the fifth shot, she'd hit the target—outer edge, but still.

"There!" I couldn't keep the pride out of my voice. "You hit it."

She lowered the gun, grinning despite herself. "I did, didn't I?"

"You did." I took the gun, ejected the magazine. "Want to go again?"

"Yes." The answer was immediate, eager. "I want to actually hit center mass."

I smiled. "That's my girl."

We spent the next hour going through magazines. Dakota's aim improved steadily—she was a quick learner, focused and determined once she got past the initial fear.

By the end, she was hitting center mass regularly at twenty feet. Not perfect, but good enough to be effective.

"You're a natural," I said, watching her empty another magazine into the target.

"I wouldn't go that far." But she looked pleased. "How often should I practice?"

"Once a week, at least. More if you want to get really good." I took the gun, made it safe. "But Dakota, remember—this is last resort. If you're ever in a situation where you need this, something has gone very wrong."

"I know." She removed her safety glasses, and her expression was serious. "But I'd rather have it and not need it than need it and not have it."

"Smart." I pulled her into a quick kiss. "Scary, but smart."

"I learned from the best." She smiled against my mouth. "Well, the scariest, anyway."

"I am not scary."

"Lorenzo, you just spent an hour teaching me how to shoot people in the chest. You're objectively scary."

"Only to people who threaten what's mine." I tucked hair behind her ear. "To you, I'm… what's the word… cuddly?"

She laughed—actually laughed—and the sound did something to my chest. "You are absolutely not cuddly."

"I could be cuddly."

"You're about as cuddly as a shark."

"Sharks can be cuddly. You just have to approach them correctly."

"That's not how sharks work."

"How would you know? Have you tried cuddling a shark?"

She was fully laughing now, and Marco glanced over from his position by the door, eyebrows raised. I'd make fun of him later for being surprised I could make my wife laugh.

"Come on," I said, taking her hand. "Let's get you home. You've earned a break."

"Can we stop for food?" She peeled off the ear protection. "I'm starving. Apparently shooting makes you hungry."

"Everything makes you hungry."

"That's not true. I wasn't hungry in Bora Bora."

"You were constantly hungry in Bora Bora. We ate like six meals a day."

"That was different. That was vacation eating."

"Vacation eating." I pulled her close as we walked to the car. "Is that different from regular eating?"

"Completely different. Vacation eating doesn't count." She leaned into me, comfortable in a way she hadn't been even a week ago. "So yes, food. Something not fancy. I want... pizza. Real Italian pizza."

"Pizza I can do." I opened the car door for her. "There's a place near the penthouse. Best in Rome."

"Better than Rosa's cornetti?"

"Different category. But yes, equally excellent."

We drove through Rome, Tony at the wheel, Marco in the passenger seat, and I tried to pretend this was normal. That I normally went shooting with my wife, that she normally asked for pizza afterward, that we were just a regular couple doing regular things.

But the guards in the car reminded me otherwise. The way Marco constantly scanned the streets. The weight of my own gun concealed under my jacket.

Nothing about this was normal.

"Lorenzo?" Dakota's voice pulled me from my thoughts.

"Hmm?"

"Why are you frowning?"

"Am I?"

"Yes. Very intensely." She squeezed my hand. "What's wrong?"

Everything. Nothing. I didn't know anymore.

"Just thinking," I said finally.

"About?"

"About whether this is fair to you. Teaching you to shoot, surrounding you with guards, making you live like this."

"It's not fair," she said simply. "But it's reality. And I'd rather face reality prepared than pretend everything's fine and get hurt."

"You shouldn't have to face this reality at all."

"But I do. Because I married you. Because I chose to stay." She shifted to look at me directly. "Lorenzo, I'm not going to pretend I love every aspect of your world. I'm terrified most of the time. But I'm also not helpless. Learning to shoot, understanding the threats, being part of the solution instead of just the problem—that helps."

"You're not the problem."

"I'm the vulnerability. You said so yourself." She said it matter-of-factly. "Calabrese knows you care about me, so he's using that. Fine. But if I'm prepared, if I'm capable, if I'm not just sitting around waiting to be rescued—that changes things."

I studied her face—determined, a little scared, but resolute. When had she become so strong?

Or had she always been this strong, and I just hadn't seen it?

"You amaze me," I said quietly.

"Because I can hit a target?"

"Because you're facing this head-on instead of running. Because you're trying to understand my world instead of just condemning it. Because you're..." I trailed off, not sure how to finish.

"Because I'm what?"

"Because you're staying. Even knowing what it costs." I brought her hand to my lips. "Even knowing what I am."

"You're not so bad." Her smile was soft. "I mean, you're a little scary, definitely dangerous, probably morally questionable—"

"This is a terrible compliment."

"—but you're also kind. And protective. And you make me feel..." She stopped, and I saw her struggle with the words.

"Feel what?"

"Safe." The admission seemed to cost her. "Even in the middle of all this danger and chaos, when I'm with you, I feel safe. Is that crazy?"

"No." My voice was rough. "That's... that's everything, Dakota."

The car pulled up to the pizzeria, and I forced myself to let go of her hand. To step back into the role of cautious husband instead of just... husband.

Tony opened the door, and I climbed out first, scanning the street. Marco was already positioning himself near the entrance.

"All clear," Tony said quietly.

I offered my hand to Dakota, and she took it, letting me help her out of the car. She looked around at the small restaurant—nothing fancy, just good food and authenticity—and smiled.

"This place looks perfect."

"Wait until you taste the pizza." I guided her inside, hand on her lower back. "Then you'll understand why I brought you here."

The owner, Giuseppe, greeted us warmly and showed us to a corner table—the one I always requested when I came here. Best sight lines, near the back exit, away from the windows.

Dakota noticed. "You always sit here?"

"Habit."

"Paranoid habit."

"Productive paranoid habit." I pulled out her chair. "Keeps me alive."

"Keeps us alive," she corrected, sitting. "I'm part of the 'us' now, remember?"

"How could I forget?" I took my own seat, positioning myself so I could see both the entrance and the street. "You remind me constantly."

"Because you keep trying to protect me from everything instead of with me."

"I'm trying to keep you alive."

"You can do both." She reached across the table for my hand. "Protect me and include me. They're not mutually exclusive."

Giuseppe arrived with wine before I could respond, and I was grateful for the interruption. We ordered—Margherita for her, diavola for me—and settled into comfortable silence.

"Lorenzo?" she said after the first glass of wine.

"Yes?"

"Thank you. For today. For teaching me instead of just locking me away." She traced patterns on the back of my hand. "I know it wasn't easy for you."

"You're right. It wasn't." I turned my hand over, interlacing our fingers. "Every instinct I have says to hide you somewhere Calabrese can't reach. Somewhere safe."

"But?"

"But you're right that you're not helpless. And treating you like you are would only make you a bigger target." I squeezed her hand. "So I'm trying. Trying to find the balance between protecting you and trusting you to protect yourself."

"That's all I'm asking." She smiled. "Well, that and pizza. I'm definitely asking for pizza."

The food arrived, and Dakota's eyes widened at her Margherita—simple perfection, fresh mozzarella, basil, tomato sauce, thin crust charred from the wood oven.

She took a bite and made a sound that I definitely shouldn't be thinking about in public.

"Good?" I asked, amused.

"Incredible." She took another bite. "Okay, you were right. This is the best pizza in Rome."

"I'm always right."

"You're sometimes right."

"I'm right about pizza."

"You're right about pizza," she conceded. "And cornetti. And—" She paused. "Actually, you have good taste in food generally."

"High praise from my wife."

"Don't let it go to your head."

We ate and talked and for a little while, I let myself pretend we were normal. Just a couple having dinner, nothing complicated, no threats lurking in the shadows.

But reality intruded when my phone buzzed.

Marco: *Calabrese's people were spotted near the range. Followed us for three blocks before Roberto scared them off.*

My hand tightened on my fork.

"What is it?" Dakota asked, seeing my expression change.

I debated lying. Decided against it. "Calabrese had people following us. They know where we went today."

She paled slightly but didn't panic. "Are they still there?"

"No. Roberto handled it." I set my phone down. "But they're watching, Dakota. Constantly."

"Then we watch back." Her voice was steady. "We're careful. We're prepared. But we don't let them control our lives."

"You make it sound simple."

"It's not simple. But it's necessary." She reached for my hand again. "Lorenzo, if we let fear dictate everything, we've already lost. Calabrese wins without ever having to actually do anything."

She was right. I hated that she was right.

"When did you become so wise?"

"I married a paranoid mafia heir. I had to adapt quickly." She smiled, but it didn't quite reach her eyes. "Can we still finish dinner? Or do we need to leave?"

"We can finish." I wouldn't let Calabrese take this from us too. "But Dakota?"

"Yes?"

"When we get home, I'm doubling the security."

"I know."

"And I'm going to be insufferable about checking locks and windows."

"I know that too."

"And I'm probably going to hover."

"Lorenzo." She squeezed my hand. "I know. And it's okay. I understand why. Just… don't suffocate me, okay? Let me breathe a little."

"I'll try."

"That's all I ask."

We finished our pizza, and I paid Giuseppe—tipping heavily, as always—and headed back to the car. The drive home was quiet, both of us lost in thought.

When we got to the penthouse, I checked every room, every lock, every window. Dakota watched without comment, understanding this was what I needed to do.

"All clear," I said finally.

"Good." She moved into my arms. "Now can we pretend for a few hours that we're just a normal married couple? No threats, no guards, no Calabrese?"

"We can try."

"Then let's try." She took my hand, leading me toward the bedroom. "Because I don't want to think about any of that tonight. Tonight, I just want to be with you."

And God help me, I couldn't resist that.

So for a few hours, we pretended.

We pretended we were normal. We pretended the world outside didn't exist. We pretended that love was simple and safety was guaranteed.

But in the back of my mind, I was already planning.

Planning how to respond to Calabrese. Planning how to protect Dakota. Planning how to end this before it escalated further.

Because pretending was nice.

But reality was coming.

And when it did, I was going to be ready.

41

Chapter Forty-One: Dakota

I should have known something was wrong the moment I saw the flower shop.

It was Tuesday afternoon, and I'd convinced Lorenzo to let me go out—just to the market a few blocks away, with Tony and one of the newer guards, Marcus. I needed to feel normal, needed to do something as simple as buy fresh vegetables for dinner.

Lorenzo had agreed reluctantly, after making me promise to stay within a three-block radius and keep my phone on me at all times.

I'd kept my promise. Had my phone. Stayed close. Didn't do anything risky.

But the flower shop had peonies in the window.

My favorite. The ones Lorenzo had sent me. The ones that meant something to us.

"Can we stop?" I asked Tony. "Just for a minute. I want to get some flowers for the penthouse."

Tony scanned the street, that ever-present vigilance that I'd learned meant he was constantly calculating threats. "One minute. Marcus, you stay with her. I'll check inside first."

He entered the shop, and I waited on the sidewalk with Marcus, looking at the display. The peonies were beautiful—pink and white, full blooms, exactly like the ones Lorenzo had given me.

197

Tony emerged. "It's clear. But make it quick, Mrs. Marchetti."

I stepped inside, Marcus right behind me. The shop was small, cramped with buckets of flowers and the earthy smell of stems and water. An older woman stood behind the counter, smiling.

"Buongiorno," she said warmly.

"Buongiorno." I moved to the peonies. "Queste, per favore?" I pointed, proud of my very basic Italian.

"Sì, sì." She began gathering stems, wrapping them carefully.

That's when I noticed the man.

He'd been browsing near the back, barely visible behind a display of roses. But now he was moving forward, and something about the way he moved—purposeful, focused—made my skin prickle.

"Marcus," I said quietly.

"I see him." Marcus had already positioned himself between me and the man, his hand moving to his jacket.

The man stopped, smiled. "Scusi. I just want to pass."

His accent was wrong. Too careful. Too practiced.

"The back door," Tony said sharply. "Now."

But before I could move, two more men entered through the front—blocking the exit, casual but clearly coordinated.

My heart stopped.

"Mrs. Marchetti." The first man spoke in accented English now. "Don't be afraid. We just want to talk."

"She's not interested in talking." Marcus had his gun out now, not quite pointing it but ready. "Step back."

"Now, now. No need for that." The man's smile never wavered. "We're just delivering a message. From Signor Calabrese."

At the name, the florist went pale and hurried into the back room. Smart woman.

"Whatever message you have, you can deliver to Lorenzo." Tony had also drawn his weapon, positioning himself near me. "Not to his wife."

"But that is the message." The man spread his hands, showing they were empty. "Signor Calabrese wants Mrs. Marchetti to understand something.

She's very exposed. Very... accessible. Despite all of Lorenzo's precautions."

Ice flooded my veins.

"If we wanted to hurt her," the man continued conversationally, "we could have. Just now. Before you even knew we were here. But we didn't. Because Signor Calabrese is a reasonable man. He just wants Lorenzo to understand the situation."

"The situation is that you're threatening his wife." Marcus's voice was cold. "That's an act of war."

"Is it?" The man tilted his head. "Or is it just... a demonstration? We're not touching her. We're not hurting her. We're simply showing that we could. If we wanted to."

"Get out of the way." Tony's gun was fully raised now. "Or this becomes a different kind of demonstration."

The tension in the room ratcheted up instantly. I could feel it—the moment before violence, the breath before everything exploded.

The two men at the door shifted, hands moving to their own jackets.

Three against three. In a tiny flower shop. With me in the middle.

This was going to get people killed.

"Wait." My voice surprised me—steady, calm, when inside I was screaming. "What's the message? Exactly. What does Calabrese want me to tell Lorenzo?"

"Dakota—" Tony started.

"I'll tell him," I cut him off, keeping my eyes on the man. "What's the message?"

The man's smile widened. "Smart. Beautiful and smart. Lorenzo is a lucky man." He took a single step closer, and both Tony and Marcus tensed. "Tell him that the offer is still open. Fifty-fifty. But the price of refusal has gone up. Way up. He has twenty-four hours to reconsider."

"And if he doesn't?"

"Then we stop being so polite." His eyes traveled over me, assessing. "And demonstrations become... actions."

The threat was clear. Unmistakable.

"I'll tell him." I forced the words out. "Now leave."

"Of course." He gestured to his men, who stepped aside from the door. "Enjoy your flowers, Mrs. Marchetti. Peonies, yes? Lorenzo's favorite for you. Sweet."

He knew. He knew about the flowers, about what they meant to us, about—

How much had they been watching?

The three men left as casually as they'd arrived, disappearing into the street like nothing had happened.

I stood there, shaking, while Tony immediately moved to the door, scanning outside.

"Marcus, call Lorenzo. Now." Tony's voice was tight. "And tell him we need immediate backup."

Marcus was already on his phone, speaking in rapid Italian.

I looked down at my hands. They were trembling.

"Mrs. Marchetti." Tony was beside me, his expression grim. "We need to get you out of here. Now."

"The flowers—"

"Forget the flowers. Move."

He guided me toward the back door, Marcus covering our exit. My legs felt like water, but I made them work. Made myself move.

We emerged into an alley, and Tony was already calling for the car. Within seconds, it pulled up, and he practically shoved me inside.

"Go. Now. Don't stop for anything."

The driver—Roberto, I realized—floored it, and we shot through Roman streets fast enough that I had to grip the door handle.

"Are you hurt?" Tony asked, finally looking at me. "Did they touch you?"

"No. They just… talked." My voice sounded far away. "They were proving a point."

"They were threatening you." His jaw was tight. "That's the same thing."

My phone rang. Lorenzo.

I answered, and before I could speak: "Are you okay? Dakota, tell me you're okay."

"I'm okay. I'm in the car. Tony and Marcus got me out."

"Did they touch you? Did they hurt you? If they so much as—"

"They didn't touch me." I closed my eyes, trying to steady my breathing. "They just delivered a message. From Calabrese."

Silence. Then: "What message?"

"He wants fifty-fifty. You have twenty-four hours. Or—" I couldn't finish.

"Or what?" His voice was deadly quiet.

"Or demonstrations become actions. Those were his exact words."

I heard something crash on his end. "Where are you now?"

"In the car. Heading home."

"Tony's with you?"

"Yes."

"Put him on."

I handed the phone to Tony, and listened to one side of the conversation—short, clipped sentences in Italian, Tony's expression growing grimmer with each word.

Finally, he handed the phone back. "He wants to talk to you."

"Dakota." Lorenzo's voice was strained. "Listen to me carefully. You're going straight home. Don't stop for anything. When you get there, you lock yourself in the bedroom and you don't come out until I get there. Understood?"

"Lorenzo—"

"Please." The word broke. "Please just do what I ask. I need to know you're safe while I handle this."

"Okay," I whispered. "Okay. I'll lock myself in."

"Thank you." A pause. "I love you. I need you to know that. Whatever happens next, I love you."

The words sent ice through my veins. "What's going to happen next?"

"I'm going to end this. One way or another."

"Lorenzo, don't do anything—"

"I'll be home soon. Stay safe. I love you."

He hung up before I could respond.

I stared at the phone, my heart racing. *I'm going to end this. One way or another.*

What did that mean? What was he going to do?

We pulled up to the building, and Tony practically carried me to the elevator, Marcus securing the perimeter. The ride up felt eternal.

The penthouse was exactly as I'd left it. Normal. Safe. Empty.

"Bedroom," Tony reminded me. "Lock the door. Don't open it for anyone but Lorenzo or me."

"What about you? Where will you be?"

"Outside your door. No one's getting past me, Mrs. Marchetti. I promise you that."

I believed him. But I also saw the fear in his eyes—the knowledge that Calabrese's men had gotten close. Too close.

I locked myself in the bedroom as instructed and sank onto the bed, still shaking.

They'd been right there. Three feet away. Could have grabbed me, hurt me, killed me—and there was nothing I could have done to stop them.

All of Lorenzo's precautions, all the security, all the careful planning—and Calabrese had still reached me. Still proven he could get to me whenever he wanted.

I thought about the gun Lorenzo had taught me to use. It was in the safe in the closet. He'd shown me the combination, made me practice opening it.

I got up and retrieved it, checking the magazine like he'd taught me. Loaded. Safety on.

Then I sat on the bed, gun in my lap, and waited.

Waited for Lorenzo to come home. Waited to find out what "ending this" meant. Waited for the other shoe to drop.

Because Calabrese had made his point. Had shown that all the guards and guns and precautions in the world couldn't keep me completely safe.

And Lorenzo was going to have to respond.

The question was: how far would he go?

How much blood would be spilled to protect me?

I stared at the gun in my hands and realized I might be about to find out exactly what kind of man I'd married.

Not the gentle one who bought me flowers. Not the patient one who taught me to shoot. Not the loving one who whispered sweet things in

Italian.

The other one. The one who gave orders that got people hurt. The one who made examples. The one who ran an empire built on violence and fear.

That Lorenzo was coming.

And I wasn't sure I was ready to see him.

42

Chapter Forty-Two: Lorenzo

I was going to kill Antonio Calabrese.

Not hypothetically. Not as a threat. I was going to actually kill him, and I was going to make sure everyone in Rome knew why.

"Lorenzo." Marco's voice was cautious. "We need to think this through."

"I've thought it through." I loaded my gun with mechanical precision. "He threatened my wife. He sent men to corner her in a flower shop. He proved he could reach her. There's nothing to think through."

"If you kill him, his family will retaliate. This becomes a full war."

"Then we go to war." I holstered the gun. "I don't care anymore, Marco. I told him—I told everyone—that Dakota was off-limits. He crossed that line. There have to be consequences."

We were in one of our secure locations—a warehouse near the docks that had seen more violence than I cared to remember. Ten of our people were here, armed, waiting for orders.

This was happening. Tonight.

My phone rang. My father.

I almost didn't answer. But ignoring him would only make things worse. "Father."

"Lorenzo." His voice was cold, controlled. "I heard about the incident with your wife."

"Then you know why I'm doing this."

204

"I know you're about to start a war over a woman." Not my wife. A woman. Like she was interchangeable. "That's not how we handle these situations."

"This is exactly how we handle these situations." I kept my voice level through sheer force of will. "Someone threatens what's mine, they pay for it. That's always been the rule."

"The rule is we think strategically, not emotionally. Calabrese is testing you, yes. But if you kill him, you prove him right—that your wife is your weakness."

"She's not my weakness. She's my line in the sand." I moved to the window, looking out at the dark water. "And he crossed it. If I don't respond, every other family will think they can use her against me. This isn't about emotion, Father. It's about establishing boundaries that no one dares cross."

Silence on the other end. Then: "What's your plan?"

"I'm going to his house. I'm going to confront him. And I'm going to make sure he understands that touching Dakota was the last mistake he'll ever make."

"And his family? His associates? They'll come for you. For us."

"Let them try." I was done being careful. Done being strategic. "I'm not losing her because we're too afraid to take action."

"Lorenzo—"

"I have to go, Father. I'll call you when it's done."

I hung up before he could respond.

Marco was watching me with an expression I couldn't quite read. "Your father's right, you know. This could go very badly."

"I know." I checked my gun again. "I don't care."

"You should care. Dakota needs you alive, not dead because you went after Calabrese in a rage."

"I'm not in a rage." I was. We both knew I was. "I'm being decisive."

"You're being emotional."

"I'm being a husband." I turned to face him. "Marco, I get it. This is risky. This could start something we can't control. But if I don't do this—if I let Calabrese threaten my wife and just negotiate like nothing happened—I lose her trust. She'll always wonder if I can really protect her. If I'm willing to."

"So you're doing this for her?"

"I'm doing this for us." I grabbed my jacket. "For our future. For the life I want to build with her. And that life doesn't exist if people think they can use her as leverage."

Marco studied me for a long moment, then nodded. "Okay. Then let's do this smart. Not just effective, but smart."

"I'm listening."

"We don't go to his house. Too many variables, too many of his people around. We draw him out. Neutral ground. Somewhere we control."

"He won't come."

"He will if the invitation is right." Marco pulled out his phone. "What if you offer to negotiate? Say you're willing to discuss new terms. He thinks he has the upper hand now. He'll come."

I considered it. It made sense. But: "I want him to know this isn't a negotiation. This is punishment."

"Then you make that clear when he arrives." Marco was already typing. "But Lorenzo, we do this with witnesses. Other families. Make it public. That way, when Calabrese dies, everyone knows why. Everyone understands the line he crossed."

That… was actually smart.

"The Rossi family," I said slowly. "They're neutral. Respected. If they witness it—"

"Then no one can claim you murdered him in cold blood. It becomes justice, not murder." Marco sent the message. "Give me twenty minutes. I'll set it up."

Twenty minutes later, we were in a private room at one of the old establishments near the Forum—technically a restaurant, but really a place where families conducted business that required… discretion.

Giovanni Rossi sat at the head of the table, old and shrewd, the kind of man who'd survived fifty years in this life by knowing when to intervene and when to watch. His nephew, Paulo, sat beside him—younger, but equally sharp.

"Lorenzo." Giovanni nodded. "This is highly irregular. A meeting on such short notice."

"I appreciate you coming." I took my seat. "What I'm about to do needs witnesses. Respected witnesses."

"And what are you about to do?"

"Defend my family's honor. And my wife's safety."

Giovanni's expression didn't change. "The Calabrese matter?"

"You've heard."

"Everyone's heard. Antonio's been quite vocal about his… concerns… regarding your marriage." He leaned back. "Tell me what happened. Exactly."

I laid it out—the demands for better terms, the veiled threats, the men cornering Dakota in a flower shop. I kept my voice level, factual, but I saw Paulo's expression darken with each detail.

"He sent men to intimidate your wife?" Paulo asked. "Directly?"

"Yes."

"That's…" He looked at his uncle. "That's beyond the pale."

"It is," Giovanni agreed. "Women are off-limits. Children are off-limits. That's always been the rule." He looked at me. "What are you asking of us, Lorenzo?"

"I'm asking you to witness what comes next. So that when I respond to Calabrese's actions, everyone understands it was justified."

"You mean to kill him."

"I mean to end this. However necessary."

The door opened, and Marco stepped in. "He's here. With two of his men."

My heart rate kicked up. "Show him in."

Giovanni raised a hand. "Lorenzo. Before this proceeds. You understand what you're starting?"

"I understand I'm ending something that never should have begun."

"Fair enough." He settled back in his chair. "We'll bear witness. But the consequences are yours to manage."

"Understood."

Marco opened the door wider, and Antonio Calabrese walked in, flanked by his enforcers. He saw the Rossis and stopped, surprise flickering across his face.

"Giovanni. I didn't expect—" He looked at me. "What is this, Lorenzo? I thought we were negotiating."

"Sit down, Antonio." My voice was cold. "We need to talk."

He remained standing. "I don't like the setup here."

"I don't care what you like." I gestured to the empty chair across from me. "Sit. Or leave. But if you leave, the next time we meet won't be in a restaurant."

He calculated for a moment, then sat. His men positioned themselves behind him, hands near their weapons. Marco and two of our people mirrored them on my side.

"Giovanni," Calabrese said carefully. "I don't know what Lorenzo's told you, but—"

"He told us you sent men to threaten his wife." Giovanni's voice was neutral. "Is that accurate?"

"I sent men to deliver a message. There's a difference."

"Is there?" I leaned forward. "You sent three men to corner my wife in a flower shop, Antonio. Away from me, with limited security, vulnerable. You proved you could reach her. That's not delivering a message. That's making a threat."

"I never touched her."

"You didn't have to. The threat was implicit." My hands clenched on the table. "You crossed a line. The one line I told you was absolute."

"I was making a point—"

"You were testing my boundaries. Seeing if I'd actually enforce what I'd said." I stood slowly. "Let me be very clear: my wife is not part of any business discussion. She's not leverage. She's not a negotiating point. She's completely off-limits. And by going after her, you've declared yourself an enemy of the Marchetti family."

"That's not—" He stood too, facing me across the table. "Lorenzo, you're overreacting. Nothing happened to your wife. She's fine."

"This time. But you made it clear there would be a next time if I didn't meet your demands." I moved around the table slowly. "Twenty-four hours, you said. Or demonstrations become actions. What did you mean by that,

Antonio?"

He glanced at the Rossis, clearly uncomfortable with the audience. "I meant we'd take our business elsewhere. Find other partners."

"Liar." The word was soft but deadly. "You meant you'd escalate. You'd go after what I care about to force my hand. And the only thing you know I care about is Dakota."

"You're reading too much into—"

"Am I?" I was close now, close enough to see the sweat on his forehead. "Then explain the flowers. Explain how your man knew she liked peonies. Explain how he knew those were significant to us. You've been watching her, Antonio. Closely. Learning her habits, her preferences, her vulnerabilities. That's not business. That's targeting."

Silence fell in the room.

"Giovanni," Calabrese said, his voice strained. "You see what he's doing. He's twisting—"

"I see a man who broke the oldest rule we have." Giovanni's voice was hard. "Women are off-limits, Antonio. Everyone knows this. Your father knew this. You should know this."

"I was just—"

"You were threatening Lorenzo's wife to gain leverage in a business negotiation." Paulo spoke up now. "That's not how we do business. That's how animals do business."

"Watch your tone—"

"No, you watch yours." I cut him off. "Because right now, in this room, with these witnesses, I'm giving you one chance. One. You apologize. You swear on your family's name that you'll never approach my wife again. You accept the current terms of our arrangement. And maybe—maybe—I let you walk out of here alive."

His face went red. "You're threatening me?"

"I'm offering you mercy. There's a difference." I held his gaze. "But it expires in about thirty seconds. So choose quickly."

I saw him calculate. Saw him weigh his options. Saw the moment he decided his pride mattered more than his life.

"I don't apologize to men who don't understand business." He straightened his jacket. "And I don't take orders from someone who lets his wife make him weak. You want war, Lorenzo? You've got it."

He turned to leave.

I moved.

One step, fast, and my hand was on his shoulder, spinning him back. My other hand came up with my gun, pressing it under his chin.

His enforcers moved, but Marco and our people were faster. Guns out, aimed, the standoff instant.

"Lorenzo," Giovanni said carefully. "Think about this."

"I have thought about it." I kept the gun steady. "Antonio. Last chance. Apologize."

"Go to hell."

I pulled the trigger.

The sound was deafening in the enclosed space.

Calabrese dropped, and chaos erupted—his men going for weapons, ours responding, Giovanni shouting for order.

But I was already moving to Calabrese's enforcers, gun trained on them.

"Drop them." My voice cut through the noise. "Drop your weapons or join your boss."

They looked at their dead employer, at the blood spreading across the floor, at the six guns now pointed at them.

They dropped their weapons.

"Smart." I lowered my gun slightly. "Now get out. Tell his family what happened. Tell them Antonio Calabrese died because he threatened my wife. Tell them that's what happens when you cross the Marchetti family."

They scrambled for the door, and I let them go.

Giovanni stood slowly, looking at the body. "Lorenzo. What have you done?"

"What was necessary." I holstered my gun. "He crossed a line. In front of witnesses, you heard him refuse to apologize, refuse to back down. You heard him declare war. I just made sure that war ended before it could really start."

"His family—"

"His family will be furious. But they'll also understand the message." I looked at Paulo. "He died because he went after what was mine. Anyone else who tries the same will meet the same fate. That's the message I need spreading."

Giovanni was quiet for a long moment. Then: "You've changed, Lorenzo. Marriage has made you… dangerous."

"Marriage has given me something worth protecting." I looked down at Calabrese's body. "And I'll kill anyone who threatens that. Anyone."

"I'll testify to what I saw," Giovanni said finally. "That he refused to apologize. That he declared war. That you acted in defense of your family's honor." He moved toward the door. "But Lorenzo? This will have consequences. His family won't let this stand, witnesses or not."

"Let them come." I was past caring. "I've drawn my line. Anyone who crosses it ends up like Antonio."

They left—Giovanni shaking his head, Paulo giving me a look that might have been respect or fear, I couldn't tell.

Marco was on his phone, already arranging cleanup. "That was… decisive."

"It was necessary."

"Dakota's going to ask what happened."

"I'll tell her the truth." I looked at the blood on the floor, felt nothing. No regret. No guilt. Just cold satisfaction. "I killed the man who threatened her. And I'd do it again."

"Lorenzo." Marco stopped me as I headed for the door. "Are you okay?"

Was I? I'd just killed a man in cold blood. Started what might become a full-scale war. Crossed lines I'd always said I'd never cross.

But Dakota was safe. No one would doubt my willingness to protect her now. No one would dare use her as leverage again.

"I'm fine." I clapped him on the shoulder. "Get this cleaned up. I need to go home. My wife's waiting."

The drive back to the penthouse felt longer than it was. I kept seeing Calabrese's face—the moment he'd realized I was serious, the split second before I pulled the trigger.

I should have felt something. Remorse. Regret. Something.

But all I felt was relief. It was done. Dakota was safe.

That's all that mattered.

Tony let me in, his expression carefully neutral. "She's still in the bedroom, sir. Hasn't come out."

"Thank you. Take a break. I'll watch the door myself for a while."

He nodded and left.

I stood outside the bedroom door for a moment, suddenly uncertain. What would I tell her? The truth? A sanitized version?

She'd know. She always knew when I was lying.

I knocked softly. "Dakota? It's me. Can I come in?"

Silence. Then: "Is it locked from the outside?"

"No. Just from the inside."

I heard movement, then the lock clicking. The door opened, and Dakota stood there, eyes wide, still wearing the same clothes from earlier. She looked exhausted.

"Are you okay?" she asked immediately.

"I'm fine."

"Lorenzo." She stepped back, letting me enter. "What happened? What did you do?"

I looked at her—this woman who'd been terrified hours ago, who'd locked herself in our bedroom with a gun, who was looking at me now with fear and hope and something else I couldn't name.

I could lie. Could tell her it was handled, leave out the details.

But she deserved the truth.

"I killed him," I said quietly. "Antonio Calabrese. He's dead."

Her face went pale. "You... killed him?"

"Yes. With witnesses. Giovanni Rossi was there, saw everything. Calabrese refused to apologize, refused to back down. He chose pride over life." I moved closer. "And I chose you over politics. Over strategy. Over everything."

"Lorenzo..." She sank onto the bed. "You killed him. Actually killed him."

"Yes."

"Because of me."

"Because he threatened you. There's a difference." I knelt in front of her. "Dakota, I know this is shocking. I know you didn't want violence. But I couldn't let him get away with what he did. I had to make a statement. Had to show everyone that you're untouchable."

"By killing someone." Her voice was hollow. "By starting a war."

"By ending one before it could really begin." I took her hands. "His family will be angry, yes. But they'll also understand. He crossed a line, and he paid for it. That's how this world works."

She looked at me, and I saw her trying to process it. Trying to reconcile the man who'd taught her to shoot, who'd bought her flowers, who'd made love to her—with the man who'd just killed someone in cold blood.

"Are you safe?" she asked finally. "Are they going to come after you?"

"Maybe. Probably. But I'm prepared for that." I squeezed her hands. "Dakota, I know this changes how you see me. I know you're probably scared of what I did. But I did it for you. For us. Because the alternative— letting him threaten you and doing nothing—that wasn't an option."

"You should have told me. Before you went. You should have—"

"If I'd told you, you would have tried to talk me out of it. And Dakota, there was no talking me out of it. Not after what he did."

She was quiet for a long time, and I waited, bracing myself for her to pull away. To tell me she couldn't handle this. Couldn't be with someone capable of what I'd just done.

Instead, she said: "I love you."

The words stopped my heart.

"What?"

"I love you." She looked at me with tears in her eyes. "I've been too afraid to say it. Too afraid to admit it. But today, when those men cornered me, all I could think about was you. About never seeing you again. About all the things I never said." She cupped my face. "And I'm not okay with what you did. I'm not going to pretend I am. You killed someone, Lorenzo. That's... that's huge. But I also understand why you did it. And I know that in your world, there wasn't another choice."

"Dakota—"

"I love you," she repeated. "Even knowing what you're capable of. Even knowing what you did tonight. I love you. And I'm staying. I'm choosing you. All of you. The gentle parts and the violent parts. Because they're all part of the same person."

I pulled her into my arms and held her so tight she gasped. "Say it again."

"I love you."

"Again."

"I love you, Lorenzo Marchetti." She pulled back to look at me. "Now and always. Even when you do terrifying things to protect me."

"Especially when I do terrifying things to protect you," I corrected, and kissed her.

She kissed me back, and I tasted salt—tears, though I wasn't sure if they were hers or mine.

"We're going to be okay," I whispered against her lips. "I promise. Whatever comes next, we're going to be okay."

"How can you promise that?"

"Because I'll do whatever it takes to make it true." I pulled her closer. "Whatever it takes, Dakota. Always."

She held me, and we stayed like that for a long time—two people who'd crossed lines they couldn't uncross, who'd chosen each other despite every reason not to, who'd found love in the least likely place.

Outside, Rome continued its eternal rhythm.

Inside, we held onto each other.

And tried to believe we'd survive what was coming.

43

Chapter Forty-Three: Dakota

I didn't sleep that night.

Lorenzo held me until dawn, neither of us speaking much, both lost in our own thoughts. He'd killed a man. For me. Because of me.

And I'd told him I loved him anyway.

Was that wrong? Should I have been horrified? Should I have packed my bags and run?

Maybe. Probably.

But when I'd seen him standing in the doorway, looking exhausted and dangerous and worried about what I'd think of him—all I'd felt was relief. He was safe. He was home.

And the words I'd been holding back for weeks had just… fallen out.

I love you.

True then. Still true now as I watched the sun rise over Rome, Lorenzo's arm heavy around my waist.

"You should sleep," he murmured against my neck.

"Can't."

"Try anyway." He pulled me closer. "Nothing's going to happen today. I promise."

"How can you know that?"

"Because Calabrese's family will need time to process. To plan. To decide how they want to respond." His hand traced lazy circles on my hip. "We have at least a few days before anything happens."

"And then?"

"And then we handle whatever comes." He kissed my shoulder. "Together."

Together. That word meant something different now. Something heavier. Something that included blood and violence and choices that couldn't be undone.

My phone buzzed on the nightstand. I reached for it, expecting Marco or Bianca.

Instead: Mom calling

My blood went cold.

"Lorenzo." I sat up, showing him the screen. "It's my mother."

"Don't answer."

"I have to. If I don't, she'll worry. She'll—" The phone kept ringing. "She might already know something's wrong."

"Dakota, you can't tell her. Not about last night. Not about—"

"I know." I answered before he could stop me. "Hi, Mom."

"Dakota!" Her voice was tight, strained. "Thank God. I've been trying to reach you since yesterday. Are you okay?"

"I'm fine. Why wouldn't I be?"

"Because it's all over the news! A man was killed in Rome last night—Antonio Calabrese. And the reports are saying—" She paused, and I heard papers rustling. "They're saying it was connected to the Marchetti family. To Lorenzo."

My heart stopped. The news already? How?

"Mom—"

"Is it true? Is Lorenzo involved in… in organized crime? Because that's what all the articles are saying. That the Calabreses and the Marchettis are both—" Her voice broke. "Dakota, please tell me this isn't what I think it is."

I looked at Lorenzo. He was sitting up now, tension visible in every line of his body.

"Mom, I can't really talk about this right now."

"That's not an answer. Dakota Marie Phillips—"

"Marchetti," I corrected automatically. "Dakota Marie Marchetti."

Silence. Then: "Oh my God. You knew. You knew and you married him anyway."

"Mom, it's complicated—"

"Complicated? Complicated is long-distance. Complicated is different religions. Complicated is not your husband being part of the mafia!" Her voice rose. "Does your father know? Did he know when he arranged this?"

The word 'arranged' hung in the air like a guillotine blade.

"What do you mean 'arranged'?" I asked carefully.

"I'm not stupid, Dakota. I know your father had debts. I know he was desperate. And then suddenly you're engaged to some Italian businessman we've never met?" She was crying now. "I thought—I thought maybe it was love. That you'd met him somehow and fallen for him and just moved fast. But it wasn't, was it? This was a business arrangement. My daughter was sold—"

"I wasn't sold." The words came out sharp. "Mom, yes, Dad had debts. Yes, the marriage was originally arranged. But I chose to stay. I chose Lorenzo. And I'm choosing him now."

"Choosing a man who kills people?"

The question hit like a physical blow.

"Mom—"

"The news says Antonio Calabrese was executed. In a restaurant. With witnesses. And those witnesses are saying Lorenzo Marchetti pulled the trigger." Her voice was shaking. "Is that true? Did your husband murder someone?"

I looked at Lorenzo again. He was watching me, face carefully blank, but I could see the tension in his jaw. The way his hands were clenched.

He was waiting to see what I'd say. What I'd choose.

"Yes," I said quietly. "It's true."

My mother made a sound like she'd been punched. "Oh God. Oh God, Dakota, you need to leave. Right now. Pack your things and—"

"I'm not leaving."

"What?"

"I'm not leaving, Mom. I know this is shocking. I know it's not what you wanted for me. But I love him. And he did what he did to protect me."

"Protect you? From what?"

"From Calabrese. He was threatening me. Sent men to corner me yesterday. Lorenzo was protecting his family. Protecting me." The words sounded hollow even as I said them. Justifications. Rationalizations.

But they were also true.

"Dakota." My mother's voice was cold now. Controlled. "Listen to me very carefully. You need to get out of there. Come home. We'll figure this out. We'll keep you safe—"

"I am safe. Lorenzo keeps me safe."

"Lorenzo is a murderer!"

"He's my husband!" The words came out fierce. "Mom, I know you don't understand. I know this isn't what you imagined for me. But this is my life now. My choice. And I'm asking you to respect that."

"Respect that my daughter married into the mob? Respect that you're living with a killer?"

"Respect that I'm an adult who made a decision. Even knowing all the consequences." My voice softened. "Mom, please. I need you to trust me."

"How can I trust your judgment when you're clearly not thinking straight? You've been in Rome, what, a month? That's not enough time to—"

"It's enough time to know what I want. Who I want." I looked at Lorenzo, saw something vulnerable flash across his face. "I'm staying, Mom. I'm sorry if that hurts you. But I'm staying."

Silence stretched between us—an ocean and a world of difference growing wider with each second.

"Then I don't know what to say to you," my mother said finally. "Because the daughter I raised wouldn't choose this. Wouldn't choose violence and danger over safety and family."

"I'm not choosing over family. You're still my family. But Lorenzo is too now. And I need you to accept that."

"I can't. I won't." Her voice broke again. "And neither will your father when he finds out you knew. When he finds out what we've done to you."

"Dad knew what he was doing. We both did."

"No. No, we thought—we thought it would be different. Safer. Not this." I heard her take a shaky breath. "I have to go. I can't—I need to think."

"Mom—"

"Don't call me until you're ready to come home. Really come home. Away from him. Away from all of this."

She hung up.

I stared at the phone, feeling like I'd been hollowed out.

"Dakota." Lorenzo's voice was quiet. "I'm sorry."

"Don't." I set the phone down. "Don't apologize. This isn't your fault."

"Isn't it? If I hadn't married you, hadn't brought you into this world—"

"Then my father would be dead. And I'd be back in Idaho, safe and miserable, wondering what could have been." I turned to face him. "I don't regret this, Lorenzo. Even now. Even after last night. I don't regret choosing you."

"You just lost your mother."

"No. She lost me." I blinked back tears. "Because she can't accept that this is my life now. That you're my life now."

He pulled me into his arms, and I let myself cry—for my mother, for the life I'd left behind, for the innocence I'd lost somewhere between Bora Bora and a flower shop in Rome.

"She'll come around," Lorenzo said against my hair. "Give her time. When she sees we're happy, that you're safe—"

"Will I be?" I pulled back to look at him. "Will I be safe? Calabrese's family is going to retaliate. You said so yourself."

"Yes. But we'll be prepared. And Dakota, I swear to you, I will never let anything happen to you. Never."

"You can't promise that."

"Watch me." His eyes were fierce. "I killed for you. I'll do worse if I have to. Whatever it takes to keep you safe."

The words should have scared me. Instead, they made me feel… protected. Valued. Loved in a way that was probably unhealthy but felt essential.

"We're so messed up," I said, half-laughing, half-crying.

"Completely." He kissed my forehead. "But we're messed up together."

"Together." I settled against his chest, listening to his heartbeat. "Lorenzo?"

"Mmm?"

"I meant it. What I said last night. I love you."

His arms tightened around me. "I know. And I love you. More than I thought I was capable of loving anyone."

"Even though I'm making your life complicated?"

"Because you're making my life worth living." He tilted my chin up. "Before you, it was just the business. Just survival. Just going through the motions. But now—now I have a reason. A purpose beyond just maintaining power."

"And what's that purpose?"

"Making you happy. Keeping you safe. Building a life with you that's more than just violence and politics." He kissed me softly. "You make me want to be better, Dakota. Even if I'm not sure I can be."

"You are better. You just don't see it yet."

"Then I'll trust your judgment." He stood, pulling me with him. "Come on. Let's get some food in you. You haven't eaten since yesterday."

"I'm not hungry."

"You're always hungry. You just don't realize it yet." He guided me toward the kitchen. "And while you eat, we'll talk about what comes next."

"What does come next?"

"We prepare. We strengthen our position. We make sure Calabrese's family understands that coming after you would be suicide." He started pulling ingredients from the fridge. "And we figure out how to handle your mother."

"She won't come around. Not about this."

"Maybe not. But we'll try anyway." He handed me a tomato. "Start chopping. You're going to help me make pasta."

"I'm terrible at cooking."

"Which is why you need practice." He kissed my nose. "Besides, it'll give you something to focus on besides everything else."

So I chopped tomatoes while Lorenzo worked beside me, both of us falling into a rhythm that felt almost normal. Almost like we were just a regular couple making breakfast together.

Except we weren't regular. Would never be regular.

My husband had killed a man last night. My mother had disowned me this morning. And somewhere in Rome, the Calabrese family was planning their revenge.

But for now, in this moment, we had tomatoes and pasta and each other.

And maybe that was enough.

Several hours later, I was on the couch, attempting to read, when Bianca arrived unannounced.

She swept into the penthouse like a force of nature, took one look at me, and crossed directly to where I sat.

"Oh, cara." She pulled me into a hug. "I heard about your mother. I'm so sorry."

"How did you—"

"Lorenzo called me. Told me what happened." She sat beside me, keeping hold of my hand. "Mothers can be difficult when they don't understand our choices."

"Did you… did you have to choose? Between your family and Lorenzo's father?"

"In a way." Her expression was distant. "My parents didn't approve of the match. Thought Vittorio—Lorenzo's father—was too dangerous, too involved in things they didn't want to know about. They told me I'd regret it."

"Did you?"

"Sometimes. Often, even." She squeezed my hand. "But I loved him. And I loved the life we built, despite its complications. And I never doubted that choosing him was right, even when it was hard."

"How did you reconcile it? The violence, the danger, the moral… ambiguity?"

"I accepted that the man I loved existed in a world I didn't always approve of. That loving him meant accepting all of him, not just the parts that were comfortable." She studied my face. "Lorenzo told me what happened with Calabrese. How you reacted."

"I told him I loved him."

"After he'd killed someone."

"Because he'd killed someone. To protect me." I looked down at our joined hands. "Is that wrong? Should I have been horrified?"

"There's no should or shouldn't in this life, Dakota. Only what you can live with." She tilted my chin up. "Can you live with knowing Lorenzo killed to protect you? Can you live with the possibility he might do it again?"

Could I? I thought about Calabrese's men in the flower shop. About the fear that had gripped me. About knowing they could reach me whenever they wanted.

And I thought about Lorenzo, standing in our bedroom last night, telling me Calabrese was dead. Making sure I was safe.

"Yes," I said quietly. "I can live with it. I don't like it. But I can accept it."

"Then that's your answer." Bianca stood. "Now, let's talk about practical matters. Your mother may have cut contact, but we need to ensure your father isn't left vulnerable. Men in his position—with debts paid but knowledge of our world—they can become targets."

"I hadn't thought about that."

"That's because you're still thinking like a normal person, not like a Marchetti wife." Her tone was gentle but firm. "Your father knows things. About the arrangement, about the families, about how business is conducted. That makes him a potential risk. Or a target for people wanting information."

My stomach dropped. "What do we do?"

"Lorenzo's already handling it. Security on your parents' home, monitoring their communications, making sure no one from Calabrese's family approaches them." She smiled at my expression. "Don't look so surprised. Protecting you means protecting what you care about."

"I care about my mother too. Even if she hates me right now."

"She doesn't hate you. She's scared for you. There's a difference." Bianca moved toward the kitchen. "Give her time. And in the meantime, let us handle security. You focus on being ready for what comes next."

"What does come next?"

"The Calabrese family will respond. Not today, probably not tomorrow, but soon." She started making tea—something I'd noticed she always did when delivering difficult news. "They'll want to make a statement. Show that killing one of their own has consequences."

"Will they come after me?"

"No. Not directly. Lorenzo made that too costly." She set the kettle on. "But they'll look for other ways to hurt him. To hurt the family. You need to be prepared for that."

"How do I prepare for something I don't understand?"

"By learning. By watching. By trusting Lorenzo and the people around you." She pulled out cups. "And by remembering that you're a Marchetti now. That comes with protection, but also responsibility."

"What kind of responsibility?"

"The responsibility to be strong when things get difficult. To support your husband even when his choices are hard. To represent the family with dignity." She poured tea, handed me a cup. "Being a mafia wife isn't just about looking pretty at parties, Dakota. It's about being a partner in a very complicated, very dangerous world."

I took the tea, letting the warmth seep into my hands. "I'm not sure I'm cut out for this."

"Lorenzo thinks you are. So do I." She sat across from me. "You faced down Calabrese's men yesterday. You didn't panic, didn't break. You told Lorenzo you loved him after learning he'd killed someone. You're stronger than you think, cara. You just need to believe it."

"What if I'm not? What if I break when things get really bad?"

"Then Lorenzo will put you back together." She said it simply, like it was obvious. "That's what partners do. They catch each other when they fall. They hold each other up when standing alone becomes impossible."

"You make it sound almost romantic."

"It is romantic. Just not in the way books and movies suggest." She smiled over her teacup. "Real love—the kind that survives in our world—it's not about grand gestures and perfect moments. It's about choosing each other every day, even when it's hard. Especially when it's hard."

"My mother thinks I'm making a mistake."

"Your mother thinks you're in danger. And she's right. You are." Bianca's honesty was almost refreshing. "But danger doesn't mean wrong. And safety doesn't mean right. Sometimes the most dangerous choice is also the most worth making."

"Was it? For you?"

"Yes." No hesitation. "Every difficult moment, every fear, every time I questioned my choice—yes. It was worth it. Because I loved him. Because we built something together that mattered."

"Even though it's…" I gestured vaguely. "All of this?"

"Especially because of all of this." She set down her cup. "Dakota, perfect marriages don't exist. Not in our world, not in any world. What exists is commitment. Choice. The decision to stay even when leaving would be easier."

"I've made that choice."

"I know. Lorenzo knows. Now you just need to believe in it enough to weather what comes next." She stood. "I should go. Lorenzo will be home soon, and you two should talk. Really talk. About what happened, about what's coming, about how you face it together."

"Thank you, Bianca. For coming. For…" I struggled for words. "For helping me understand."

"That's what family does, cara." She kissed both my cheeks. "And you're family now. Whatever you need, you have us."

After she left, I sat with my tea and thought about everything she'd said.

Choosing each other every day, even when it's hard.

Was I ready for that? For a lifetime of hard choices and dangerous situations and loving someone who lived in violence?

I looked around the penthouse, our home now. Saw Lorenzo's jacket draped over the chair. His espresso cup from this morning, still on the counter. The peonies he'd sent me, wilting now but still beautiful.

Evidence of a life being built. Evidence of choices being made. Evidence of love that existed despite every reason it shouldn't.

My phone buzzed. A text from Lorenzo: Coming home. Need anything?

I typed back: Just you.

His response was immediate: Always.

And somehow, that simple exchange, that promise, made everything else bearable.

My mother might not understand. The Calabrese family might seek revenge. The world might think I was crazy.

But I had Lorenzo. And he had me.

And maybe, just maybe, that was enough to survive whatever came next.

44

Chapter Forty-Four: Lorenzo

Three days after I killed Antonio Calabrese, his family made their move. I'd been expecting it.

Waiting for it.

Had security doubled, tripled even. Had people watching their operations, their movements, their communications.

But they were smarter than I'd anticipated. They didn't come after me. They didn't target Dakota directly. They didn't do any of the obvious things I'd prepared for.

Instead, they went after our shipments.

"Four locations." Marco spread photos across my desk. "Hit simultaneously. Two warehouses, one transport truck, one distribution center. All of them torched. Millions in losses."

I studied the photos—charred buildings, destroyed cargo, our operations literally going up in smoke.

"Casualties?"

"Three injured. None dead, thank God. They waited until the buildings were mostly empty." Marco pointed to one photo. "This was deliberate, Lorenzo. They're sending a message without crossing the line into outright war."

"The message being?"

"That they can hurt us without directly attacking you or Dakota. That killing Antonio has consequences beyond just his death." Marco leaned back. "It's smart, actually. They're not giving you justification to escalate further."

He was right. If they'd gone after Dakota, I could have retaliated with full force. But attacking our business? That was just… business. Unpleasant, expensive, but not grounds for a war.

"What does Giovanni say?" I asked.

"That the Calabrese family is within their rights to respond. That we killed their leader, they destroyed our property. From his perspective, it's almost even."

"Almost."

"Almost."

Marco watched me carefully.

"Lorenzo, we could walk away now. Take the loss, rebuild. The other families would accept it. Honor satisfied on both sides."

I should have agreed. Should have seen this as the off-ramp it was—a way to end things without further bloodshed.

But I couldn't shake the feeling that walking away would be seen as weakness. That other families would look at this and think: Lorenzo Marchetti can be pushed.

His wife is still a vulnerability.

"No." I stood, moving to the window. "We don't walk away."

"Lorenzo—"

"They burned our operations, Marco. Destroyed months of work, millions in revenue. If we just accept that, what's to stop them from doing it again? Or the Rossettis? Or any other family that thinks they can take a piece of us?"

"So what do you want to do?"

Good question. I couldn't kill another Calabrese—that would definitely start a war. But I also couldn't do nothing.

"We hit them where they hurt us. Their operations. Their warehouses." I turned back to him. "Equal response. Show them we're not backing down, but we're not escalating either." "That could still spiral."

"Then we make sure it doesn't." I was already planning. "We hit them, we make it clear it's proportional response, and then we call for mediation. Get Giovanni involved. Make it official that this is done."

Marco considered it, then nodded slowly. "That could work. If we're smart about it."

"We will be." I checked my watch. Three PM. Dakota would be having tea with my mother right now—a weekly ritual Bianca had insisted on.

"Set it up for tonight. And Marco? No casualties. Property only. I don't want to give them an excuse to escalate."

"Understood." He gathered his papers. "What are you going to tell Dakota?"

"The truth." I'd promised her that. No more secrets, no more half-truths. "She deserves to know what's happening."

"She's handling all of this remarkably well."

"She's stronger than anyone gives her credit for." I smiled slightly. "Myself included." After Marco left, I sat at my desk and thought about Dakota. About how she'd reacted to everything—the threats, the killing, her mother's rejection.

She'd wavered but never broken. Had been scared but never run.

I love you.

She'd said it while knowing what I was.

What I'd done.

What I was capable of.

That kind of love—the kind that existed despite knowing the worst—that was worth protecting.

Worth fighting for.

My phone buzzed.

Dakota: Your mother is trying to teach me Italian swear words. Should I be concerned? Despite everything, I smiled. Very concerned. She knows some colorful phrases. She says they're essential for a Marchetti wife.

She's not wrong.

How's the lesson going?

I can now tell someone their mother was a hamster and their father smelt of elderberries. In Italian.

I laughed out loud.

That's Monty Python, not Italian.

Your mother finds it hilarious.

My mother has a strange sense of humor.

I'm learning that. When will you be home?

The question made my chest tighten.

Home.

She called it home now, not just the penthouse or Lorenzo's place.

Home.

Few hours. Need to handle some business first.

The Calabrese situation? Always so perceptive.

Yes. I'll tell you about it when I get there. Be safe. Always. Love you.

Love you too.

I pocketed my phone and got back to work.

The hits went exactly as planned. Two of their warehouses—torched. One transport truck—destroyed. Property damage matching almost exactly what they'd done to us.

No casualties. Clean. Proportional.

I stood in my office at midnight, watching the reports come in, feeling the satisfaction of a message sent and received.

My phone rang.

Giovanni Rossi.

"Lorenzo." His voice was neutral. "I heard about the fires."

"Proportional response. Property only. No casualties."

"I know. Very professional." A pause. "The Calabrese family is requesting mediation." There it was. The off-ramp I'd been hoping for.

"When?"

"Tomorrow. Noon. Neutral ground. My restaurant." He was choosing careful words. "Lorenzo, they want this done. They've made their statement, you've made yours. Now it's time to end it."

"I agree. What are the terms?"

"No more retaliation from either side. You both accept the losses. Business returns to normal, separate territories." He paused. "And you never speak of Antonio Calabrese again. His death is… forgotten."

"Forgotten." The word tasted bitter.

He'd threatened Dakota, and I was supposed to just forget? But this was how it worked. This was how we avoided wars that destroyed families.

"Fine. I agree to the terms. But Giovanni? Make it clear to the Calabreses that Dakota is still off-limits. Permanently. Non-negotiable."

"I'll make it clear." His tone suggested he understood. "Noon tomorrow, Lorenzo. Don't be late."

He hung up, and I stood there for a moment, processing.

It was over.

The Calabrese situation, the retaliation, all of it.

We'd paid our prices, made our statements, and now we were walking away.

Dakota was safe.

The family was secure. The business would recover.

I should have felt relief. Instead, I felt… empty. Like I'd been running on adrenaline and violence for so long that stopping felt wrong.

I called Dakota. "Lorenzo?" She answered immediately, voice heavy with sleep. "What time is it?"

"Late. I'm sorry, I didn't mean to wake you."

"It's okay." I heard rustling as she sat up. "Are you alright?"

"Yes. It's done. The Calabrese situation. We're meeting tomorrow to formalize the end of it."

Silence. Then: "It's really over?"

"It's really over." I leaned against my desk, suddenly exhausted. "No more retaliation, no more threats. We both walk away."

"And me? Am I still—"

"Off-limits. Forever. I made sure that was in the terms." I closed my eyes. "You're safe, Dakota. Finally safe."

"Then why do you sound so sad?"

Because I was. Because some part of me had wanted to keep fighting. Had wanted to burn the entire Calabrese operation to the ground for daring to threaten what was mine.

But that would have made me a monster.

And Dakota didn't deserve a monster for a husband.

"I'm just tired," I said instead. "It's been a long few days."

"Come home." Her voice was soft. "Stop working and come home. I'll be waiting."

Home. To her. To safety. To a life that was more than just violence and revenge.

"I'm on my way."

I grabbed my jacket. "Dakota?"

"Yes?"

"I love you. So much it scares me sometimes."

"I know." I could hear the smile in her voice.

"I love you too. Now hurry home before I fall back asleep."

When I walked into the penthouse an hour later, I found Dakota in one of my t-shirts, curled on the couch, trying to stay awake. "

You should have gone to bed," I said, dropping my jacket on the chair.

"I wanted to wait for you." She stood, moving into my arms.

"You look exhausted."

"I am." I buried my face in her hair, breathing in her scent—familiar, comforting, home. "But I'm here now."

"Tell me what happened."

So I did. Told her about the retaliation, the mediation, the terms.

Told her it was over, that she was safe, that we could finally breathe.

She listened without interrupting, her hands tracing patterns on my back.

"How do you feel?" she asked when I finished.

"I don't know." The honesty surprised me. "I should feel relieved. But mostly I just feel… tired. Like I've been carrying something heavy for so long that putting it down feels strange."

"That's normal." She pulled back to look at me. "You've been in crisis mode since the flower shop. Your body doesn't know how to relax yet."

"When did you become so wise?"

"I married a paranoid mafia heir. I've learned a few things." She took my hand, leading me toward the bedroom. "Come on. You need sleep."

"I need you." The words came out rougher than intended.

"You have me." She turned at the bedroom door. "Always. But right now, you need rest." She was right. But when we got into bed and she curled against me, I found I couldn't sleep. My mind kept racing—replaying the past few days, calculating what could have gone wrong, planning for threats that were already resolved.

"Lorenzo." Dakota's voice cut through the spiral. "Stop thinking."

"I can't."

"Yes, you can." She shifted, moving to straddle me. "Look at me."

I did.

Found her looking down at me with determination and something else. Something heated.

"Dakota—"

"You've been taking care of everyone else. The business, the family, me. Now let me take care of you." S

he kissed me before I could respond, slow and deep, and I felt something in me finally let go.

The tension, the hypervigilance, the constant calculation—it all fell away until there was just her.

Just us.

She took her time, learning what made me groan, what made my hands tighten on her hips, what made me forget everything except the feeling of her skin against mine.

When she finally took me inside her, moving slowly, deliberately, I felt something close to peace.

"I love you," she whispered, hands on my chest, dark hair falling around her face.

"I love you, Lorenzo Marchetti. All of you. Even the complicated parts. Even the violent parts. All of you."

I pulled her down, kissing her desperately, pouring everything I couldn't say into the contact.

Thank you for staying.

Thank you for choosing me.

Thank you for loving someone who probably doesn't deserve it.

After, when we were tangled together, both breathing hard, she traced patterns on my chest.

"Better?" she asked.

"Much better." I captured her hand, kissed her palm. "You're dangerous, moglie."

"Me? I'm not the one who killed someone."

"No, you're worse. You made me fall in love with you. Made me care about something beyond just survival and power." I pulled her closer. "That's far more dangerous than any violence I'm capable of."

"Good." She settled against me. "Someone needed to civilize you."

"I'm not sure I'm civilizable."

"Then I'll just have to keep trying." She yawned. "Starting tomorrow. After the mediation. After everything's really, truly over."

"And then what?" I asked. "After everything's over? What do we do?"

"We live." She said it simply. "We have dinner with your family. We explore Rome. We fight about stupid things like who forgot to buy milk. We have sex. We sleep in on Sundays. We live, Lorenzo. Like normal people."

"We're not normal people."

"Then we live like us. Whatever that looks like."

She tilted her head up to look at me.

"We've survived the hard part. Now we get to figure out what comes after."

What came after. A future. A life together that was more than just crisis management and survival.

The thought was terrifying and exhilarating in equal measure.

"I like the sound of that," I said quietly.

"Good. Because you're stuck with me." She kissed my chest.

"For better or worse. Till death do us part. You said the words."

"Best decision I ever made."

"Even though you didn't really have a choice?"

"Especially because I didn't have a choice." I kissed the top of her head. "The best things in life are the ones we don't plan for. The ones that just... happen."

"Like falling in love with your arranged wife?"

"Exactly like that." She laughed softly, and the sound filled something in me I hadn't known was empty.

We lay there in the darkness, holding each other, and for the first time in days—maybe weeks—I felt something like contentment.

The mediation would happen tomorrow.

The Calabrese situation would officially end. And then... Then we'd figure out what normal looked like for a mafia heir and his American wife.

We'd build something that was ours—not defined by violence or threats or the expectations of others.

We'd live. And maybe, just maybe, we'd be happy doing it.

"Lorenzo?" Dakota's voice was sleepy now.

"Mmm?"

"Thank you."

"For what?"

"For choosing me too. Every day. Even when it's hard."

I tightened my arms around her. "Always, amore. Always."

She drifted off then, her breathing evening out, body going soft and relaxed against mine.

I stayed awake a little longer, watching her sleep, marveling at the fact that she was here. That she'd stayed.

That she'd chosen this life, this world, me—despite every reason not to.

I'm the luckiest man alive, I thought. And for once, I let myself believe it.

*

The mediation the next day was exactly as formal and tedious as I'd expected.

Giovanni presided over it like a judge, laying out the terms both families had agreed to. The Calabrese representative—Antonio's younger brother, Felipe—looked at me with pure hatred the entire time.

I didn't blame him.

I'd killed his brother.

That wasn't something forgiven easily.

But he signed the agreement. Acknowledged the terms.

Agreed to the ceasefire.

"It's done," Giovanni said finally. "The matter between the Marchetti and Calabrese families is settled. No further retaliation from either side. May we all move forward in peace."

Peace.

What a concept.

Felipe Calabrese stood, buttoning his jacket.

"Marchetti." His voice was cold. "Calabrese."

"My brother made mistakes. I acknowledge that." He moved closer, and my people tensed. "But know this: if you ever threaten my family again, ceasefire or not, I will respond. Decisively."

"Understood." I held his gaze. "And know this: if anyone in your family approaches my wife again, agreement or not, I will respond. Permanently."

We stared at each other for a long moment—two men who would probably never be friends, barely even allies, but who understood the rules of this world

. "Agreed," he said finally.

He left without another word, his people following.

Giovanni approached me.

"That went better than expected."

"Did it?"

"No one died. In our world, that's a victory."

He clapped my shoulder. "Go home to your wife, Lorenzo. Let this be the end of it."

"I intend to."

When I got back to the penthouse, Dakota was in the kitchen, attempting to cook something that smelled vaguely like it might be edible.

"You're cooking," I observed.

"Badly." She turned, spatula in hand. "But I'm trying. Your mother said a Marchetti wife should know how to make at least one traditional dish."

"And you chose...?"

"Carbonara. How hard can it be?"

I looked at the stove—eggs that were slightly scrambled, pasta that was probably overcooked, bacon that was definitely burned.

"Very hard, apparently."

She threw the spatula at me. I caught it, laughing.

"Don't mock me. I'm learning."

"You're adorable when you're learning."

I moved behind her, wrapping my arms around her waist.

"But maybe we order in tonight?"

"Probably a good idea."

She leaned back against me. "How did it go? The mediation?"

"It's done. Officially over. The Calabrese family agreed to the terms."

"So we're safe? Really safe?"

"As safe as we can be in this world."

I kissed her temple. "But yes. The immediate threat is over."

She turned in my arms. "Then what do we do now?"

"Now?" I smiled. "Now we live. Just like you said."

"Starting with ordering food because I've ruined dinner?"

"Starting with ordering food." I pulled out my phone. "And then maybe we watch one of those terrible reality shows you like."

"You said you'd never watch those with me."

"I lied. I'll watch anything if it means sitting on the couch with you."

"Who are you and what have you done with Lorenzo Marchetti?"

"He fell in love and became soft." I kissed her nose. "Your fault, really."

"I'll accept responsibility." She wrapped her arms around my neck. "As long as being soft includes cuddles."

"It can include cuddles."

"And letting me pick the show?"

"Within reason."

"And admitting I was right about staying?"

"Don't push it."

She laughed, and I kissed her, and somewhere in the background the carbonara continued to burn.

But it didn't matter. Because this—this moment of normalcy, of laughter, of love—this was what I'd fought for.

What I'd killed for. What I'd risked everything for.

And it was worth it. Every terrible, violent, complicated moment had been worth it. Because it led to her.

To us.

To this.

And I wouldn't change a single thing.

45

Epilogue

One Year Later
DAKOTA

Elissa Marie Marchetti was born on a Tuesday morning at 6:47 AM, screaming loud enough to wake half the hospital.

"She has your lungs," Lorenzo said, exhausted and awestruck, as the nurse placed our daughter in my arms for the first time.

"And your stubborn chin." I traced the tiny, perfect features, still not quite believing she was real. "Look at her, Lorenzo. We made a person."

"We made a perfect person." He kissed my forehead, then Elissa's. "The most beautiful person in the world."

"You're biased."

"Completely." He didn't take his eyes off her. "But I'm also right."

That had been three months ago. Three months of sleepless nights, endless diaper changes, and a love so fierce it sometimes scared me.

Now I stood in the nursery of our new house—not the penthouse, but an actual house with a yard and security that was subtle rather than obvious—watching Elissa sleep in her crib.

"You're staring again," Lorenzo said from the doorway.

"I can't help it. She's perfect."

"She is." He moved behind me, wrapping his arms around my waist. "But she's also asleep, which means we should also be sleeping."

"I know. I just—" I leaned back against him. "Sometimes I still can't believe this is real. That she's ours. That we're… this."

"This?" His lips brushed my temple. "You mean deliriously happy and severely sleep-deprived?"

"Exactly that." I turned to look at him. "Are you happy? Really happy?"

"Dakota." He cupped my face. "I have you. I have Elissa. I have a life that's more than just the business. Yes, I'm happy. Happier than I thought I could be."

"Even though I made you watch six seasons of reality TV?"

"Even though." He smiled. "Though I maintain that show is terrible."

"You cried when they voted off Sarah."

"I did not cry. I had something in my eye."

"You cried."

"Fine. I cried." He kissed me. "But only because you've made me soft."

"Good." I rested my head on his chest. "Someone needed to."

Elissa made a soft sound in her sleep, and we both froze, waiting to see if she'd wake up. She settled, and we both exhaled in relief.

"We should really sleep while we can," Lorenzo whispered.

"Five more minutes. I just want to watch her."

"Five minutes." He tightened his arms around me. "And then we're both going to bed, and we're sleeping until she wakes up demanding food."

"So like an hour."

"Optimistically."

We stood there in the soft glow of the nightlight, watching our daughter sleep, and I thought about everything that had brought us here.

The forced marriage. The fear. The violence. The choice to stay. The choice to love him.

All of it had led to this moment. To this life. To this tiny person who was half me, half him, and completely perfect.

"Lorenzo?"

"Mmm?"

"I'm glad it was you. The arrangement, the marriage, all of it. I'm glad it was you."

He kissed the top of my head. "Me too, amore. Me too."

LORENZO

The doorbell rang at exactly noon, and I checked the security feed before answering.

Dakota's parents stood on the doorstep, her mother holding a wrapped gift, her father looking nervous.

It had taken months. Months of Dakota calling her mother, leaving voicemails that went unanswered. Months of her father trying to mediate. Months of patience and persistence and hope.

But finally, two weeks ago, her mother had called back.

And now they were here. Meeting their granddaughter for the first time.

"They're here," I called to Dakota.

She emerged from the nursery, Elissa in her arms, and I saw the nervousness in her eyes. "How do I look?"

"Beautiful." I kissed her cheek. "They're going to love her. And they're going to remember why they love you."

"I hope you're right."

"I'm always right."

"You're sometimes right."

"I'm right about this." I squeezed her hand. "Ready?"

She nodded, and I opened the door.

Dakota's mother saw Elissa and immediately started crying. "Oh. Oh, she's beautiful."

"Mom." Dakota's voice broke. "I've missed you so much."

Her mother crossed to her, carefully, like she was afraid Dakota might pull away. "I've missed you too, sweetheart. So much. I'm sorry. I'm so sorry for—"

"It's okay." Dakota shifted Elissa so her mother could see better. "Would you like to hold her?"

"May I?"

"Of course." Dakota carefully transferred the baby, and I watched her mother's face transform as she held her granddaughter for the first time.

"Hello, little one," she whispered. "I'm your Nana. I've been waiting so long to meet you."

Dakota's father stood awkwardly in the doorway, and I moved to shake his hand. "Robert. Thank you for coming."

"Lorenzo." His grip was firm but cautious. "Thank you for… for taking care of them. Both of them."

"Always." I meant it. "They're my world."

He studied me for a moment, then nodded. "I can see that. I'm sorry it took us so long to—" He glanced at his wife, at Dakota. "To accept this. To accept you."

"You were protecting your daughter. I understand that."

"Still." He cleared his throat. "I'm sorry."

Dakota had moved to stand beside her mother, both of them cooing over Elissa. Watching them, seeing the tears and the smiles and the healing beginning—it made something tight in my chest finally ease.

This. This was what I'd wanted. What I'd fought for. Not just Dakota's love, but her happiness. Her wholeness. Her family reunited, even if that reunion had taken a year and the birth of a child to accomplish.

"Come in," I said, stepping aside. "Please. Let's have lunch. Get to know each other properly."

We moved to the dining room, where I'd had staff prepare everything perfectly. Nothing too formal, nothing that screamed "mafia wealth," just a nice family lunch.

Dakota's mother couldn't stop holding Elissa, passing her to her grandfather only reluctantly. Robert held his granddaughter with careful wonder, tears in his eyes.

"She has your nose," he told Dakota. "And your stubborn expression."

"Lorenzo says she has his chin."

"Maybe she has both." Her mother smiled. "The best of both of you."

We ate and talked, carefully at first, then more naturally. Her parents asked about the house, about Rome, about our life here. I answered honestly— within reason. They didn't need to know everything about my business, but I didn't lie about who I was or what I did.

"Is it safe?" her mother asked finally. "Raising a child in your… world?"

"I've made it as safe as possible," I said. "Security is discreet but thorough. Elissa will grow up protected but not imprisoned. She'll have as normal a childhood as we can give her."

"But it won't be completely normal."

"No." I wouldn't lie about that. "But it will be full of love. And safety. And two parents who would do anything to protect her."

Dakota's hand found mine under the table, squeezing.

"That's all any parent can ask for," her father said quietly. "Love and protection. The rest… the rest we figure out as we go."

After lunch, while Dakota and her mother caught up in the living room, I found myself on the terrace with Robert.

"I owe you an apology," he said without preamble. "For the debt. For putting Dakota in that position. For—"

"You don't owe me anything. You did what you had to do to survive. I understand that."

"Still. My daughter shouldn't have been the price."

"No. But she also wouldn't be my daughter if I hadn't agreed." I looked through the window at Dakota, laughing at something her mother said. "And I can't imagine my life without her now."

"You really love her." It wasn't a question.

"More than I thought I was capable of loving anyone." I turned to face him. "Robert, I know you have concerns. I know my world is violent and dangerous and not what you wanted for Dakota. But I swear to you—on my life, on my daughter's future—I will keep them safe. Both of them. Always."

He studied me for a long moment. "I believe you. I see the way you look at her. At Elissa. That's not a man playing a role. That's a man who found something worth living for."

"I did. They're everything."

"Then I suppose I can't ask for more than that." He offered his hand. "Welcome to the family, Lorenzo. Officially."

I shook it, feeling like I'd finally been granted something I hadn't known I needed. Her father's approval. Her family's acceptance.

"Thank you."

DAKOTA

My mother held my hand as we watched Elissa sleep in her crib later that afternoon.

"I'm sorry," she said quietly. "For cutting you off. For not being there when you needed me. For missing so much of your pregnancy."

"Mom—"

"No, let me finish." She squeezed my hand. "I was scared. Terrified, actually. When I found out what Lorenzo was, what his family did—all I could think about was losing you. You dying because of that world. So I pushed you away, thinking somehow that would protect you."

"It just hurt."

"I know. And I'm so sorry, sweetheart." She turned to face me. "But seeing you now, seeing you with Lorenzo, with Elissa—you're happy. Really happy. And I was wrong to think you couldn't be happy in this life."

"It's not perfect. It's still scary sometimes. But yes, I'm happy." I smiled. "He's a good man, Mom. I know it's hard to see past what he does, but he's good. He takes care of us. He loves us. And he's an amazing father."

"I can see that." She wiped her eyes. "The way he looks at Elissa—my father used to look at you that way. Like you were the most precious thing in the world."

"She is. To both of us."

"I'm glad." She pulled me into a hug. "I love you, Dakota. I never stopped loving you. I just—I lost my way for a while."

"I love you too." I held her tight. "And I'm so glad you're here. That you get to know Elissa. That we can fix this."

"We'll do better. Your father and I. We'll visit more. We'll be part of your life, part of Elissa's life." She pulled back, smiling through tears. "If you'll let us."

"Of course. She needs her Nana and Papa."

"Nana and Papa." She tested the words. "I like that."

We stood there, watching my daughter sleep, my mother's arm around me, and I felt the last piece of broken things inside me finally heal.

I had my family back. I had Lorenzo. I had Elissa.

I had everything.

LORENZO

That evening, after Dakota's parents had left with promises to return soon, I found Dakota on the terrace, looking out at Rome as the sun set.

"Penny for your thoughts," I said, wrapping my arms around her from behind.

"Just thinking about how much has changed in a year." She leaned back against me. "Last year at this time, we were dealing with Calabrese. I was terrified. My mother wasn't speaking to me. I wasn't sure we'd survive."

"And now?"

"Now we have a daughter. My parents are back in my life. The business is stable. We're happy." She turned in my arms. "We survived, Lorenzo. We actually survived and came out better on the other side."

"We did." I kissed her forehead. "Though I maintain you did most of the surviving. I just killed people."

"You protected us. That's different."

"Is it?"

"Yes." She was firm about that. "You protected your family. That's what good men do."

"Good men." I smiled. "A year ago, you wouldn't have called me a good man."

"A year ago, I didn't know you yet." She cupped my face. "But I know you now. And Lorenzo? You're a good man. A complicated, dangerous, occasionally terrifying man. But good. Where it matters."

"I love you." The words still felt new, even after saying them hundreds of times. "So much."

"I love you too." She kissed me softly. "Thank you."

"For what?"

"For being patient when I couldn't say it. For protecting me even when I didn't understand why. For being a better husband than I ever imagined."

She smiled. "For giving me Elissa. For giving me this life."

"I should be thanking you. For staying. For choosing me. For loving me despite everything."

"We can both be grateful." She rested her head on my chest. "That's allowed."

We stood there as Rome lit up below us, the ancient city glowing in the twilight. From inside, I heard Elissa starting to wake up, making those little sounds that meant she'd be demanding food soon.

"I'll get her," Dakota said. "You've been dealing with family all day."

"We've been dealing with family all day." I pulled her back for one more kiss. "But I'll come with you. I want to see her."

"You saw her ten minutes ago."

"And I want to see her again. Is that a crime?"

"You're obsessed with our daughter."

"Guilty." I followed her inside. "But you're equally obsessed, so you can't judge."

"I'm not judging. I think it's adorable."

"I'm not adorable. I'm terrifying."

"You're adorable when you're with Elissa. You make these faces—"

"I do not make faces."

"You absolutely make faces. You go all soft and—"

Elissa's cry interrupted us, and we both hurried to the nursery.

Dakota lifted her from the crib, and immediately Elissa quieted, recognizing her mother's scent, her warmth. I watched them together—my wife, my daughter—and felt that familiar tightness in my chest.

Love. This was what love looked like. Not grand gestures or perfect moments. But this—sleepless nights and tiny hands and a woman who'd chosen me despite every reason not to.

"What?" Dakota asked, seeing my expression.

"Nothing. Just… this. You. Her. Everything." I moved closer, wrapping them both in my arms. "Just being grateful."

"Sentimental Lorenzo. Who are you?"

"A man who got lucky." I kissed her temple, then Elissa's head. "Impossibly, undeservedly lucky."

"We both got lucky." She leaned into me. "Even if it started terribly, even if the path was hard—we got lucky in the end."

"Yes. We did."

Elissa grabbed my finger with her tiny hand, holding on with surprising strength. A future mafia heir, I thought with amusement. She'd be running this city someday.

But for now, she was just our daughter. Just Elissa Marie Marchetti, three months old, perfect and loved and safe.

And that was more than enough.

"Lorenzo?" Dakota's voice pulled me from my thoughts.

"Yes, amore?"

"Thank you for giving me this. For being patient. For fighting for us." She looked up at me with those eyes that had captured me from the first moment. "For loving me."

"Always." I kissed her, careful not to jostle Elissa between us. "Always and forever, Dakota. That's a promise."

"I'll hold you to it."

"Please do."

We stood there in the nursery, the three of us together, and I realized this was what I'd been looking for my entire life. Not power or respect or fear.

Just this. Just love. Just family.

Just home.

And it had started with a forced marriage, a woman who hated me, and a debt that needed paying.

Funny how the worst beginnings sometimes lead to the best endings.

Or maybe not endings at all.

Just new beginnings.

Better ones.

Ones worth fighting for.

Worth killing for.

Worth living for.

"I love you," I whispered to both of them. "Both of you. My whole world."

Dakota smiled, Elissa yawned, and somewhere in Rome, the city continued its eternal dance.

But here, in this moment, in this room, with these two people who'd changed everything—

Here, I was finally, truly home.

THE END

46

Author Biography

Maura-Ann is the author of the haunting 'A Love Written in Blood' trilogy and several dark, twisted standalones. She is currently working on her next high-stakes series

As a neurodivergent writer with dyslexia and a processing disorder, Maura-Ann knows what it means to be underestimated. More than once, she's been told her writing felt "too good" to be hers but every word comes from her own hands, heart, and sleepless nights. Her stories are her truth, and she's proud to be telling them.

When she's not writing, she's sipping tea, spoiling her guinea pig, or losing sleep over books that break her heart (in the best way).

She's just getting started, expect more twisted love stories and characters who live in the shadows. Find her on Instagram and TikTok @authormaura anncairns.

www.ingramcontent.com/pod-product-compliance
Lightning Source LLC
Chambersburg PA
CBHW051442050726
47593CB00005B/1898